WITHDRAWN

D1546423

I've travelled the world twice over,
Met the famous: saints and sinners,
Poets and artists, kings and queens,
Old stars and hopeful beginners,
I've been where no-one's been before,
Learned secrets from writers and cooks
All with one library ticket
To the wonderful world of books.

THE LOOKING-GLASS

Gregg MacIvor glanced in the mirror before stepping into the elevator. Her reflection glowed back at her, the shining red hair framing the fine features and the wide luminous eyes. Suddenly she was stunned with sick, paralysing terror as the face of the man behind her came into slow agonising focus. Their eyes met for one lingering moment and he was gone. Was it possible? The chill fear she had believed long buried, once again enveloped her. . . .

VIRGINIA COFFMAN

THE
LOOKING-GLASS

Complete and Unabridged

ULVERSCROFT
Leicester

First published in Great Britain in 1984 by
Judy Piatkus (Publishers) Limited,
London

First Large Print Edition
published October 1985
by arrangement with
Judy Piatkus (Publishers) Limited,
London

British Library CIP Data

Coffman, Virginia
    The looking-glass.—Large print ed.—
    Ulverscroft large print series: romance suspense
    I. Title
    813′.54[F]   PS3553.O415

    ISBN 0-7089-1360-1

Published by
F. A. Thorpe (Publishing) Ltd.
Anstey, Leicestershire
Set by Rowland Phototypesetting Ltd.
Bury St. Edmunds, Suffolk
Printed and bound in Great Britain by
T. J. Press (Padstow) Ltd., Padstow, Cornwall

For DONNIE MICCICHE *and*
BEV MONJAR,
the Saturday Lunch Gang

1

HURRYING into the lobby of the ancient, Lower Manhattan skyscraper, Gregg MacIvor cried, "Hold it!" to the elevator doors which quietly closed upon her groping fingertips. Not for the first time, she damned the tyranny of mechanical objects, none of which were created to handle people late for appointments.

Then, as usual, she turned to the mirrored wall which reflected the elevator doors, and began to check the damage the wind had done to her rich auburn hair. While she was combing her hair into some kind of order, the far elevator rising from the underground garage opened briefly for its lobby stop. Caught half-combed, Gregg glanced into the looking-glass, and seeing a man in the elevator cage, yelled, "Wait for me!" and in her hurry dropped her comb.

During the few seconds it took to pick up the comb, the mirror in front of her revealed the man in the elevator. He was a little taller than she was, which meant he was quite tall. She was caught by the horrid familiarity in the deep-set dark eyes and the chiseled, squarish chin. She blinked, looked again. Surely, the mirrored image showed the same mouth she had once called "stubborn" in the days and nights of her girlhood illusions. "Cruel," she reminded herself now. Ugly and cruel. And sensuous? Or just sensual.

Curious that he didn't seem to have grown older. She had not seen Martin Helm for eleven years. Since, in fact, she failed to show up for their wedding. He must be nearly forty now. Was this youngish man actually Martin Helm?

In an icy panic she kept her back to the elevator, waved it on. This was hardly necessary. The elevator doors had already begun to close without her. As for the man inside, he glanced her way but then his view of her was cut off by the elevator doors.

As if she had been hit in the stomach, Gregg found herself still hunched over while she watched the elevator's old-fashioned floor indicator in the mirror.

2

. . . Not the twelfth floor, please, she prayed.

Twelfth floor it was.

What the devil did Martin Helm want with the Oliver Sills Publishing Company, whose offices occupied the twelfth, fourteenth and fifteenth floors? He must have tracked her here. But why, after more than ten years?

Maybe he knows I've made a little money.

The past fiancées in Martin Helm's life had been "well-to-do," as those old newspapers put it long ago when Gregg was shown the stories about him.

Years afterward, with the horror fading, she occasionally told herself that Martin Helm's love for her had been genuine. She was not an heiress. Her parents had left her enough to see her through college, but that was it.

Martin Helm knew that. He must have checked on her. Maybe he intended to use the few thousands of her college money and then leave her. Or murder her? It was his thing. But somewhere, deep within, he must have cared a little for her. And Gregg had betrayed him, jilted and then betrayed him. He would certainly want to murder her after that, if he could find her. And she had thought she'd made fairly certain he would not find her.

How maddening that he should look more attractive than ever! She had always been afraid of her own weakness in the face of his oddly dark Teutonic charm. She shivered to think of that weakness, when she remembered the fate of the women who had preceded her in his affections.

She was already late for her lunch date with Oliver Sills, but she wanted to be certain he did not tell Martin Helm (if indeed it *was* Martin) where to find her. The lobby itself was large, high-ceilinged and empty. No telephone. She hurried out into the breezy September daylight and found a telephone in the drugstore on the corner.

Patty Bergstrom, Oliver's receptionist, heard Gregg's voice and cut in with her usual complaint, "Honey, you know you're late?"

"Patty, you aren't listening to me. This is important. Is anyone in your office now? A man—he looks European, maybe

4

German. Attractive, with dark hair and eyes?"

"You've got to be kidding! Can I expect one?"

"It may be someone I know, and I don't want to meet him. Does Oliver have an appointment with anyone right now?"

"Yes. You. Honey, this isn't a put-on?. . . Well, you want the truth, I've been on my coffee break up in publicity, but I sure would've remembered seeing anything like your gorgeous friend."

"He's not my—forget it. Did Oliver have another appointment this morning, somebody he's seeing before he goes to lunch?"

Patty reached for her appointment pad. "Nobody unless—Oh, Miss MacIvor! He's been anxious to get hold of Eric Raeder, who wrote that weird best-seller originally published in Germany. It was called *Doppelgänger*; that's some strange word that can't be translated, so in English it's just called *The Looking-Glass*. Anyway, he's due in this afternoon. We're all dying to see him. And *he's* German."

Gregg's fingers were sweating and she

took the receiver in her other hand. "What does this Eric Raeder look like?"

"Who knows? There was no picture on the jacket and you never see him during his TV interviews. It's his thing. 'Author unknown,' you know? Heard but not seen. A German with a sense of humor. Speaks pretty fair English, too."

"Eric Raeder! Just another phony with a gimmick."

"Now, Miss MacIvor, your funny little travel books are great, but you mustn't expect to compete with an operator like Eric Raeder. He's riding a freak success. The hardcover of his book was on *The Times* list for months."

"Okay, okay. If no one is there now, I'll come on up and meet Oliver in his office."

"Great. And if I see any good-looking males, besides the boss, of course, I'll hold them for you."

"Don't do me any favors. Bye."

After a quick glance outside, Gregg went back up the street and managed to find one of the elevators in the publisher's building waiting for her. While she rode up, a horrifying idea occurred to her. Eric Raeder, the new glamour boy of the literary world, was thought to be German, but couldn't he be Swedish, as she knew Helm to be? She had not read his suspense novel, partly from sheer stubbornness, because everyone was talking about it and speculating wildly on the writer's identity. But now, as she tried to recall bits and pieces she had heard about *The Looking-Glass*, it did seem that Eric Raeder might be Martin Helm. Or was her imagination running away with her?

She looked up. Too late now. The twelfth floor. Patty Bergstrom's desk and a small switchboard took up most of the floor space in the little, inner reception room with its tubes of neon light the color of nonfat milk. Everyone who stepped out of the elevator almost fell into Patty's well-endowed lap.

Gregg could see that the receptionist was ready to burst with her news.

"Miss MacIvor! He's here now. He was in talking to the boss all the time I was on the phone to you. Mr. Raeder. Right there in that room. I just brought coffee to him and the boss."

Gregg stiffened. Her fingers closed around the spine of the huge, new, sexy

7

novel by the hottest selling female author in Oliver Sill's stable. Patty twisted it out of her hand.

"Watch it, honey. I'd hate to tell you what that gold jacket set us back."

"What is he like?"

Patty didn't even pretend to misunderstand. "Attractive. Not movie-star handsome or anything, and dark like you described him. Sexy, I thought."

"Martin Helm."

"Who? No. I heard our mystery boy tell the boss to call him Eric. I'm not supposed to let it out, but—" She leaned forward over a glue pot and a huge pair of shears. "They were talking about his hometown. Some place on the Rhine. And some of his family live in Geneva. The boss actually knew Mr. Raeder's aunt. Isn't that a riot? And everybody's guessing he was an ex-Nazi, or an ex-convict, a loony or a movie star, and I don't know what all."

Gregg sat down abruptly on the corner of Patty's desk, winced and removed the shears from under her all-too-thin skirt. "I thought—God knows! The most preposterous thing—"

"Such as?"

"He just might be a murderer I once knew."

The sight of Patty's slightly protuberant eyes broke Gregg up. She laughed. "Don't worry. It can't be the same man." She paused.

"He could be a murderer, at that," Patty decided, considering her meeting with the author. "They say murderers charm their victims. Boss is trying to get him signed to do a new chiller. Would you believe it? Raeder's first book was a one-shot deal. Even London hasn't been able to sign him for the next, though *Looking-Glass* was published there right after the Berlin edition. He yaps about privacy, but that's all part of the publicity buildup."

Gregg got up, walked the length of the narrow room, past the office of Oliver's elderly female assistant and back, her long stride taking her closer to Oliver Sill's elegantly paneled door each time. Patty pantomimed for her to listen at the door, but Gregg frowned, playing it nobly, pretending an elaborate indifference.

"Talk about *my* being late!" she remarked after a few minutes. She had barely gotten out this complaint when she and Patty heard Oliver Sill's urbane voice as the door opened.

"Quite right. No pressures, but one final thought. Sills Publishing asks to meet any offer you get elsewhere. We are a small house, but we can give you special attention."

"Frankly," said a voice from inside the room, "now is the time I would like to play. Not work."

Gregg backed away from the opening door. In spite of the excellent English, the accent was there and, as Patty Bergstrom indicated, not unattractive. It was not the voice of Martin Helm, who spoke more deliberately, with lower-pitched tones that she now thought of as sly. She muttered, "Vive la difference!" and saw Patty Bergstrom look up in surprise.

Gregg watched Oliver Sills emerge first, rangy and tweedy, like the English country gentleman with the white mustache he stroked complacently. The publisher stood aside, and that celebrated unknown, Eric Raeder, came out into the reception area. Once more Gregg felt the shock of the man's superficial resemblance to Martin Helm. . . . But unless Helm had found a

10

handy fountain of youth, this Raeder could not possibly be the same man. His unruly black hair was thicker than Martin Helm's faintly graying hair. And then there were Eric Raeder's scars, a faint white thread across his forehead, cutting into the widow's peak of his hair. And those nasty, crisscrossing white scars across the knuckles of his right hand. . . .

He turned slightly, saw Gregg and looked her up and down without a sign of recognition. Not with the slumberous eyes and careful, seductive effort of Martin Helm, but with raised eyebrows and an obvious, unconcealed interest. He seemed to like her legs, which was not surprising. When she went to lunch with men she seldom wore pants suits. Her hair and her long, nicely proportioned legs were her particular physical assets, and she liked to display the latter when the time seemed especially right.

Oliver said quickly, "Gregg, dear girl, I would like you to know . . . may I say who you are, Raeder?"

The German was caught in a position where he could hardly say no. Gregg smiled, her relief so great she would have liked him no matter how he regarded her, but she found that his answering smile was worth waiting for, in spite of that stubborn, almost cruel mouth.

He held out his hand to Gregg. "Eric Raeder."

His grip was strong but he made no effort, as Martin might have done, to prolong the moment. He nodded to Patty, shook hands with Oliver and walked out after another glance at Gregg and the brief valedictory, "A pleasure, Miss MacIvor."

Twenty minutes later, in the cab headed uptown with Oliver Sills, Gregg asked the question that should have occurred to her in his office.

"Ollie, how did Mr. Raeder know my name?"

He nodded knowingly. "Likeable chap, and no mistake."

"Don't be silly. But how does he know? You didn't have any occasion to mention my name, did you?"

"No, but I do have that autographed picture of you in the office. And if I had known he was going to catch your wandering eye, old girl, I certainly wouldn't have mentioned you." He considered the subject more seriously. "I don't think we're going to get his next book."

Gregg said, "I should have read that book of his. I suppose there was just too damned much talk about it. And all that phony publicity. Masked interviews—"

"Not masked. He just sits near the cameras and answers questions. It's the usual publicity gimmick, but it works. He begun by refusing to be interviewed, but after the paperback came out last month and there was such a hullabaloo, the book went back on the best-seller lists again, and, if you want to know the truth, I think it's the money that's getting to him now. There are a few relatives, an aunt, cousins, nephews, et cetera. So he's out publicizing the new paperback edition. You hear him during his interviews. You just don't see much of him. By the way, they're calling the proposed movie 'greater than Jekyll and Hyde.' Shows you."

"It all fits too well," she murmured, while her mind dovetailed all these similarities and coincidences. Puzzled, Oliver Sills watched her but did not press. They had reached the dark, popular little bistro on

Fifty-first Street, and while her companion ordered Bloody Marys, still with an inquiring eye on her, Gregg explained, "I knew a man eleven years ago who was a ringer for this Eric Raeder. It strikes me that our oh-so-secretive Dr. Jekyll just might be trying not to expose Mr. Hyde."

That stunned him. He studied his celery swizzle stick and asked, carefully nonchalant, "I take it the fellow you knew eleven years ago was Mr. Hyde."

She shrugged. "Mr. Hyde, suitably masked."

"Know him well?"

She bit the celery with a hard crunch. "You won't believe this, but we met on a cruise."

"Good God! All the clichés."

"In every way. I'll never forget our midnight sailing out of Port-au-Prince harbor. Ollie, you've never seen such a moon. And the waters! All sparkling, and black as ink. When we came into our cabins—" She grinned, a wry little grin that ridiculed herself and always intrigued him. "Clichés. Right down the line. He was a good lover. Not the greatest, but more than efficient. I didn't know any better anyway. I had just turned eighteen. I went home to Chicago thinking I was engaged to him. I lived with my uncle and aunt. My mother had left a trust fund to take care of me until I was twenty-one. Believe it or not, Ollie, my Mr. Hyde really did come to Chicago to marry me."

Oliver Sills finished his drink, choking on an ice cube in his surprise and shock.

"You mean you married him?"

"It was all set. Aunt Mona thought he was numero uno. What a charmer! He talked to her long distance, wooing her, you might say, courtesy of Ma Bell, and didn't even reverse the charges. Uncle George wasn't quite so thrilled. He's a newspaperman and he kept telling me he had seen my beloved Martin Helm before. Of course I had a dozen Polariods of him. It might have been the fact that Uncle George first saw him as a photo, so to speak. Two days before our wedding, Uncle George dragged me down to his newspaper morgue. There it was in a New York paper of eight months earlier. A nice little picture of Earl M. Haverill. His fiancée had fallen—or had been pushed—

out of a hotel window. The seventeenth floor, yet."

He whistled. She looked around quickly but there were so many conversations going on around them that he assured her no one was listening to them. "They are all too busy cutting each other up to hear us. But how was this Haverill involved in the woman's death?"

"She had made guess-who her beneficiary. And the day of her death they quarreled madly. The chambermaid heard the woman threaten to cut him out of her will. A male guest in the next room saw Haverill leave the woman's suite around the time she. . . fell."

"Then why wasn't he charged?"

She laughed. "An alibi, of course. Somebody named Alys Lane. It was her word against the hotel's male guest."

"But—"

"—who had been drinking several highballs."

This raised his eyebrows. "Good Lord, old girl! Did you face this Haverill with it?"

She shook her head. "Uncle George had a few connections and we talked to the

16

detectives in New York. The case was still open. They were trying to tie Haverill to a Max Harville in New Orleans. No evidence there. Not even a snapshot. Nothing but a wife who disappeared off a cruise ship. On their honeymoon."

Gregg took a fork to her quiche Lorraine when it was brought to her, and seemed engrossed in shifting bits of it around the dish. Oliver Sills watched her, his own thick onion soup growing cold in it's bowl. After several throat clearings he said plaintively, "You can't leave me dangling like that. You don't mean to tell me you think our Eric Raeder is this monster! His family seems to exist, and in an area I know rather well."

"No," she agreed in a low voice, without looking up. "It was only certain outward features. When he spoke, the way he looked at me, and then his smile were nothing at all like Martin Helm, the man I knew. And there are his scars." She raised her eyes so suddenly their green depths startled him. "He *has* had them a long time, hasn't he?"

"Seems to me someone in London told me. A plane crash on takeoff from some airport. Basel, I think. He was a young newsman. Did some work for Reuters out of London."

"How old do you think those scars are?"

He shrugged. "God knows. They certainly aren't recent. My dear Gregg, he is *not* your monster."

"I know he isn't," she admitted. "He is nothing like Martin, except in the most superficial way. The really weird coincidence is that novel of his. All about a Jekyll and Hyde, as if he might, at one time, have known a man like—"

"He is not Martin Helm . . . Haverill. Or whatever. He is Eric Raeder. Take my word for it."

"I know. I know."

"Incidentally, what happened to your Martin Helm?"

Gregg hesitated. "Not very courageous of me, I admit, but I wrote him a letter and left it with Aunt Mona. I said it had all been a ghastly mistake, that I had my career to think of. I wanted to be an actress, if you can imagine! And I left for New York. I figured he would never come here because of . . . of that business about the woman's suicide. Aunt Mona told me he was overcome, as she put it. He managed to wink a few tears, and kiss her good-bye, much to Uncle George's horror. I suppose the police must have kept an eye on him. But Uncle George couldn't learn anything more. He just vanished. We never heard from him again, or saw him, until I looked in your lobby mirror today."

"The looking-glass, he called it."

"What!"

"Nothing. Do you feel like dessert?"

She said abruptly, "I feel as though I've been stepped on. My insides hurt."

Her free hand was on the table. He tapped her knuckles with his finger.

"Know what I think? You ought to settle all those little crawling doubts in your head right now. Raeder is staying at the Berkeley Lane. Why don't you go over sometime during the weekend and see if he doesn't look harmless? He's sure to eat his meals there. Seems to be a very private fellow."

"What? Me go chasing after that man? He'd think I was one of his fans, or something."

He laughed and pointed out frankly, "It has nothing to do with your murderous Mr.

Helm. I believe you're jealous of those sales Raeder has piled up."

She ducked and clutched at her heart. "You got me where it hurts, pal."

But he thought she still looked uneasy.

2

GREGG MacIVOR had lived in midtown Manhattan for the last five years, between her frequent trips to spots around the globe that would make amusing or titillating articles about Traveling Singles. Except for infrequent love affairs, usually foreign and temporary, she liked her own company.

She rented a second-floor apartment on a tree-lined street off Third Avenue because she had come upon the street suddenly one evening, after buying odds and ends from a gourmet delicatessen, and been caught by its resemblance to an old MGM movie set. The series of shoulder-to-shoulder brownstones was painted white, the trees near the curb looked so green under the streetlights she thought at first they were fake and she never walked along that unreal block without expecting Gene Kelly to come zipping down the front steps to swing her across the sidewalk.

On Friday evening, prompted by her

lunch with Oliver Sills, she called her Uncle George's home in the Chicago suburb where he had lived since he returned from World War II. It was four years since Aunt Mona's death from emphysema, but he had never given up the seven-room, weathered-brick house. Like his niece, he could live comfortably alone, but unlike Gregg, he was an excellent cook. He had been retired from the newspaper at sixty-five but worked twice as hard nowadays in the healthier environment of his vegetable garden. It took him awhile to reach the telephone from the backyard, and then he wanted to know what had called him away from his green peppers.

"They're growing all year round, I swear. Did I send you any tomatoes this season? Those Early Girls have been popping up all over the place."

She rightly guessed that the Early Girls were tomatoes and not sexy neighbors, although Uncle George had his share of "lady friends," as he still called them.

"Marvelous! I hate to hint but I could certainly use some tomatoes. Or peppers. Anything. You should see the prices here. And I just mailed you a box of new Westerns and whodunits. Hope you like some of them."

"More the better. I give 'em to the library when I'm through. Say, Gregg, honey, would you do me a big favor? I can't seem to get it here at Slagel's. That's the only hardcover bookstore within walking distance, and I don't like to leave the garden here till I get it dug up for winter."

"Uncle George, are you overworking again? Do you want to slip a disc? What is the book? I'll send it air-special tomorrow morning."

Uncle George knew his niece well enough not to mince words. "I started the thing in paperback, but the print's so damned tiny! They call it *The Looking-Glass*. All about this guy who keeps seeing some creep behind him in the mirror, and when he looked around—"

"Nobody is there. Uncle George, they wrote that plot in Mark Twain's day. And Edgar Allan Poe, and God know's how many others. Probably Cain saw Abel in a looking-glass."

"Vice versa, honey. But Cain didn't write a best-seller."

She sighed. She knew perfectly well that

23

her dislike of *The Looking-Glass* was based on jealousy of an author who had come up from nowhere to write a best-seller his first time out. But since meeting Eric Raeder, she found her feeling ambivalent. She was dying to read his book, and yet afraid of it at the same time. Since her first sight of the dark man in the elevator, she had been haunted, as the author clearly was, by the identity of that face in the mirror. It was not, it could not be the same man she had known so many years ago, but how strange that a German newsman should write this tale which could so easily explain the aberrations that formed the murderous and greedy Martin Helm!

And the business about Eric Raeder's anxiety not to show his face on television . . . . Was it merely a publicity gimmick? Or was Eric Raeder afraid of his own Mr. Hyde?

"All right," she gave in. "I'll get a copy first thing tomorrow and send it." She laughed with a little effort. "I only wish you felt as pressed to read one of my books."

He chuckled. "You get on the 'Today Show,' and I will, honey."

She was trying to figure out some way of

moving on to the real subject of her phone call, and finally plunged in with the flat-out question, "Have you ever heard anything about Martin Helm?"

Obviously, his mind had been far away from her old love affair. "Martin who? What'd he write? Now, wait. That sombrero Western you sent me last month. Wasn't that by Martin Somebody?"

"Martin Helm. Eleven years ago. I almost married him, remember?"

"Not that actor from L.A., the one you got engaged to and canceled out before you got my congratulations card and all?" Then it came back to him. "Oh. Bluebeard. Not a word about him. Of course, I stopped checking after a year or two. Holy Jesus, honey! You haven't run across him, have you? Now, look here. No matter how he wriggled out of those other cases, he was guilty as hell, and you know it."

"Don't worry. One case might be explained. But two! And I'm not about to make myself number three. It's just that I saw a man who looked like his double from a little distance. But he is younger than Martin would be now, and different in other ways. His voice, his manner, some scars . . . And he's German."

He didn't console her in the least. "Helm might have been German. We only had his word that he was Swedish. He didn't look like any Swede I ever knew. And the only time I met him I didn't notice he had an accent."

Gregg listened in memory to Eric Raeder's voice. The accent had certainly seemed genuine, slight, but adding a definite charm to his speech pattern, as he probably knew. She could not remember exactly how Martin Helm had sounded. Fear and the old, painful sense of loss had blurred her memories of everything except his features. At this minute she couldn't even recall why he had seemed the romantic lover of her eighteen-year-old dreams. Other men since had been just as exciting. But, of course, he was the first. It must be that.

Uncle George broke in upon her jumpy thoughts.

"Well, honey, if you're sure that Bluebeard guy isn't back on your trail, I'll be hanging up now. Save you a nickel. And I want to get up early, so's I can turn over that strip of ground against the fence. Mona set a lot of store by those sweet peas, but they never did amount to anything. Night, kid."

"Good night, Uncle George."

"Don't forget that whodunit about the mirror, will you?"

"I promise."

She slid the green phone to the far end of the table which served as her desk under the long front windows, pulled over her big yellow pad and a Lindy pen and started to work on her new Traveling Singles article which dealt with the resurgence of cruises as a setting for male-female encounters. Three quarters of the encounters and flirtations had been culled from her own experience, and she thought it would be great fun recalling them now, for none of them had been serious and most were happy times.

A tease, she thought, correctly categorizing those semiaffairs. Could she thank Martin Helm for turning her away from serious entanglements? How easy it was to blame others, not herself. Yet, surely, today had been different. When she decided that Eric Raeder was not that murderous first love of hers, she had definitely felt an attraction to him.

The glow from the streetlights poured in through the windows like spotlights on a stage and roused her from her reverie. She got up, snapped the venetian blinds shut and went back to work. But the spell was broken. Her thoughts skipped over all the pleasant encounters of recent years, hurrying back to that time eleven years ago which she had buried, but not deep enough, it seemed, in her subconscious.

The September night was too warm, too sultry. She slipped off the flame-shaded chiffon djellaba she wore over her matching nightgown and wrote a few paragraphs before one of the frequent night sounds, a series of shrieks, startled her into dropping her pen. Frightened, she opened the blinds with one hand while the other grabbed the phone. But the shrieks were the raucous laughter of a drunken neighbor on her way home with her boyfriend.

Now a complete bundle of nerves, Gregg gave up for the night, turned her yellow pad facedown and went to run her bath. Tonight she would at least get to bed at a decent hour, and maybe a long, uninterrupted sleep would give her back that cool, nonchalant self-confidence which she had found so useful these last ten years.

But four hours later, a little after two in the morning, she got up, her entire body tingling with the aftereffects of a nightmare she couldn't recall, and fumbled around in her tiny, three-cornered kitchen overlooking an alley and the dingy rear of a series of brownstones facing the next street. She seldom took pills and had even written an article, tongue in cheek, detailing the ways to avoid pills in overcoming insomnia, including a careful choice of bed companions, a snifter—not too large—of Courvoisier, and other salable methods which she herself did not frequently rely upon.

On the other hand, she had an Enarax prescription for the aftermath of an ulcer attack, and now she took one of these little pills which, because of their infrequent use, knocked her out until late into the next morning. However sound her sleep had been, she was still conscious of dreams, curious dreams that left her with a memory of sensuous moments that ended in terror.

Damn it! she thought as she showered

with a spray as cold and sharp as she could stand it, I'll get his stupid book and read it. Why not? I have to get a copy for Uncle George anyway.

She was appalled to discover that it took a little courage even to think of leaving her apartment. Allowing for the fact that Eric Raeder was probably a nice, innocent German, where was Martin Helm himself? He could be anywhere. Even New York.

3

TO combat the muggy autumn heat and her own depression, she wore a new raw-silk pants suit whose butter-yellow color soon raised her spirits as she walked rapidly over to Fifth Avenue. Two shops were out of hardcovers but had the paperback version of *The Looking-Glass*, which was selling briskly.

She tried the third bookstore on the avenue and, as she put her hand out to the glass doors, saw the big placard announcing that mystery man Eric Raeder would be autographing copies of *The Looking-Glass* from noon to three o'clock today. She glanced at her wristwatch: 11:38. Barely enough time before the Big Mystery Man would arrive.

She hurried past little groups of Eric Raeder's giggling, whispering fans, mostly female, and a surprising number of them over fifty. Their comments made it clear that his publicity gimmick had paid off:

"I could tell by his voice on TV. Might be twenty-five but not a day more."

Don't bet on it, lady, Gregg thought. You're off by eight or ten years.

Another giggler said she knew for a fact that Eric Raeder might have been Robert Redford's twin.

"He's gotta be light-haired, with a kinky mustache. He's German, isn't he?"

Gregg smiled at these wild inaccuracies, and wondered if the author would disappoint them. Not if he gave them that funny, crooked smile, she suspected. Her friend, the middle-aged male clerk who usually waited on her, managed to squeeze out of a circle of Raeder fans and lead Gregg off to the Mayan jewelry exhibit where they could have a little privacy.

"Thought you'd like to know, Miss MacIvor, we've sold three more of your books in the last two days."

She appreciated his efforts on her behalf and said so warmly, but with a laugh at herself. "I don't think I offer Eric Raeder any competition."

"Maybe next time. These foreign authors—just a flash in the pan. I admit, though, I'm curious to see him. There's a rumor, just one of those things, that this Raeder is a neo-Nazi and all that *Doppelgänger* business is the fight within himself. You know, democracy versus fascism."

She burst into her contagious, gutsy laughter.

"Mr. Mendelsohn, my last book talked a lot about how women could see and be seen in sidewalk cafés all over Europe. But of course, I was secretly warning my readers that America must beware of Soviet or Peking strollers who may seduce poor little Ms. America."

He laughed on her signal, but she suddenly realized an appalling fact. He was half inclined to believe her. The world's sense of humor had certainly gone all to hell.

A women clerk stuck her head around the corner of the glass case and hissed, "Please, lower your voices. Our author is coming."

"That puts me in my place," Gregg remarked humorously. "Can I have two hardcovers of Mr. Raeder's book?"

"I think I can locate a couple. This Author Jamboree is for the paperback version, you know. But I'll get him to autograph them. Who is the other for?"

She was ashamed of her own pettiness as she said airily, "Don't bother. It's mainly for my uncle and he doesn't know one author from another." She moved away from the jewelry case, toward the less congested wing leading to the shop's side door. "You get me the hardcovers if you can find them, and I'll just slip out this way and avoid the mob."

"Whatever you say. If you will excuse me—"

She moved along the aisle, only half aware of the crowd's chatter in the front wing of the store. She examined the cookbooks, household hint books, the less salable novels and, for her own amusement, tried to figure out how much money she had made on kindly Mr. Mendelsohn's three sales of her latest book.

"Pardon. May I have your autograph?" It was a male voice behind her. The man must have come in through the side door. Without thinking, she waved him away. "He's over there in front of the shop, autographing books."

"*Bitte*, I have met Miss Gregg MacIvor. I would never confuse her with that fellow."

She swung around. Eric Raeder stood before her, with a mischievous gleam in his eyes that did not quite fit his innocent manner. He looked a little windblown as if he had been hurrying. He held out one of her own books, turned to the dedication page on which was printed: FOR THE DELIGHTFUL COMPANIONS WHO INSPIRED THIS BOOK. As the book was called *Brief Love Is Best*, she felt a slight, unexpected embarrassment, but managed to joke about it.

"I hope you don't believe everything you read, Mr. Raeder," and taking the heavy gold pen he offered, she signed her name with the prosaic addiction, "My best wishes always, your friend, Gregg MacIvor."

He tried to read it upside down and seemed inordinately pleased. "Friends? You mean that? It is good of you, Miss MacIvor." He took back the book, read the autograph again. Then he held out his hand.

These Europeans, she thought. One long series of handshakes. But she found his firm clasp so stimulating that she looked into his eyes, startled, her hand still in his.

"Who *are* you?"

His eyelids flickered. She thought for a few seconds that he had not understood her. His smile came belatedly, a little forced, as he freed her hand. She had a chilling notion that he was angry.

"You are joking? I met you yesterday."

She knew her behavior had been inexcusably rude. He might even think it came from her professional jealousy. She backtracked hurriedly.

"Of course, I know you, Mr. Raeder. It was only that you reminded me of someone I knew a long time ago. I'm awfully sorry. You must think . . . I'm terribly sorry."

He was angry. He did not like to be compared to someone else. Like everyone, he wanted to be unique. She could not blame him, and was enormously relieved to see Mr. Mendelsohn approaching with her two books. He greeted their meeting heartily.

"Mr. Raeder! Or should I say—Herr Raeder? I see Miss MacIvor has introduced herself to you. They're all clamoring for you up in the front of the store, but if I could just take a second to have you auto-graph one of these for Miss MacIvor. . . She's something of a celebrity herself, you know."

"I know. I have been asking her if—"

She cut in: "I'll take those now, Mr. Mendelsohn. I know how busy Mr. Raeder must be."

Mr. Mendelsohn watched her take, or snatch, the books from his hands and head for the side door. She waved back to him and called a good-bye to Eric Raeder. She saw the author immediately surrounded by advancing fans from the front of the store. Mr. Mendelsohn simply stood there, stupefied by her hurried exit.

Clutching her two copies of *The Looking-Glass*, Gregg found herself out on the sidewalk in a daze.

"Well, I didn't handle that too well," she admitted, and then started walking without the least idea of where she was going.

She had an early cocktail date with an old friend from Hollywood-TV, as he called his career, thus mockingly separating himself from the elegant if faded glory of the handful who could label themselves Movie-Hollywood; so she hurried to her hair appointment and then to the Overseas Press Club, and managed to get the author of *The Looking-Glass* out of her mind.

It wasn't too hard with Duane Colt, whose conversation, not uninteresting, was confined to complaints on his residuals, the breaks other actors had gotten and the way luck was perennially against him. Duane's agent, Sherry Silversteen, had begun with Gregg as an Off-Broadway hopeful and moved on to more likely fields, along with a huge, no-nonsense husband who was business agent for the local of a powerful labor union. Gregg and Sherry remained friends, partly because Sherry's husband had a lot of night work and, according to Sherry, would break her jaw if she spent her evenings with lone males, even clients.

It was Gregg who had introduced a capable young soap opera star named Duane Colt to Sherry as a client, and Gregg somehow felt a certain responsibility for Colt's professional future.

Duane's conversation today began with the boredom of a second banana role in a hit TV series, and the lack of females worth bedding in what he called Sun-Beach West. But once in a while a rather nice, wide-eyed boy would peer out from behind the pseudosophistication he thought necessary to maintain his image.

"They're not like you, Red," he reminded her as he signaled the waiter for his third Rob Roy while Sherry Silversteen stuck to a vodka on ice and Gregg nursed her second vermouth cassis. Duane Colt was obviously under the impression that at one time he had made it with Gregg, and after he had built on this false memory for a few years, there was no talking him out of it. "They're not like you out there on the Coast, Gregg." He clutched his new drink as if it were an oasis after forty years in the Negev.

"I'm different, I know."

Sherry grinned at her but did not interfere with her client's line. There was always the touching little notion that somewhere, far underneath, he really did care for Gregg, and no woman could despise a man for that.

"Well, you *are* different," Duane insisted, completely oblivious to the other female present. "No ties. No strings. And you're beautiful. Can't beat that combination. Red, why don't we rustle on up to your place?" He saw her smile and added, stammering in his eagerness, "It's business too. Sherry's got a brainstorm about a test for me. Got to get a connection, and you're it. Why don't you and I hop up to your place?"

"And Sherry?"

He grinned. "Oh, Sherry's a good kid. She's got a million things she can be doing."

"Yeah," said Sherry broadly.

"Besides," he went on, "I don't have much time anyway. Got to dude up for one of our sponsors and his wife."

Duane Colt had been a visitor in her apartment several times and never yet made it to her bedroom, though there was once a rather amusing tussle in her living room, during which he rolled off the too-small and slippery surface of the love seat and landed hard on the floor. But apparently the experience didn't bother him.

"Duane," Gregg said briskly, "go roll your sponsor's wife. I'm busy tonight."

"Who is he? Anybody I know? What're his credits? Nothing but Off-Broadway walk-ons, I'll bet."

Sherry sighed. "Shall I dunk this doll in

his Rob Roy? Duane, honey, you've got to be sober for that sponsor's wife. Remember? So why don't you rehearse with Gregg here?"

He raised a hand subconsciously and pinched his thick eyelashes between thumb and forefinger, a mechanical gesture taught him by his makeup man, on the theory that the more he pinched them the longer they might grow. "Gorgeous and bristly," one of the fan mags described them. He had begun by thinking the idea was revolting, but after three years it became purely a subconscious gesture. He looked at Gregg with some difficulty, his lashes seeming to have gotten in his way. She couldn't help thinking how very handsome he was. But she'd had a cat once that she liked in the same way, and for the same reasons.

He said, "I suppose this date of yours is one of your Commie writer friends."

As a matter of fact she was spending the evening alone, to make up for the work she had not gotten done last night, but she said, "One or two of my friends aren't Commies. They might even be fascist, for all I know."

"Very funny. Say, Gregg—" He leaned forward in the semidarkness and then had to rescue her drink just before it spilled. Sherry, too, looked as if there might be business on her mind, and she was waiting for her client to broach it. He lowered his voice. "Red, I've gotta know. How well do you. . ." For some reason, he lost his courage and went on: "How did you get those hollows beneath your cheekbones?"

"I suck in my cheeks."

Sherry was amused, but Gregg knew she expected him to say something else. Duane had the grace to laugh at himself. "Too bad. I thought it might give me a different image. Roles pass me by because I look too all-American boy."

"Darling," Sherry assured him, "if there is one thing you don't look like it's an all-American boy. Miss America, maybe, but—"

"Easy, girl," Gregg murmured. Even in the dark of the bar, Gregg could see his dark flush of anger or embarrassment as his agent shrugged.

"I just can't stand it when a man looks better than I do."

Duane tried to pass it off. "You really are in a stinking mood today, Steeny. All

42

right, Gregg, there's one other favor you can do me."

"This is your lucky day," the agent put in, to Gregg.

After a struggle, Duane managed to ignore that. "All you writers know each other, Red."

"All us Commies."

He pretended to appreciate her humor by a quick on-off smile. "Yes. Well. Somewhere in your travels you must've come across the fellow who wrote that smash book about Jekyll and Hyde. Raeder, his name is."

She must be hexed by the fellow. It was impossible to escape Eric Raeder, even here where the subject of most of Duane's conversations was Duane Colt.

"You could have seen him in person today, if you're collecting autographs. He was up Fifth Avenue."

"No, no. *Variety* says they're talking terms on the movie rights. I've got to have some inside clout. Raeder could help me. Just a test for the lead. The Jekyll type. They've got the idea of playing it with two actors. I want that test. Afterward—" He left unsaid the obvious, starlit result.

She could only stare at him, avoiding Sherry Silversteen's eyes, and recognizing that there were some put-downs involving the ego which even she could not utter.

"I don't see how I can help you, Duane. I'm not likely to see him again."

"Gregg," Sherry put in, trying to play it light, "it might help. Just a word from you, if you know him."

Duane said quickly, "If you just give me this break, I'll never forget you, Red." He caught at her hands. She thought he would squeeze them dry in his excitement, and remembering her own early ambitions as well as those magic days when she believed Martin Helm loved her, she became aware of a genuine sympathy building up in her.

"Maybe my publisher could help you. I can call him. He knows where Raeder is staying."

"Look, Red, you're terrific! I always knew I could count on you. But this publisher—well, why should Raeder pay any attention? He isn't even contracted to your publisher. No, Gregg, you're the one. It isn't much I'm asking. Just for you to put in a word with this guy."

He saw her features harden and rushed

on: "God! You don't know. You never wanted anything so bad in your life. Whatever you want, you just get. You're not human."

She felt for him and actually understood his despair. The fact that it was purely selfish and based upon what might be an overview of his own talents did not make it any less painful. She sipped her drink, while her green eyes studied Duane Colt over the edge of her glass. He became uneasy under that stare and said defiantly, "I've got as much right to test for it as Redford or Pacino or Newman."

Sherry Silversteen added, "That's true enough, Gregg."

"I know. Duane, I really do know. Where can I reach you late tonight?" As he sat forward, perking up, she went on with a smile, "By phone." And to Sherry, "I'll do what I can. If I can't reach Duane tonight, maybe I can try your number."

"I'll be home all evening. Or better yet —But you have a date tonight, you said."

"Nothing I couldn't break. Go to dinner with me, and I'll see if I can't get hold of Raeder. You can take over from there."

Gregg knew they would spend the

45

evening talking about men, but what other subject was quite so engrossing? Meanwhile, Duane Colt convinced himself that the role, and with it international fame, were his. He began to make plans. "Do you realize what this means for me, Red? Maybe a series. Along about the second, maybe third, season, forty thousand per. Maybe fifty thou . . . Ma would flip. She loves getting gussied up and telling everybody in the supermarket who her son is."

Gregg tried to think up new ways of saying, "Right!" "No doubt" and "How true!" But in spite of all her efforts not to cut him short, she finally had to interrupt his fantasy world. "Duane, you really should be on your way. You've got to look your best for that sponsor's wife."

"My God! Is it that late? Look, I'm going to leave you wonderful girls but only because duty calls. Promise to talk about me when I'm gone." He kissed each of them and beat a retreat, passing under the rainbow lights behind the bar so that a pair of middle-aged females sitting there got a good look at his profile and buzzed between themselves, arguing over his identity.

Gregg and Sherry laughed with a

common understanding. The agent remarked wryly, "I see he's left me with the check, as usual. But he's really kind of pathetic. Anybody is, with all that ambition and no talent."

Gregg shivered. "Sherry, your truths are depressing. I hope he surprises us both and hits it big. Let's get out of here and find someplace to eat. What do you feel like?"

"To tell the truth, I feel like one order of Eric Raeder. Served up any way he comes."

Sherry threw some bills down, made a few squiggles in her little Mark Cross notebook and they went out into the early evening crowd to scramble for a taxi.

While Sherry looked up the Berkeley Lane Hotel number in the phone book at the midtown restaurant, Gregg held the phone, mentally composing an apology to Raeder for her peculiar manners in the bookstore.

The subject of Eric Raeder led her, as always, to the dangerous subject of Martin Helm. While Sherry muttered, "Lane . . . Lane . . . Berkeley Lane, where are you?" Gregg thought of the woman who had given Martin Helm his alibi long ago for the New York murder. She couldn't help being curious about what Alys Lane could tell her about Helm.

The agent shook her out of these unpleasant memories. "Here we are. Berkeley Lane." She read off the number of the big midtown hotel and Gregg dialed. After she gave Raeder's name to the Berkeley Lane operator and waited for someone to answer in his room, she was aware of an excitement, a tension that had been building since their meeting in Oliver Sill's office. First of all, she must excuse herself for her rude attitude, and then what would she say?

"I'd better ask to see him tomorrow," she suggested aloud.

"Sunday?"

"Why not? Maybe he'll meet me for breakfast somewhere, or lunch."

The operator at the Berkeley Lane cut in. "The party doesn't answer. Is there a message?"

"No!" She was startled at her own sharp denial. But she did not want to leave her number. Her phone had always been unlisted, and in the back of her mind she knew the reason was because she was afraid of being tracked down by Martin Helm.

Even her name, Mary Gregg MacIvry, had been altered to Gregg MacIvor. Only Oliver Sills, of all her New York friends and associates, knew that she was Mary G. MacIvry of Chicago. The past wouldn't let go.

"I'll call back," she told the operator at Eric Raeder's hotel.

Sherry said, "Well, that does it for now. Can we try later?"

"Why not?" She wondered where he was tonight, if he was with a woman, and what type of woman it was that Eric Raeder preferred. Were his preferences anything like those of his look-alike, Martin Helm?

4

BY eleven that night even Sherry Silversteen agreed there was no use in pursuing Eric Raeder until tomorrow. Gregg was enormously relieved that he hadn't answered her call to the hotel. All evening she had rehearsed her conversation with him and still felt all the humiliation of asking a favor only hours after she had practically insulted him. If only there could be an opening, an excuse to approach him, something that would save face for her.

Gregg and Sherry were picked up at the restaurant by Mike Silversteen who looked the women over carefully, wanted to know what "characters" they had met during the evening.

"You with Sharon the whole time?" he asked Gregg as they drove home.

"The whole time."

"Met a lot of your boyfriends, I suppose." Even he must have thought this a bit blunt, so he added the salve, "You always were popular, Gregg."

Although Sherry laughed and Gregg pretended to, Mike Silversteen's jealousy and possessiveness did not seem as romantic to Gregg as they apparently were to Mrs. Silversteen.

"My jealous lover!" Sherry teased, hugging Mike's huge shoulders. "Don't you adore a jealous lover?"

Gregg said lightly, "If there's one thing I don't need, it's a jealous lover. Oh, there's my corner. Thanks, Mike. Just let me off here."

She tapped Mike on the shoulder, waved to Sherry and promised, "I'll contact you tomorrow about the Raeder thing."

The car started off but not before Gregg heard, and was amused by, Mike Silversteen's comment, "Dame's too fickle to give a guy time for jealousy."

She laughed to herself, but all the same she had told the Silversteens the truth when she indicated she wouldn't put up with pathological jealousy. She had a fierce, passionate belief in the private ownership of her own brain and her own body. No man had ever held automatic rights to any part of her since the days of Martin Helm.

She took her usual long-legged strides along the street and into the house she shared with an interior decorator and an actor and his wife. As she unlocked the door, she heard her telephone ringing. There was no reason to think it was an important call, but she rushed into her living room, reaching the green phone at exactly the instant the ringing stopped.

"Damn!"

The tyranny of inanimate objects never failed to surprise her. You couldn't fight them. Or A. T. & T.

Gregg turned on the desk lamp, closed the blinds and opened her purse to put away her key ring. Her fingers closed around a pen far thicker and heavier than her own. Puzzled, she pulled out the gold pen and belatedly recognized it. A German make, it was the pen she had taken from Eric Raeder to scrawl her dedication in the book he had placed before her, and she had never given it back to him.

Her mood suddenly lightened. This expensive pen gave her a perfect excuse to call on Eric Raeder tomorrow, without completely losing face. She could have kissed the pen.

Thinking about him, she asked herself just what her interest was in the German writer. Was she anticipating a relationship with Raeder—a sincere, even serious relationship totally unlike the disastrous liaison she'd had with Martin Helm? Was she trying to undo the past? A terrible thought. Terrible because it admitted that the influence of Martin Helm had dominated her life for over ten years. Terrible for Eric Raeder because it indicated that he was the mere looking-glass image of the man she had loved for all that time.

Stimulated by the very excitement of her thoughts, the torn emotions—had she actually loved Martin Helm so much that after eleven years he influenced her interest in a complete stranger?—she got through her day's stint of writing and was satisfied. While she lay soaking lazily in her Norell-scented bath, she knew that her fear of Martin Helm had its foundation in her attraction to him. Always in the back of her mind was the frightening thought that she might love him enough to forgive his terrible crimes. And now she had met an

53

innocent man in whom she found Martin Helm's warm, sensuous, positive qualities without the monstrous evil that blackened Martin Helm. Where would it all lead her?

Afterward, she could not recall any of her dreams, though there was seldom a night when she did not dream. Was it simply that she had been so content on this night, so sure of a future involvement with Eric Raeder that she could sleep without any problems, any of the hunger for that first, passionate love she had known at the age of eighteen?

She was awakened Sunday morning by Duane Colt, one of the few people who had her phone number. She fumbled for the phone beside her bed and listened while she opened one eye and tried to read the numbers on the digital clock beside her bed.

"No, Duane, I didn't reach him. Of course, I tried when I got home," she lied, and agreed to call him the minute she contacted Eric Raeder. She heard his wildly grateful thanks, and, promising again to do her best, she found herself hoping she might actually work up Raeder's enthusiasm for the young actor.

Shortly before noon she walked into the Berkeley Lane Hotel and discovered in the elegant lobby terrace all the pleasant, nostalgic accoutrements of a Viennese coffeehouse. The highly reputed Sunday brunch had attracted a crowd. Gregg heard the piano and violin segue from Lehár to Romberg. This European atmosphere was the one in which Gregg was happiest, and, if pressed, she might have admitted that beneath all the modern sheen, the romantic soul of eighteen-year-old Mary Gregg MacIvry lived on.

Flashing her best smile, she asked at the desk if Mr. Raeder had come down yet, citing an imaginary lunch date with him. The clerk and the cashier checked with each other. The cashier knew the author by sight, and told Gregg, "I changed some foreign traveller's checks for Mr. Raeder when he was going out this morning. He came back an hour or so ago, so he's bound to be along any minute. Or would you like his suite number?"

Gregg decided against it. Raeder might be old-fashioned and she didn't want to ruin her chances and, with them, Duane Colt's wild hopes.

She crossed the lobby and went up the steps to the Terrace Room. The headwaiter seated her at a table for two not far from the pianist and the strolling violinist. She faced the lobby, but so many people were coming and going that she wasn't sure she'd be able to spot Eric Raeder when he came down.

She ordered a martini with a twist and sipped it, wondering whether Eric Raeder had found female companionship in New York. In fact, she mused as she played with the lemon twist, was he married perhaps? Engaged? It was surprising to think how little she knew about him when she considered how often he'd been interviewed lately. Of course, there was all the secrecy, the publicity gimmick. Or was it only publicity?

Some lilting notes from *The Count of Luxembourg* caught her in their familiar golden web. She remembered her first trip to Europe after she'd broken off her marriage plans. Every time she had turned around on that romantic French liner, the orchestra played one of the tunes she had always associated with Helm: "If Ever I

Would Leave You" or "As Long as He Needs Me"—

Once she landed in Le Havre she had run from country to country, trying to escape those songs, remembering with anguish how she and Martin Helm had danced to their tunes. And finally she came to Vienna where it seemed that no one had ever heard of *Camelot* or *Oliver*! She was taken to the Volksoper by a very nice man she had met on shipboard, and she saw *The Merry Widow* and *Countess Maritza* in German and banished all painful, sad songs. She blessed Franz Lehár for the pleasure and harmony of his music and the uncomplicated plots. No heartbreak there.

The Terrace Room was getting crowded. She saw the headwaiter pass and glance her way. She signaled, and when the waitress came, she ordered the elaborate shrimp salad, croissants and coffee. She was not hungry and would merely pick at the salad, but it gave her something to do, and she wanted to keep her table as long as possible.

Before her lunch came, she felt something brush the back of her hair and a man's hand touched the nape of her neck. She started. Eric Raeder took a lot for granted! Or was he used to strange women coming after him? She looked over her shoulder and then saw who it was.

"Oh, my God! You!"

Duane Colt looked hurt, but he managed to smile.

"Just thought I'd make it easier for you. He can sort of get a good look at me, and see if I've got what the part needs."

She felt so guilty at her previous greeting that she almost gushed an invitation. "You're right. Come and sit down. If he refuses to help, we'll try whatever studio has the rights."

"The *Hollywood Reporter* says it's between Universal and Paramount. The top bid hasn't come in yet. Should I pull up a chair? What do you think? I promise to do what you tell me."

It was too late to tell him not to stay. She signaled the headwaiter again. He came over and started to draw out the chair opposite Gregg, then looked a little surprised when Gregg explained that the chair was being held for someone else.

Gregg buttered another section of the croissant, raised it to her lips then saw Eric Raeder stepping down into the lobby from

58

the cashier's cage. She put down the croissant, ran a hand quickly over her hair and had half risen in her chair when she saw that he was not alone.

The woman with Eric Raeder was tall, elegant, blond and beautiful. Wouldn't you know it? Gregg thought. They seemed to be having an animated conversation. They must be very close. Was she his wife?

Somewhat to her own surprise, they headed directly toward Gregg. Gregg pretended to see them for the first time and gave the writer a flip little wave. Eric spoke first and, fortunately for Gregg's pride, he seemed happy to see her.

"Ah! Here you are, Miss Mac—that name!"

"Gregg. Please. Won't you join me . . . us?"

"Ursula, this is my favorite author, Gregg Mac—MacIvor. I have her autograph. Gregg, I present my sister-in-law, Ursula Raeder."

Gregg hoped she did not reveal the exact reason for her pleasure at this relationship. During the last ten years, either by design or chance, she had only been involved with men she could dominate. She could not imagine a woman dominating the German author. His eyes might laugh but his mouth, like his handclasp, was hard. She suspected it could be ruthless in certain situations.

Mrs. Raeder found Gregg an interesting study, and Gregg returned the doubtful compliment. As for Eric Raeder, like most males, he clearly enjoyed the women's rivalry. Gregg unbuckled her handbag, took out his heavy gold pen and offered it to him.

"I'm so sorry. You must have missed your pen. I'm afraid I walked off with it yesterday."

He said, "I know. I knew when you took it."

"Then why didn't you stop me?" Gregg glanced at Ursula Raeder whose attention was diverted to the young actor.

Raeder took Gregg's arm. "Because it seemed the easiest way to see you again."

She glanced at his sister-in-law. He said quietly, "It will be difficult to separate Ursula from your friend. She's a great admirer of the all-American boy."

Gregg thought this was a trifle frank considering he scarcely knew Gregg, bu she could see that it was true, all the same. Duane Colt had turned his charm on the impressively beautiful Ursula Raeder, who murmured in a seductive accent that Gregg envied, "I would have known you anywhere, Mr. Colt. I adore you in your television series. But you will forgive me if I think of you as the hero. Not your friend, the other star."

"Oh, he's a good fellow," Duane tossed off generously, beaming at these magic words. "Not too versatile, but, well, a guy can't be everything."

Seeing that Ursula and Duane were engrossed in conversation, Eric Raeder asked Gregg, "Is he an intimate friend of yours, this boy?"

There was a little edge to the word *boy*. Gregg smiled. "A friend, let's say. How do you like New York, Mr. Raeder?"

"Better than I had expected." In spite of the light, airy response she found his clipped Germanic accent and his gaze disturbing. From that fixed gaze she could not doubt that he was telling her more than the words suggested. She did not want to rush into anything. On the other hand, in her seesaw fashion, she was again satisfied that he was totally different from Martin Helm. There was never anything light or teasing about Helm. He had been smooth in his advances and an absolute 1920s Valentino in his seduction. Unlike the twenties hero he had lacked a sense of humor. That was the essential difference, she thought, between this man and Martin Helm. Eric Raeder didn't quite possess Helm's extreme good looks; there were imperfections other than his scars, but there could be no denying that he was a very attractive man.

They had been looking at each other without saying anything, as if some sort of communion existed between them. It was strange. She wanted to cling to the almost sensuous feeling between them, but the mood was broken by Ursula Raeder who clapped her hands and cried, "Eric! Do you not see it? But it is so plain. Herr Colt, turn the profile to my brother-in-law. Now, the full face. My dear Eric, the young man *is* your Hans Pogge."

Gregg was puzzled, then realized too late that Ursula Raeder had done what she herself promised and failed to do. She had suggested Duane Colt as the hero of Eric Raeder's book.

Eric Raeder explained to Gregg unnecessarily, "Pogge is the protagonist of my novel. The positive force."

Somewhat late, Gregg put in her support to Ursula's suggestion. "Mr. Colt certainly has the innocent look of your character. If by positive, you mean innocent. And he is an experienced actor. He has been high in the popularity ratings for several years."

The author was amused, even interested in the suggestion, but as he watched Gregg's defense of Duane Colt, he appeared far less enthusiastic. A notion occurred to her that he was jealous of Duane, but she dismissed the idea quickly. In the first place, he hardly knew her, and in the second, he cut off her praise of the actor to remind them all, "It is the company buying the book that will make decisions. Thank God, it is not my problem."

Duane Colt reminded him eagerly, "But a word from you might get me a test."

The author, however, barely nodded. "What do you recommend on the menu?" he asked Gregg.

She said the salads were very good, but

he chose the wiener schnitzel, complete with dumplings, and a slice of Black Forest cake for desert.

Gregg could not help asking, "How do you stay so thin? I'd gain ten pounds on half that menu."

"Ten pounds would be very good on you," he assured her.

"How long are you staying in New York? Do you like it here? Or did I ask you that? I suppose everyone does."

"How long? I fly to Vienna on Wednesday. I do not think I liked New York much before. This time I do." So he had been here on other occasions. How long ago? she wondered.

"You Europeans are more direct than you are credited with being."

"It is the quickest way. All the words winding, winding . . . a waste of time. Like taking what you call a detour. Not for me. Do you like me?"

She blinked, tried to joke her way out of any flat commitment even to this ingenuous question. She countered lightly, "Why not?" and added with an abruptness that surprised herself, "When did you first see New York?"

He raised his eyes from her hands, which had intrigued him, and she found his direct gaze disconcerting, as if he would read her soul. Was it her imagination, or did it seem to her suddenly that Martin Helm was facing her across a table in his sensuous, upsetting way? Eric Raeder must be very much aware of his own attraction. Certainly Martin Helm had been aware, and had used his weapons constantly.

"Yes," Raeder said, "I first saw New York long ago, when you were very young. But we are talking about a dull fellow. Tell me about the exciting Miss Gregg."

The way he had turned off her curiosity might be flattering, but she recognized that he was as secretive with her as he was before his public.

Smilingly, she shook her head. He went right on. "You are not married. You live alone. You are from Chicago which is in Illinois. And you are twenty-eight years old."

"Twenty-nine. I have all my own teeth, which contain four fillings. I like the theater, especially old-fashioned things with happy endings."

"Yes. Me too. Like that music they are playing now."

They were playing selections from *Camelot*. How odd! It was the first time in over ten years that hearing it had not depressed her. As a matter of fact, she hadn't even noticed it.

"What are you doing Monday night?"

"I have a date," she said automatically.

"Break it?"

Her eyebrows lifted. She said nothing and he shrugged. "I am sorry. But it is the only time to see you, and we must see each other again. You know it."

She gave in but then rose. "I must go now. I've returned your pen and I have several things to do today."

"I know. Wash your hair. American women always wash the hair when one particularly wishes to see them. I'll call for you on Monday. Eight-thirty. What is your address?"

"No! I'll meet you. Where do you want to go?"

He watched her trying to gather up her handbag and napkin. He rescued the napkin as it fell, and stood up, offering it to her with a flourish.

"You are a very mysterious young lady. What are you hiding? I know. A deadly past. You are a famous ax murderess. You have killed seven lovers because they ask too many questions." She laughed edgily as he went on. "But I will hunt you down and put you in a book. How would you like that?"

"Not at all. Why don't I meet you at a little bistro on Fifty-first Street? Oliver Sills and I eat there often. It is called the Blue Pheasant."

He saw that she was actually leaving and started around the table to join her. "I'll get you a taxi."

Seeing the commotion, Duane Colt scrambled to his feet, apologizing to the beauteous Mrs. Raeder. Hoping to save the author any trouble, he offered, "You needn't bother. I'll take Gregg home."

Gregg could see that, contrary to Duane's hopes, this did not endear him to Eric Raeder. "Then you know where Miss Gregg lives?"

"Well, of course, I do. Been there dozens of times."

"Plainly, you have the advantage of me," Raeder said in unmistakably frigid tones.

He took Gregg's hand. "Until Monday. Eight-thirty."

"At the Blue Pheasant," Gregg added and gave him a warming smile to thaw him out. Since Duane had probably ruined his own chances by his gallantry, she tried to help him out by refusing his escort and insisting that he finish his conversation with Ursula Raeder, who patted the chair beside her and invited him to remain. Gregg did not know if she had mollified Eric Raeder, but he was still watching her when she had crossed the lobby and looked back before going out into the muggy September heat.

By the time she reached home she wanted nothing so much as a shower and a few restful minutes alone. She undressed, snapped on the little radio in her dressing room and, while a symphony orchestra played Mozart, she let her body be pelted by the cool, sharp spray of the shower. She turned off the shower and began to towel herself dry just as the music was interrupted by the hourly news.

As usual, there was trouble abroad and in Washington, but she was struck by a local tragedy.

". . . fell four stories to her death. The

window-washing cloth and a plastic spray bottle were found beside her. The long, bay windows of her brownstone apartment were in the process of being washed. A neighbor reported that Alice Lane often washed her own windows . . ."

Alice Lane? Or *Alys* Lane? Could it be the woman who had given Martin Helm his alibi long ago? A common enough name, except for the unforgettable spelling. Gregg drew the terry-cloth robe around her and listened with growing fear.

". . . Police are investigating witnesses' reports that loud voices were overheard in the apartment earlier in the day . . . This concludes the news as of this hour, and now, back to the all-Mozart concert by the Concertgebouw Orchestra of Amsterdam . . ."

5

DURING the next thirty hours Gregg went out only once, to a gourmet shop on Third Avenue where she loaded up a shopping bag with everything that would keep. She hurried home, looking all around her, suspecting every passerby until she reached her tree-lined street. There she was sure a bearded stranger followed her to the front steps, and when she got inside and locked the street door, she sighed in relief.

She couldn't shake the uneasiness that she felt, even though she knew nothing for certain that would connect the woman in the news bulletin with the Alys Lane of years ago.

She tried to write, but she had the living room television set on most of the time and also an FM radio to catch any information the television might fail to give out. She heard nothing more about the woman's fall from the windowsill after a brief follow-up to the first report. She had apparently been alone at the time of her accident. The cleaning rag was found beside her body, and the long, bay windows were partially washed. Everything fitted.

"Maybe it *was* an accident," Gregg told herself several times. "People do wash windows. And they occasionally fall out of them. What I want to know is whether or not this is *the* Alys Lane."

But the news bulletins contained only the further remarks of a Mrs. Zelasky, Miss Lane's landlady in the building on Eighty-fifth Street.

"She always paid her rent in cash. Either she turned her annuity into cash the minute she got it, or it came to her in cash. She didn't work at any job. She didn't have visitors, except one gentleman. She told me he was a former boss. Sometimes he wouldn't come around for months. Then he'd be back."

A description followed: forty to fifty, graying mustache. Miss Lane had said the gentleman was Finnish. The landlady never got too good a look at him. He visited in the evenings and didn't stay long . . . "Just friends," Miss Lane had told her landlady.

All the same, the "accident" fell into the

same pattern as the others maneuvered by Martin Helm. And the description might easily be that of Helm.

But why had he waited so many years to kill his former protector? And where was he now, at this minute? Outside in the street somewhere, watching, waiting for Mary Gregg MacIvry? But if he didn't know her whereabouts and she went to the police, she would at once announce to the world her connection with his other victims, and he was bound to find out. No matter how hush-hush the police might keep her name, there would always be some wiseacre reporter who would slap her name, and probably her picture, all over the newspapers.

After that? She looked out through the slats of the blind. Martin Helm could hardly depend upon killing her in a "fall" from one of her second-story windows. But there would be some other way. He had always managed in the past.

During these hours, she found her thoughts of Helm and of Eric Raeder hopelessly woven together. She loathed Martin Helm but was drawn by the irresistible sensuous appeal of Eric Raeder. If they were the same man—Impossible! She tried to recall some physical detail that one of the men possessed to set him apart from the other. There must be some major difference, aside from the matter of age.

She called Oliver Sills on Monday and asked him, "Have you given out my phone number to anyone lately?"

Oliver was understandably surprised. "No one. You and your secrecy! You're as bad as that Raeder chap. I'm fond of you, Gregg, old girl, but no one is beating down my doors to get at your phone number."

Her laugh was a bit hollow. "Thanks a whole heap. You're sure no one has been prowling around asking questions?"

"Not a one. Look here, Gregg. You have nothing to hide that I know of. Don't you think you'd better calm down and take it easy?"

"Never mind that. I haven't killed anybody, if that's what you mean. But remember, I knew someone once who turned out to be—well, he wasn't the man I thought he was."

"Gregg, look here. . ."

"Just tell me if anyone has been around inquiring about how to get hold of me."

His sigh was audible over the phone. "Eric Raeder wanted to know. I'd like to get you two together sometime. You're both nice people."

Gregg hardly heard this. "How long have you known Raeder? Or known of him?"

"Met him Friday, as you know. Before that? I'd say I never heard of him until a little over a year ago when his book came out. He had a brother who died about three years ago. There is a sister-in-law. A dazzler, they say."

"I've seen her, and she is," Gregg remarked dryly. An idea surfaced. "You've never seen a picture of this dead brother, have you?"

"Good Lord, no! Why would I?"

"I'd give anything to see a picture of him. Snapshot. Whatever. You don't know how he died?"

Oliver Sills was completely confused. "What the devil is going on? Is all this for some new book of yours? If so, I think we should discuss it before you plunge into it too deeply. We've been doing very well with your feminist angle. I don't know if you should sacrifice that for a—what will it be? A suspense novel? Foreign intrigue? Gothic?"

"All of them," she lied, since this seemed to be the only way out of the mess. "You'll do what you can, won't you? If you have any way of finding out what Raeder's brother looked like or how he died, it's awfully important."

"I can see that it is. Damned if I know why. Let's get together in the next few days and you can tell me your thoughts on this new idea of yours."

Nervously, she began to make excuses, as she was thinking about leaving town on another trip. She had convinced herself that the Lane woman was murdered, and if so, all signs pointed to Martin Helm. There was always a chance that Helm might cross her path, or vice versa, if she remained in New York, where she believed he had been as recently as early Sunday morning. The old, familiar method, apparently foolproof, had been used again. And the "Finnish" friend? He fitted an older image of Helm.

Several times during those nerve-racking Monday hours, she remembered that she had agreed to meet Eric Raeder that night at the Blue Pheasant. Well, it was out of the question now. She sat at her table writing for most of the day, and, oddly enough, the chapter she completed read adequately when she reviewed it at dusk. There were even a few sparkles, a certain lightness that was the secret of her modest fame.

Every twenty minutes or so she looked out of the window, keeping behind the old-fashioned scrim curtains. There were few people outside. Once she suspected something sinister from a man in a black turtle-neck sweater and slacks, and a golf cap that seemed ludicrous on a man with such a powerful build, but he turned casually toward her and it was clear he looked nothing like Martin Helm.

Satisfying herself that no one who could be mistaken for Helm had passed along her street, Gregg left her work. She went into the kitchen, produced a glass ice bucket and some tongs and carried them to her little dry bar in the living room. When she had made herself a tall gin and tonic, she settled back to take it easy. It was past the time of her date and she wondered vaguely what Eric Raeder had done when she did not show up, or—if he actually was Martin

76

Helm, would he guess why she was avoiding him now?

Peering thoughtfully into the tall glass, trying to spear the holes in the ice cubes until they were all strung together on her stirrer, she wondered what to do. The only answer would be to leave New York for a few months and see to it that Martin Helm had no idea when and where she went. Dreamily, over her second gin and tonic, she tried to decide where she would go this time. It seemed preposterous that Martin Helm could follow her; it would take intimate knowledge of her life to do that.

A trash can on the top back step rattled as if scuffed by a hard shoe sole. Gregg sat up straight, listened. She heard a scuffling noise, then silence. She got out of her chair, moved quietly toward her bedroom where she could catch a view of the steps below. She knew that even if someone were on the back steps, it would be next to impossible for that person to even reach her second-floor apartment, no less break in. And all of her windows were either barred or locked, but she couldn't shake off the nervous feeling. Then she saw beside the trash can a boy of about sixteen or seventeen was curled up in a fetal position. Probably trying to sleep off a few too many beers—or worse, she thought, and stepped away from the window.

Her movement had disturbed the sleeper. He untangled himself, staring wildly at the curtained window, and before she could reassure him, he scrambled down the steps and shot off into the alley beyond the radius of the single globe that lighted that back steps. Night had fallen while she fussed about the boy and her trash can, and as he ran up the alley she lost sight of him.

She went into the kitchen, made iced tea and thought about arranging a plate of cold cuts and fresh tomato slices. She was just carrying a tomato and a knife to the sink in the kitchen when the front doorbell rang. By the time she carefully set everything down, the bell had rung again.

Trying to decide which of her friends could be calling at nine-thirty, she wondered also how he, or she, had gotten this far inside the building; probably the tenant on the first floor had let him in. She finally reached the door and looked through the little peephole that would give her a look at her uninvited guest. Apparently the caller had decided to do the same thing, and she found herself staring through the hole at a large, dark eye.

Martin Helm's?

She moved backward, away from the door, holding her breath and wondering if he might have heard her footsteps approaching. He rang once more, then gave up and went down the stairs to the street door. Gregg rushed to the window and squinted out between the slats of the blind.

He stood under the streetlight looking up and down the street as if lost, or perhaps trying to decide if he had the right address. He was clearly unsure of himself, not at all the smooth, all-knowing Martin Helm. In fact, his quick, lithe movements were also unlike Helm's. And he could not be much over thirty.

Eric Raeder had come to see why she had stood him up. She hesitated, studying him. He looked disappointed and obviously puzzled. If he had been Martin Helm and knew where she lived, he would probably have tried to kill her before this. He wouldn't come walking up the street for all the neighbors to see him, nor would he stand in front of the house, a visible target for any spying neighbor.

He was not Martin Helm. He was an innocent European name Eric Raeder.

She watched him. He had a cab parked and waiting fifty feet or so down the street. Martin Helm would never have added this extra witness against him. Raeder raised his head, studying the front of Gregg's building. He must have noticed the light behind the blinds and known that she was there, even if he hadn't seen her through the peephole. After a minute or two he shrugged and gave a sign to the cab which backed up to meet him.

On an impulse she opened the slats of the venetian blind and rapped sharply on the window.

The driver said something to Raeder as he was getting into the cab. He turned, looked up and saw her. She waved to him. There was a brief conversation between him and the driver, then he got back out of the cab and started up the front steps of her building. He had to wait while she pressed the button that opened the street door. She wondered again how he had reached her door the first time and asked him abruptly as he came up the stairs, "How did you get in before?"

He grinned, apparently not the least bit surprised at this odd greeting. "A very kind gentleman on the third floor. He asked me if I knew him. Should I?"

"Sh!" When he reached her door she whispered, "He is a TV actor. Did he know you?"

"I hope not. My sister-in-law insists there is only one actor for my poor hero, Hans Pogge. That is your friend Doone Colt."

"*Duane*. Come in."

He obeyed her, at the same time asking blandly, "Do you always receive guests in this odd way? Not that I object. Please understand. I only ask out of curiosity."

She looked behind him, as if she still expected to see a ghost of Martin Helm, his *Doppelgänger*, in the shadows somewhere. He took all this in stride, walked into her living room and glanced around like a prospective tenant.

"You live here? Now, I will always picture you in these rooms."

To her surprise and amusement, he went through the hall to her bedroom, looked in, giving it a nod of approval, then stuck his head into the triangular kitchen which was the size of a small closet. She caught his wide-eyed disbelief as he tried to praise it politely.

"What we call . . . er . . . *gemütlich*. You know. Cozy."

"All of that," she agreed. They caught each other's eyes and both laughed. It was pleasant to share a sense of humor, a happiness not always possible between Gregg and her previous male friends. Often, like the ambitious young Duane Colt, they were too serious to appreciate an absurdity.

He looked into her bedroom with its big double bed whose mattress, during the past five years, she and a few very select guests considered the most comfortable in New York. He remarked, "Ah, another *gemüt*—"

She cut him off with the tart, "Not necessarily."

He surprised and pleased her by not pressing the matter. He became all business, the efficient businessman. "Now. We are old friends. We go to dinner and maybe then you will stop being afraid of me."

Affronted by the truth, she reminded him, "There are other reasons for breaking a date."

"A headache?" he teased her with bland innocence.

"Well—yes."

"Come out with me. I will cure your headache."

"You are awfully sure about your powers of persuasion."

His eyebrows expressed more sarcasm than his flat assertion.

"I am sure I can persuade your headache to go away. Don't waste time. Get ready. I'll be here reading . . . let me see"—he read the top page of her completed chapter —"that you expect women to enjoy cruises again because there are more men. Is this true?"

"Sometimes."

"More males now on cruises. It does not intrigue me. You mean you sell this kind of thing?"

"It is not supposed to appeal to you. It's aimed at women," she told him as she walked into her bedroom to change her clothes.

Suddenly, she wanted to go out with

him. She was tired of feeling imprisoned—
by fear—in this little apartment. And she
could not deny the attraction she felt for
him.

The cabdriver outside honked insist-
ently, as a reminder, as she selected a cool,
green dress and hoop earrings that glittered
through the thick auburn waves of her hair.
She made up carefully but quickly and in
an understated way, and was rewarded by
the excitement in Eric's eyes as he looked
her over when she emerged.

He opened the door, made a sweeping
gesture and watched her walk out onto the
stair landing. The cabdriver honked again.
Without quite knowing why, Gregg and
Eric Raeder found themselves laughing
together as if on cue. They went downstairs, still laughing.

On their way to an Italian restaurant
which the cabdriver guaranteed would
serve fresh-made spaghetti and ravioli at
midnight, Gregg asked her companion,
"How did you get my address? Oliver, I
suppose. He told me he wouldn't ever give
it out, but you can't trust anybody
anymore."

"You may still trust the human male. He gave me nothing."

"Then how—?"

"His receptionist. A young woman named Bergstrom." He grinned, watching her with his head cocked on one side. "She was surprisingly easy to seduce."

"Ah!"

"With words."

"More and more dangerous. I must watch myself."

"If it makes you happy. But I think you are a person who might enjoy a little danger."

"What do you mean?"

"Only to warn you that I may try to seduce you. With words."

He watched her widening smile. It was nice to know someone with whom she could tease and talk and flirt, a man who was not always serious and who knew when to laugh. She had been a fool to suspect him because of a fancied resemblance. If only she could erase the memories.

The cabdriver proved to be right. Pasta at Vario's was something special and, washed down with a dark Burgundy, made a wonderful meal.

"I still think we could have had Moselle wine, my dear Gregg. I was born in Koblenz, you see, where we had the good Rhine wines in our blood. Do you know Koblenz at all?"

"Only from when I was a child, in the early fifties. It was so devastated! I think I remember it more than the other places because the manager of our hotel was kind. Very warm and wonderful."

"My brother—he was five years older than I—used to tell me how it was before the war. He was not like me. He laughed and joked a lot and, always, the days before the war sounded very pleasant. You would have liked Rolfe."

She stared at him. For a few seconds she thought this was a part of his dry humor. She had already begun a disclaimer, almost a laugh, before she realized he was deadly serious.

"And I suppose you were the sober, substantial citizen," she went on hurriedly, "but you have a marvelous sense of humor. It must have been a happy family in spite of the bad times."

He shrugged. "There were good and bad times. Rolfe was the popular fellow. I envied him his easy ways, but I couldn't be like him, so I became ambitious. I tried to be as different as possible. Then I was caught in an accident. A plane crashed on takeoff." He rubbed his forehead where the scar cut parallel to his hairline. He laughed abruptly. "All this time, Rolfe was a great success. A comedy actor in the new film industry in Berlin. I was laid out for a time—"

"Laid up."

"Yes. All that year I thought when I recovered I would change. Be like Rolfe. Carefree. Laugh a great deal. But when I was well, I was my old stuffy self again, until Rolfe died. That was three years ago."

She resented the dead, jolly brother without even knowing him. "I am sure you are every bit as charming as your marvelous brother. Why you think you're stuffy is beyond me."

He reached across the table and took her hand.

"Thank you. Do men often tell you that you are very understanding?"

She tried to make a joke of it. "Rarely, if ever. But I like it." Seeing that his good spirits were returning, she reminded him,

"And now, thanks to your own career, you are more famous—more popular—than your marvelous brother ever was."

His smile was lopsided and a bit rueful. "Even that I owe to Rolfe."

"Now you are really joking. How could your success as a writer be due to your brother?"

He took her hand, twining his fingers around hers in a hard grip. "You see, I used Rolfe as my *Doppelgänger*."

"Why not?" she asked calmly, playing down the obvious importance he attached to the announcement. An idea occured to her, a way in which she might see a photograph of that overwhelming fellow, Rolfe Raeder. "I still say you were lucky to have a brother. I was an only child and, being a typical redhead, I was always in a fight with someone or other. I used to wish I could whip out one of those little wallet photos of me and my big brother—to scare off the opposition."

That made him laugh, but there was a tender note in his voice. "I wish I had been there."

"To watch me fight the enemy?"

"To scare off the opposition."

She was enjoying herself and her companion so much she hated to turn once again to business, but she felt it absolutely imperative to know what Rolfe Raeder had looked like.

"And I suppose, like all families, you had your snapshots. Did you use your big brother's picture to scare off your own enemies? I'd love to see a picture of your family."

He considered her for a minute. "You are curious to see Rolfe, of course."

He had completely misunderstood her interest. She tried to get him off that track. "What I really am curious about is you. What kind of person are you? How many are there in your family? Where do you live and write? Things like that."

She was sure now that his absurd jealousy of the dead brother had brought on this sudden moodiness. It seemed to be a struggle for him, but he accepted her questions for what they were.

"I am afraid I do not carry pictures of my family. It did not occur to me." He tried to make a joke of it. "You see, in spite of the publicity for my book, I am not at all mysterious." He satisfied himself that she was genuinely interested and explained, "I have a sister-in-law, as you know. Ursula has two children, a girl and a boy. And, of course, there is my aunt, the Baroness de Lieven."

"Ah! A baroness."

He grinned. "I have impressed you at last. Well, that is my harem."

"Three females? Does it ever bore you?"

He shrugged. "I like women. And Ursula is engaged. The less said about that, the better. She is out with your friend Doone tonight, by the way."

She knew better than to agree with him when he criticized another woman. "But these men are her choices, after all."

He had held her hand so long it felt cold and numb when he let it go. He was being suddenly casual. Too casual, she thought. Reaching for the Italian bread, he broke off a piece and seemed to find the ragged surface fascinating.

"You have not told me why you broke our date. Or why you watched me from behind the window blind. What are you afraid of?" He looked up suddenly, staring straight at her. It was a trick, she decided but startling enough to give her a momentary chill.

"A man I once knew. Many years ago. Somebody said he was in town. I wanted to avoid him."

"Is that all? It was nothing then. Nothing to do with me."

"Of course not."

His tense, alert expression vanished. Then, suddenly he asked, "Do you like this Doone Colt?"

"He's very young." She had given up correcting him on the name. Nor did she care what they talked about, so long as she sat here looking at him and enjoying his company. There was another reason which she tried to blank out of her mind, but it remained, both sensuous and sinister: being with Eric Raeder, she satisfied the passions that had been twisted and nearly destroyed long ago when she realized she loved a murderer. A murderer had made love to her. But here before her was the murderer's face and all of his charm; yet she was free to enjoy his company, because the man within was quite different.

6

IT was difficult for Gregg to believe, when she said good night to Eric Raeder at the foot of the stairs in her apartment building, that five hours ago she had been terrified of him. When he kissed her good night, taking her in a firm grip, his mouth on hers before she could make the expected feeble protests she felt the same pressure of his hard body against hers and knew that she wanted to be with him that night.

He made no move to stay, though, and she remembered then that he was leaving New York the next day. He probably had a good many things far more important than Gregg MacIvor on his mind. Hoping for the promise of another meeting, she wished him a good trip, and added, "Where are you off to this time?"

"Home to Switzerland. That family of mine I told you about. They live nea Geneva." He added only one encouraging thing as he opened the front door.

"You would like Geneva. Well—*auf Wiedersehen*."

Then he was gone.

Gregg took a cold shower and went to bed.

The cold shower did not quite serve its purpose, and several times during the night she awoke to picture what might have happened between them. She felt again in memory the tight, muscular pressure of his body against hers. No other man had affected her with this sense of leashed force and the ability to control that force. How different from the lazy, persistent lovemaking of Martin Helm which he had insisted upon performing before mirrors, obviously with the intention of admiring his own image.

His looking-glass image? She sat straight up in bed and slapped the sheets hard. No! She would not again confuse Eric Raeder with the detestable and horrifying Martin Helm.

It was hard to get back to sleep after that, and she was relieved when the smoggy autumn morning came at last and she could shake off both dreams and nightmares.

Her next few days were filled with

thoughts of Eric Raeder, particularly after a pretentious pile of kitchen utensils and appliances was delivered to her with full instructions on German cooking.

"I'll be as fat as a pig if I cook all these recipes," she told the delivery boy.

"You musta' ordered 'em. Name's on 'em," he insisted.

"Yes. Thank you. Just keep piling them in."

Afterward, looking inside the microwave oven, she found the envelope containing a note from Eric Raeder. She broke open the stiff, cream-colored envelope and read quickly,

My dear Miss Redhead:

When I am in New York next, you will owe me wiener schnitzel mit spatzel.

But New York is very crowded, not like Europe. The individual is special here. Come and see?

Until we are together again, in your ridiculous little kitchen, and elsewhere, remember,

Eric Raeder

She laughed, caressed the note and carefully put it away in a table drawer with other souvenirs. Someday—maybe—he would meet her again. She had a feeling—or maybe it was just a hope—that their lives were intertwined, one in the other.

On the day she brought her completed manuscript to Oliver Sills, she was surprised to be told that Mrs. Raeder had invited her and Oliver to a cocktail party at the apartment she was occupying opposite Central Park.

"Not Ursula Raeder!"

"Why not?"

"But I thought she had returned to Europe with Eric—Mr. Raeder."

Oliver eyed her interestedly. "You liked that fellow, didn't you?"

She started to lie, thought better of it and admitted, "He was nicer than I expected, and not at all conceited. Did you manage to sign him?"

"No. But maybe I wasn't persuasive enough. Isn't it about this time that you usually go over to Europe?"

She caught her breath and volunteered before he could ask, "You want me to be persuasive? I'll do it." Then, recovering, she added with a sly grin, "But only to please you."

"Very likely. Then you'll come with me tonight? You will be meeting the fair Ursula's fiancé."

The man Eric seemed to dislike. Gregg wondered why. She was undeniably curious and agreed to go, promising herself to look her very best. Ursula Raeder was beautiful enough to give any woman an inferiority complex.

Gregg dressed carefully that afternoon, but found herself more nervous than she had been in days. She did not want Ursula Raeder to guess how much Eric remained in her thoughts.

The evening promised to go well. Oliver Sills was always a distinguished and entertaining escort. He said all the right things to Gregg, but he couldn't help betraying his real interest as the cab dropped them off before the canopy of the apartment house.

"Do you suppose this Nordic bombshell of a sister-in-law has influence with Raeder? I could certainly use his next book as the lead title for our spring list."

Startled, Gregg asked, "Do you know then that there *is* a new book?"

"No, but he did say an idea had occurred to him during his stay in New York. About someone afraid. You know: locked doors, peepholes, psychotic fear. The symptom of the age we're living in, he said. He also claimed to be jotting down notes. I think it all turns out to be fear of failure, or of some imaginary ills. I didn't quite absorb the whole thing.'

"And is his protagonist a male or, by any chance, a female?"

Hearing her voice raised, the doorman looked surprised as he ushered them into the lobby of the building. She paid no attention to him. Oliver said easily, "Who knows? I don't pretend to understand the workings of any author's mind."

Though she did not feel too high-spirited, this made her laugh, the pleasant sound calling the tall, dark doorman's attention to her again. He examined her with new interest.

Oblivious, she remarked to Oliver, "I think I know where your precious Raeder got the germ of his idea. That's why he made such a fast play for me. Any author likes to observe his protagonist at close range."

"What!"

"Like watching ants in a jar. I was the ant."

Before the doorman could hear the end of this interesting argument, Oliver and Gregg were in the elevator with the doors closed. Oliver was amused at Gregg's unfounded opinions.

"Gregg, old girl, in the first place, friend Raeder's interest in you involves assets quite aside from your similarity to an ant in a jar. Look at yourself in the nearest mirror. He is young, vital and so far as his reactions are concerned, a typical male. Be honest, Gregg. Did he spend his time studying you?"

She thought back, recalled his examination of every room in her flat, all the details that seemed to fascinate him. Then there were the hours at the Italian restaurant, the way he kept watching her, questioning her, analyzing. She had often done the same thing herself when working up a character for a short story, or even for the travelers she sometimes invented for her books and articles.

She said, "I wish you were right."

They had reached the ninth floor and

stepped out directly in front of an open apartment door through whose black and white foyer they could hear the familiar party sounds: women's voices, ice cubes clinking in glasses, laughter and somewhere, low but still adding to the jumble, music.

"This has got to be our destination. It even smells like a cocktail party," Oliver announced, ushering her through the little foyer.

At the far end of the big, corner living room Ursula Raeder was the center of a fascinated group of men and women, including Mike and Sherry Silversteen, and Duane Colt. A powerful, good-looking man with a heavy face and the air of a born host strode toward the newcomers with hand outstretched. His English was impressive, with only a certain baroque richness to his enunciation that suggested this was not his native language.

"More of Ursula's good friends. Welcome, welcome. Let me present myself. Heinz Albrecht. Call me Henry. I am, as you say, engaged to my lovely Ursula. I cannot tell you the honor of meeting you. You are Mr. Oliver Sills, the publisher, of course! And you must be Miss MacIvor."

Both Oliver and Gregg were surprised at his fawning admiration of Oliver, and when Albrecht had shaken hands with both of them and gone off to get their drinks, Oliver whispered, "Ten to one, he's got a manuscript tucked away somewhere."

Gregg laughed. "Maybe you can make a better deal with him than with his future brother-in-law."

"Hush! Here he comes—Thank you. Yes, the Bloody Mary is mine."

Their host elaborately handed the smaller glass to Gregg. "And the dry vermouth on ice is, of course, for Miss Gregg. Poor Eric spoke of you so highly, I feel I am entitled to call you Gregg. No?"

What was this "poor Eric" business? Gregg resented it on principle, and in her fiery way would have revealed her resentment except for a warning look from Oliver Sills, who knew her all too well. She changed her mind but pursued the subject, though obliquely.

" I hear that Mr. Raeder's book is an enormous success in Europe. And he has certainly aroused interest here. There was a great crowd to see him in the bookstores last week."

"Oh, well, as to that, there are opinions and then—" He broke off. Heinz, no, Henry Albrecht, saw his fiancée crossing the room to greet the newcomers. Clearly, he had been about to put down his future brother-in-law, and was stopped either by Ursula's opinion or discretion. The Silversteens and Duane Colt waved to Gregg, and she went to join them after a quick exchange of greetings with Ursula Raeder. But her attention was divided. She was curious to know what Ursula and her fiancé had to say about Eric Raeder.

Sherry Silversteen and her excited young client both began to talk at once, explaining as Gregg finally gathered, that Eric Raeder had made a call to the studio which put in the highest bid for the movie rights, and it looked as though Duane would get a chance to test for the role of Hans Pogge, the hero of Eric's novel.

Gregg was impressed. "I can't believe it. He seemed so—" She was about to say "jealous" but changed her mind. At the same time, she realized what must have happened. Her own influence had nothing to do with it. Undoubtedly, it was Ursula Raeder whose persistence decided the matter. She said aloud, "It was lucky you met Mrs. Raeder that day at the Berkeley Lane. She seems to have been very kind. Not," she added quickly, "that you don't deserve the break, Duane. I know you will make the most of it. It's wonderful, Sherry. A real opportunity."

"Thanks to you, Red," Duane put in, bestowing a wet, Scotch-scented kiss on her cheek.

Ursula Raeder turned at that moment and caught the gesture. She seemed oddly interested in Duane's relationship with Gregg, yet her little smile was not jealous in the least. For some reason, she was pleased, Gregg thought.

"Don't thank me," she said quickly. "I wish I could take the credit, but it must have been Mrs. Raeder."

Sherry and Duane disclaimed together.

"Not on your life," the agent insisted. "Raeder himself called and told me. It was the day he flew to Geneva. Said he'd spent a delightful evening with you and that you had persuaded him."

"Well, I'll be damned!" Gregg felt her cheeks heat up, to her own surprise.

The small groups shifted, reformed in different patterns and conversations broke off, to be succeeded by other subjects which, in their turn, were left unended, as if no one really cared about the subject itself but only the vocal exercise as drinks were refilled. Oliver approached Gregg when Ursula and Henry Albrecht went to greet newcomers drifting into the foyer, loudly complaining about something.

Oliver said, "I've forgotten, old girl. Did you and I make a bet? Ten to one, wasn't it? You owe me a dollar."

"What on earth for?" Then she remembered. "Don't tell me he has a manuscript?"

"So he says. Wants to see me tomorrow at the office."

Gregg asked brightly, "A history of his family's intense sufferings during the war when he was a child, of course?"

"Fooled you. A story of the god Wotan, who came down to earth and wooed a young beauty with an impotent, ancient husband. The child of this interesting affair becomes a dictator—well, a prince, I think he said—and somehow manages to kill his mother, and—"

"Spare me!"

"Oh, no!" Oliver insisted. "He didn't spare *me*. Not one single detail. If I suffered, you are going to."

The voices of the newcomers came through their discussion and Gregg turned to see what had happened. An attractive man and woman, both unknown to Gregg, were describing their entrance into the building.

"Not a soul, I swear. Isn't that true, Eddie? The doorman was gone. Nobody was in the lobby. We banged around awhile and then a nice old couple leaving for the theater opened the doors, and that's how we got in. What kind of attendants do you have in this building, darling?"

"Actually, I am subleasing from some friends of Henry's," Ursula apologized. She added, "I love places where there are handsome appendages."

"Appendages?" one of the guests echoed, with a sly look at her male companion.

"Take our new doorman, for instance. Divinely amusing. So quiet. So subdued.

He hardly ever looks you in the eye. But he is quite attractive. In fact, he reminds me of—" She glanced at Albrecht. "Sorry, Henry. Am I talking out of school? Heinz doesn't see the resemblance. Come along, you two. Martinis for both of you, I take it?"

All this, along with his wife's business dealings, was boring to Mike Silversteen who had begun to urge Sherry, "Let's go, damn it!"

Sherry Silversteen made a face at Gregg and muttered, "I'd better do what Papa says. God knows he didn't want to come here in the first place. What do you think of this setup?"

"Our hostess?" Gregg whispered.

"Blondie and our Nordic muscle man. Tell me, have you any use for Eric Raeder?"

Gregg looked at her sharply. "Why? What has that to do with anything? But— yes, I like him."

"Well, then, I'd be careful of those two. They don't have much use for Raeder. One dig after another."

"Thanks. I'll remember that."

She watched them say their brief thank-yous and good-byes and was thinking of getting Oliver to do the same when she found herself surrounded by Ursula Raeder and her fiancé who, despite Gregg's protests, brought her a refill and some hors d'oeuvres.

"Gregg, forgive me, but I feel as if I know you well. Such praise as your friend Mr. Colt heaps upon you, and my poor brother-in-law too! Eric is a dear fellow, as I am sure you found him. It is such a pity. Is it not too bad, Henry?"

Having just been warned, Gregg promised herself that whatever happened she would not lose her temper, but it was hard going. Her smile felt taped to her mouth.

"What is a pity? He seems very healthy to me. And anyone with such success in his career would hardly be 'poor.'"

Ursula's pale eyes regarded her for an uncomfortably long time.

"I'm sorry. I thought, naturally, that he had told you. He is such a naughty boy, our Eric. I would not for worlds have you think the less of him. No! It is better he tells you."

Bitch! thought Gregg furiously . . . I'd

like to scratch that plaster face of yours clear to the bone!

She wanted desperately to know what Ursula Raeder was dying to tell her, but she would not give the woman that satisfaction. She raised her eyebrows instead, sipped her drink and remarked to Albrecht, "I'm afraid this is sweet vermouth. Do you mind?" and held out the glass.

He chewed his lip, probably in disappointment that their unpleasant gossip hadn't sunk in, and said, "Sorry. I will change it. It takes only a minute."

"Darling!" Gregg called, looking over Ursula's head. Oliver looked around, got the signal and came to her just as Ursula twisted her head around to see who had broken up this little tête-à-tête. She laughed, raised her own glass in salute to Gregg who said sweetly, "We really must be going now. I'm afraid we promised to see one of Oliver's authors tonight. You know how that is."

The look on Ursula Raeder's face was one of disappointment, or even distress, as if her purpose in inviting them had not yet been accomplished.

"But you mustn't go yet. Henry wanted

107

to talk to Mr. Sills about his allegorical novel. You see, it can be of immense significance. It explains the rise of Adolf Hitler through the allegory of the god who destroys his mother."

Oliver said hastily, "Send it over care of my assistant, Miss Plumb. Happy to read it. Anytime."

Albrecht was already before him, and to Gregg's amusement, he had two huge loose-leaf notebooks, some of whose pages looked a trifle dog-eared.

"But, my dear fellow, it must be read in my presence. Tonight. Surely you have an hour or two for a manuscript of this importance? There are things it is necessary to explain. For example, all of the subject matter dealing with the god Wotan is in red, but very clear. I used the ball-point. The rest is typed."

Gregg avoided Oliver's anguished eyes. "Ollie, we really are late now. Dear Ursula, how good of you to invite us! Thanks again."

Albrecht was still talking as they shook hands with him and moved to the door. "If I could read it aloud to you, Oliver—Mr. Sills."

"Afraid not tonight," Oliver cut him off in the doorway.

"Do you wish us to call a taxi for you?" Ursula wanted to know.

"We'll have the doorman get us one. Thanks all the same."

By the time they were alone in the elevator Gregg began to laugh. "Ollie, you couldn't even wait for her to call a cab."

"Good Lord, no! That fellow was just about to start reading his manuscript. In red ball-point yet!"

"Only Wotan's part."

"Very funny."

She remarked edgily, "That woman was certainly anxious to have us think Raeder is on his last legs."

"Probably doesn't want him involved with other women. If they can keep him from marrying, she or her children are bound to be his heirs, and that would involve upward of three million Deutsche Marks, even after taxes. He'll make at least two million dollars, what with the movie and paperback sales. The European sales are phenomenal. In Europe it's being called an allegory of the German mind."

"And here you are, turning down another allegory, from Albrecht."

He laughed, threw up his hands in horror.

"God forbid!"

They stepped out into the lobby. Straight ahead, toward the front doors, there were the usual bright pools of light, but a small section of the lobby beside the elevator shaft and around the staircase door was in shadows. Ursula Raeder's guests had been right, Gregg thought. Not only was the doorman gone but the light failure apparently had not been reported.

Oliver Sills used the doorman's telephone to call out for a cab. Afterward, while they waited, he noted Gregg's depressed mood and guessed what troubled her.

"I wouldn't think too much about any of this 'poor Eric' bit. He's healthy enough to all accounts. Flew back to Geneva, then to Vienna, next Berlin and Scandinavia. According to Miss Plumb, who is quite a fan of his, next week he'll be autographing in Denmark and Sweden. Doesn't sound as though Eric Raeder might be ill, poor or otherwise in need of pity."

"I thought so. Thank God for it! That hateful woman!"

He looked at her curiously. "And still you were afraid of Raeder. I hope you've gotten over the notion that he resembled that murderer you once knew."

She was watching for the cab in the bright mid-evening darkness outside.

"There is still a resemblance, but Eric behaves so differently. I'm satisfied there's no connection. Besides, he's much younger than Martin—than the other one."

"You and your dark past! Gregg, has it ever occurred to you that you should have reported everything you knew about that ex-lover of yours?"

"Uncle George and I told the police everything we'd discovered eleven years ago. There was nothing to hold Martin Helm on then, and all he's done since, so far as anyone can tell, is keep a low profile. I have no proof of the other things—if there indeed are any. If I could prove something against him, it would be different. I certainly don't want him hot on my own trail, after what happened to that poor Alys Lane. He's far too clever with windows."

"With what?"

Something seemed to stir in the silent, shadowed corners of the lobby behind them. A footstep on the tile floor. Or nothing. Merely the night air, the creaking of wood somewhere. It was too dark to make out anything, but Gregg, ever on edge, cut in quickly, "Never mind. Here's the cab."

They stepped out of the lobby, into the welcome noise of the street.

7

DURING the next few days Gregg persuaded herself that her nerves would not stand any more of her paranoia, this nervous feeling that she was being watched, or followed. She looked into strangers' eyes a hundred times, always fearing that Martin Helm had found her.

"I admit I've got to get out of this town for a while, or I'll go crazy; so I'm going to Europe," she explained to Duane Colt who was trying to persuade her that a trip to Hollywood with him was just what she needed.

Duane had come to her flat, making a considerable stir in the neighborhood, though not in Gregg's house where the actor and his wife on the third floor snubbed him on the stair landing. He had arrived all in white with white mink trim on his sweater and his jacket cuffs. Gregg had pronounced that he was a sight to behold, which he optimistically took for a compliment.

"I don't get it, Red. If you want to get out of town, why not go to the Coast with me? Look! You go with me, and I'll pick up the tab. Charge it to my expenses for the year. How about it?"

She was touched, within reason, and kissed him. He blushed, but demanded why she kept getting up and peeking out through the venetian blinds. She had curled up on the stiff, satin love seat with her legs under her and Duane beside her, but she was so nervous she couldn't sit still and she perfectly understood poor Duane's objections. It was only a little after noon and the street was crowded. At the corner to her right she could see busy Third Avenue. She couldn't possibly know if one pair of eyes was focused on her house, but she couldn't free herself of the feeling that Martin Helm was out there somewhere.

How do I know it? she thought. In the last few days he had seemed horrifyingly close. Was there still a tie between them that made her know . . . a hideous, blood-red tie that she thought had been broken years ago?

There was one consolation. Even if Martin Helm *was* somewhere in New York, that meant that he could hardly be in Europe masquerading as a popular German writer. The thought appealed to her and made her think more than ever about Eric Raeder. She wanted desperately to believe he had no connection with Helm.

"I'm sorry, Duane, dear. I simply can't write any more articles about Hollywood. I did that bit a long time ago. Wrung it dry."

His eyes were shining with the thought of future career prospects, and under that momentum he caught her hands and drew her nearer. She let herself be pulled down beside him on the love seat. He was warm and endearing, and as she considered him, she knew that she loved him in a way. Not sexually, but in the way one loves children or puppies.

He said persuasively, "You'll be surprised. I can be quite good for you if you'd just give me a chance. Why can't you be nice to me the way you are to others, Gregg?" He was obviously sincere, a little hurt, and she wondered if he guessed her thoughts.

"My dear boy," she began, borrowing Oliver's usual preface, "you know perfectly well if you had your way with me, you'd drop me like a hot potato."

"I wouldn't. I would not! A lot you know about me. I need somebody like you. To keep me in line."

She was amused at this less than romantic argument, but leaped onto it as her way out.

"But I would try to dominate you, Duane. I'd be frantically jealous. I'd never let you even look at another woman. I'm afraid it wouldn't work."

He began to exert those beautifully developed muscles that were so photogenic beneath his silk sweaters. "Oh, but I know you, Gregg. You like a little fun." He was stronger than she had remembered. "You call it flirtation. Okay. Somebody like you isn't going to be too rough on me. Come here to me."

The telephone buzzed. "Saved by the bell," Gregg muttered, and scrambled out of his arms to reach the green phone on her desk. It was Oliver Sills.

"You're all set, Gregg. You fly out tomorrow for Copenhagen. They've got a World Bank Conference or something going on and the hotels are over-booked.

But we got you into the Danemark. I've often stayed there."

"About—you know—"

"He is due in Copenhagen on Thursday. Meanwhile, why don't you see what ideas you can pick up there for a few articles?"

"Sure. Sure. Thank you, Ollie. You're a darling, as always."

"All Miss Plumb's doing. You may have competition for our boy's attention, though. I just had a call from some writer. Said he's from *People* mag. He wanted to do a cover story on your mystery author. Wanted to know where to find him, not an hour from now but right this minute."

She laughed. "Did you tell him?"

"In general. He asked me about you, too."

"*People* magazine asked about me?"

"Well, in a way. He asked me if you were a writer."

"Damn him! Don't tell him a thing."

Oliver was amused at this reaction of an injured ego. "You'll have to forgive me, dear girl, but I did tell him, with pride, that you were on your way overseas to get material. About European men. He said he guessed you would want to interview the mystery man, Raeder."

"He's mighty inquisitive. What's he doing? Spying on us?"

Duane Colt's moving shadow interrupted her. "I just might go to Europe myself. But I can see that you couldn't care less. Bye."

"No, wait. Duane, don't run away mad. Duane—" He was already on the stairs. She turned back to the phone. "Duane Colt is off to the wars."

She thanked Oliver Sills again, hung up and hurried out to salve Duane Colt's wounded feelings, but he merely waved back without looking around, called, "See you!" as he walked toward Third Avenue.

She was sorry. Though she was used to laughing at him, he had been a friend for several years and she was ashamed of herself for leading him on.

Meanwhile, however, there was tomorrow's trip to prepare for. She scrambled around, packing and repacking, and occasionally remembering the *People* magazine interviewer who had asked if she was a writer.

She said good-bye to Oliver Sills at lunch the next day; she had a superstition about having people see her off at the airport, ever since she saw Martin Helm for the last time as her plane took off for Chicago long ago. Now, each time she boarded a plane, she could not help looking back, always wondering if one day she would again see the ghost of her past life standing there.

There was no handsome, sinister figure waving good-bye to her on this trip. The plane was only half full, and she settled back down with a paperback, to read and sleep away the boredom of the flight.

Somewhere out over the North Atlantic and halfway through her mystery novel, she felt the stewardess close above her shoulder.

"Excuse me, miss. I wondered if you would like the gentleman to take the vacant seat beside you."

"Who?"

"He's come past you so often, and seemed to know you. I beg your pardon. I thought he might be a friend of yours."

Gregg looked around. Most of the passengers were male, and asleep. None seemed familiar.

"Can you point him out?"

But the stewardess had already shaken her head. "Sorry. I don't see him now."

"I'm sure I don't know anyone aboard." Her grin was ingratiating. "But thanks for trying." Then she had a quick, uneasy idea. "What was he like? His description. Is he dark and clean-shaven? Rather tall, slightly foreign."

The stewardess smiled. "I'm afraid not. Tall and graying, I would say, with a moustache. I believe he may be European, but—he is not the friend you are expecting."

"I'm not expecting anyone. Thank you."

All the same, at Kastrup Airport Gregg watched the various passengers as they approached Danish customs. She knew by this time that none of them could be the man she remembered so vividly and painfully, Martin Helm. Three of the passengers resembled the man the stewardess had mentioned. Probably all three were Danes. She could not make a close study of them, but none had the dash and flair, the frighteningly sensuous appeal of the man she had once loved.

By the time she reached the Hotel Danemark facing one of Copenhagen's busy, historic old squares, she had almost forgotten the little episode on the plane. The hotel itself was crowded with tour groups and a few of the distinguished members of something called the World Monetary Conference. It occurred to Gregg that, with any luck, she might get a couple of interviews out of these men. On the other hand, the men in the tour groups might give her a more realistic view of the European approach.

She liked her room. The bathroom was small and old-fashioned, but the room itself was charming. There was a small bed in the corner, but also a couch, and in front of it a long table, as well as a three-mirrored dressing table in one corner, and several windows. The windows opened on two sides onto the wide court.

She looked out onto a court that took up the center of the L-shaped hotel. Her room was four floors above the lobby, or perhaps the dining room. She tucked her head in again. Every time she looked out of a high window, she got vertigo, remembering the fate of Alys Lane.

Had that actually been a coincidence, a purely accidental tragedy? Was it possible

Martin Helm had never returned to New York? What was truth—and what was her imagination?

Gregg unpacked and hung up her clothes, proud of the careful planning and long experience that enabled her to remove her well-coordinated outfits wrinkle-free. After a bath in the too-short tub whose shower hose opened up full force on her head, she put up her hair and went to bed.

She did not sleep long, but awoke to a cold, clear northern afternoon and wondered what noise had aroused her. She sat up, breathed the crisp air from the open windows and discovered the noise had been children's voices arguing. Gregg turned over in bed, wishing their shrill voices wouldn't cut into the pleasant silence in the court.

Then, realizing that she could no longer sleep, and that there was a great city to examine, she got up. While she was washing and making up, the children's voices seemed to get a little closer. Curious, she went and knelt on the couch under the south windows to see where they came from.

She was shocked to see a young girl

dancing on a windowsill across the court, holding precariously onto the window frame over her head. She was all legs, wearing knee stockings in the European style and a plaid skirt. Her hair, in tight braids, was not at all flattering to her thin, freckled face. But she was spirited, daring and obviously willing to take a dare. A boy stuck his head out the window and spoke to her harshly in either German or Danish. It sounded like German.

With nothing on above the waist but her bra, Gregg leaned out and called as gently as she could, "Hi! You speak English?"

The girl was not disturbed. She peered across at Gregg between raised arms, "Certainly, Fräulein. You should not let people see you half naked like that. It is not nice. Pauly," she said to the boy, "don't look."

"Come inside. And stop giving me orders," the boy demanded, speaking in English, no doubt to impress Gregg.

"I'll go in if you'll go in," Gregg proposed.

The girl was duly impressed by her power over a grown-up, and looked up at her own fingers, still clutching the window frame over her head. She removed one hand and flexed the fingers as one of her feet reached behind her, feeling its way into the room with no help from the boy. Having safely ducked back into the hotel room, the girl called across the intervening court, "Good-bye, Fräulein!"

Enormously relieved that the girl had gone inside, Gregg called, "Good-bye," and waved across the court.

The girl said, "My name is Marlene Raeder. My brother—" she cocked her head toward the dark, serious boy with glasses, "he's Pauly. *Auf Wiedersehen*, Fräulein."

Raeder. Not an uncommon name, but Ursula Raeder had two children, and Eric was expected to arrive soon in Copenhagen. Couldn't the children be here to meet their uncle? And, of course, with the subtlety of a sledgehammer, Oliver Sills had managed to book Gregg into the same hotel. Oliver was getting to be quite a busybody.

Gregg left the window and, taking young Marlene's advice, got dressed. She liked the children, especially the daring girl, and hoped they would turn out to be Eric's niece and nephew.

Gregg readied herself for a pedestrian's look at the city, fortunately remembering that there was more of the arctic chill in the air than one might suspect after a look at the blue sky and the bright sun. Armed with pamphlets and maps she had found on the dressing table, she thought of having lunch at the hotel, but changed her mind when she saw the two Raeder children, together with a middle-aged woman, probably a governess, crossing the street and the big, busy square beyond.

Feeling like a CIA agent, Gregg followed the children and their escort at a short distance. At the next corner they turned to the right, onto a shop-lined street twisting away into the distance. Though free of automobiles, it was jammed with pedestrians, and Gregg thought for a minute or two that she had lost sight of the children.

There were a hundred items in the first block of shops that she would have liked to buy, but the displays of pastries and other delicious foods in shop windows topped all her interest in Royal Copenhagen china, the glassware, stainless steel, clothing and furniture. She was beginning to remember

125

that she hadn't had a decent meal since yesterday's lunch. She was, in fact, so interested in the food and the children ahead that she scarcely noticed whether the sexual fame of Copenhagen lived up to its reputation. The street seemed full of beautiful creatures with wavy, shoulder-length hair and a unisex look that certainly did not arouse her libido.

One sight of Eric Raeder, she thought, and her libido would go soaring. Vive la difference!

Striding along rapidly against the stiff breeze, she caught sight of a mouth-watering window display of Danish pastry. There on the tray were the favorites she had adored as a child, the custard centers. Damn! she decided. I don't care whether meet those children or not. I'm going in and eat a dozen fattening pastries! Well two or three, anyway, she thought.

She walked in, past the pastry and after noon tea section, ordered three of the pastries and then went up to the Strøget eating the custard-centered Danish. The pastry itself was heavenly. It was even more delicious, buttery and rich than she had imagined it would be. She stopped t examine a window full of Royal Copenhagen china and heard a familiar young voice call out in English,

"Oh, look, Miss Tibbs, it's the Fräulein at the window."

As she might have guessed, an even younger voice, and male, contradicted her immediately. "No, it isn't. She looks different."

By the time Gregg had turned to greet them, secretly delighted that they spoke to her instead of the other way around, Miss Tibbs was scolding the children in a querulous but not really angry voice.

"That will do, children. You know better than to annoy strangers."

Gregg apologized for the children. "Please, we are not really strangers, madam. An hour ago I met the young lady in—" She caught the girl's pleading gesture and quickly changed her remark. "—in her window. We talked for a few minutes. I am staying at the same hotel."

"She was climbing out of the window, Marlene was," young Pauly cut in.

Gregg saw Marlene pinch Paul and said hastily, to prevent further hostilities, "May

I offer the young people a pastry? I just bought them."

Miss Tibbs coughed behind her hand. "Thank you, miss. You are too kind. But I think—"

"Oh, please, Miss Tibbs!" Marlene cried, and her brother, after owlishly studying Gregg through his big, horn-rimmed glasses, decided her pastries were edible and added his plea to Marlene's.

Gregg asked Miss Tibbs's permission by raising her eyebrows, to which the little woman smiled her consent, and as the children ate the delicious pastries, Miss Tibbs asked Gregg where she came from and how long she expected to be in Denmark.

"I am a writer. I expect to interview several of the international figures who are here for the monetary conference."

"Ah! Of course." Miss Tibbs was a plain woman whose smile canceled out the cautious look in her eyes. "You should have been here last night. Riots all over town. Bank windows broken everywhere. By radicals, you know."

Gregg was a little surprised. Like many others, she had thought that sort of violence was a thing of the past. She was also impressed when the governess added, "I took the children back to the hotel at once but between you and me, as terrible as it was, I found it rather exciting. If only I could write! My dear, the things I've seen!"

The children finished their pastries, and as the group had now reached the big central square of Kongens Nytorf, little Miss Tibbs said they must turn back. Much as the children and Miss Tibbs seemed to like her, they did not persuade her to return with them. They all waved good-bye to her, leaving Gregg to her own resources.

There was a modern glass department store across the busy square, and Gregg strolled over to buy a few souvenirs for Uncle George, among them some presents for females. He had told Gregg that nothing impressed his lady friends like gifts from abroad. As usual, she roamed through the book section on the street floor, this time looking for, and finding, displays of Eric Raeder's book.

It was almost a shock to see the book in its German guise, with that curious and somehow frightening word: *Doppelgänger*. She studied the jacket, noting how the silver lettering of the title bled into a gray, shadowy repetition of the word, while below it on the jacket, a young blond man looked into a mirror and saw a reflected face essentially like his own, yet with all the features out of focus, exaggerated. Evil. Was it the soul that looked back at poor, young Hans Pogge, the protagonist, or was it, as the author indicated in his melodramatic way, the Mr. Hyde side of Man?

On an impulse, she bought the German original of the book in order to have the dust jacket. With clues like this she thought she might learn to understand Eric Raeder, and then was amused at her own naiveté. Raeder, of course, had nothing to do with the jackets, which were created by total strangers.

"Gregg!"

She heard the voice and knew it very well. She had been thinking of little else since she arrived in Copenhagen. She hugged herself mentally, in anticipation.

"Gregg?"

Package in hand, she turned around. A half-dozen tall customers had poured in through the street doors, all looking a bit like Eric Raeder at this distance. She swung the other way. An elderly man stood nearby, examining the Psychology/Psychiatry section. Sensing that he was under scrutiny from some direction, he raised his head, stared at her haughtily and returned to the excitements of his reading. Several women were discussing luggage or handbags farther along the floor.

She shook her head at her own mistake. I must need a hearing aid, she thought.

She decided finally that there must be dozens of Danish words that could sound like "Gregg" if spoken rapidly. It was disappointing, but she hadn't really expected to meet him today.

"Gregg! Over here."

This was maddening. She found herself surrounded by shoppers pouring through the main floor exhibits, but not one of them appeared to be the man she hoped to see.

She decided that someone in this crowded department store had the same name as her own. But it shook her up badly and she couldn't forget it. She walked through the store, along every aisle, until, satisfied that she knew no one there, she walked out the corner door into the traffic of the big square and started back toward her hotel.

When she heard her name called once more, about three blocks from her hotel, she was furious. A joke was a joke, but this ceased to be funny. She kept walking, faster than ever, unwilling to give this joker the satisfaction of seeing her turn around. Suddenly, her upper arm was caught in a steely grip and turning her head, she saw Eric Raeder, his face close enough so that her lips almost brushed his cheek.

He looked marvelous, healthy, vigorous and excited, with what she thought of as a sexy gleam in his dark eyes. "You walk very fast. Are you running away from me?"

She stopped, causing other pedestrians to detour around her and Raeder. She said, "You devil!" but she smiled.

She thought he looked a little puzzled. "For chasing you? But it was a surprise. A beautiful surprise to find you here. I was in that shop at the corner when you passed. I could not believe it."

Startled, Gregg stared at him. "But you saw me in the department store near Kongens Nytorf. You called to me."

"If I had been there, I would certainly have called you," he assured her. "But how could that be? I have only just arrived. My

132

niece and nephew left a note for me. They are waiting for me to buy them souvenirs at Illums store. Will you go with me and meet them?"

She began to think that the two children she'd met that day were indeed Eric's niece and nephew.

It was curious about that voice in the big department store. Eric seemed utterly sincere when he denied having been there, yet, only minutes later, he imitated the sound of that other voice. Had that original voice in the store been his *Doppelgänger*, acting out a scene that would occur later?

It was an alarming idea, and though she did not believe in the occult, she found herself looking behind Eric Raeder, as if she expected his shadow to have a mind and will of its own.

8

SHE decided during the next half hour that the greatest actor in the world could not put on the pretense of general innocence that Eric Raeder presented. It was impossible to believe now that Raeder had been haunting the department store and senselessly calling out her name. She reverted to her original conclusion, that she had mistaken some Danish name or word for her own name.

But she had not been mistaken about the two children she'd met with their governess. When Gregg and Eric walked into the Illums store, the two same children immediately ran to Eric and surrounded him, hugging him and demanding that he come to see what they had bought.

"We bought a scarf for Mama and a pin for Great-Aunt Alexandra and Pauly bought—"

"I can tell. I can tell!" young Pauly insisted. "I bought notebooks to write like you, Uncle Eric. I am writing what they call a police novel, Uncle. You can read it."

Gregg watched Eric answer everything, examining Marlene's packages, promising Pauly, ". . . and I will read your *roman policier* tonight before you go to bed. And how are you, Miss Tibbs? You are looking very handsome."

Miss Tibbs blushed, fluttered and said brusquely, "Thank you, sir. I am sure the baroness will be pleased with the children. I have had them studying Danish history all week, after the Tivoli Gardens closed."

"I am sure she will be pleased." He smiled as he took Gregg's hand. "These are my unruly charges, Marlene and Paul, and our good friend, Miss Tibbs. Now then, I want you children to know a very lovely lady, my friend, Fräulein Gregg MacIvy."

"MacIvor. But I beat you. We are old comrades. We met this afternoon."

Miss Tibbs nodded pleasantly. "Indeed, we know this kind lady." She would have gone on to explain, but the children told him first, and rivaled each other in describing how big the Danish pastries she'd given them had been.

"Bribery," Eric pronounced, and wanted

135

to know what evil doings this covered. Amused as he was, his gaze did not miss the quick look exchanged between Gregg and the nervous Marlene, who relaxed and grinned when Gregg did not betray her secret balancing act.

Eric Raeder doesn't miss a trick, Gregg thought, and was pleased to find out how popular he was with these fatherless, and very nearly motherless, children.

While Ursula Raeder remained in New York, throwing cocktail parties with her fiancé, Henry Albrecht, her children made the best of their own lives far away in Europe. The fair Ursula did not seem to be a very devoted mother.

Nevertheless, her children didn't look the worse for it, and whatever the problems in their lives, they seemed at ease with grown-ups, which she found a welcome change from many other children she had known.

"I met your mother in New York," Gregg said, partly to make conversation. "We had a lovely time."

Marlene said, "*Ja*. She gives good parties. People always say so."

"Isn't she pretty? Isn't she the prettiest

lady you ever saw? Like a cinema star," Pauly raved.

"Indeed, she is," Gregg began but was interrupted by Eric.

"That would not be my choice. I would say Miss Tibbs and Miss Gregg are far prettier, and you may tell your mama I said so, when she returns."

Gregg and the governess laughed, but young Pauly, surveying the two women out if his enormous glasses, was very grave.

"I think Uncle Eric is right. Miss Gregg is very pretty, as pretty as Mama. And Miss Tibbs—" That lady pursed her lips so that all the wrinkles showed, and Marlene said, "Miss Tibbs has a very nice nose."

Everyone was hungry, and a lively discussion ensued when Eric asked where they wanted to eat dinner. Gregg insisted that she was on her way back to the hotel and could not possibly go with them, and Eric tried to persuade her when Miss Tibbs reminded them, "Miss MacIvor gave up her pastry to you two, so I think we owe her something for that."

Gregg saw that Eric Raeder was pleased, and Marlene capped the invitation by saying in her decisive way, "She must come with us. You can trust her."

This made Eric's left eyebrow go up, and he glanced at Gregg to let her know that the secret between her and Marlene had not gone unnoticed. Only sober young Pauly looked at Gregg and said nothing.

Well, we can't win 'em all, Gregg thought.

The debate about where to eat then raged all the way back to the hotel. Marlene wanted a "beautiful, glamorous restaurant, like the one in the hotel. I want to feel like a queen." Her brother, on the contrary, wanted to eat "like the natives," whatever that meant, so Eric left the decision to Miss Tibbs and Gregg.

In the end, they went to a small restaurant off the Strøget where everyone watched to see what the neighboring Danes ordered and then did likewise. They were seated at a horseshoe-shaped banquette generally used with three tiny plastic tables. The tables were now joined—as well as round tables can be joined—and everyone prepared to enjoy the dinner.

Eric ordered schnapps for Gregg and himself. Miss Tibbs stuck by her tea, and

138

the children insisted on an unappetizing bubbly orange concoction. Over the schnapps, Eric asked Gregg how she happened to find herself in Copenhagen.

"Not that we grudge our luck in having you here," he added, saluting her with his glass raised gallantly.

"She's here to interview important people in banks," Marlene said. "If you were in a bank, Uncle, she could interview you."

Gregg straightened this out, assuring Eric that she would make an exception and interview him, even if he didn't belong to international monetary circles. "Of course, I must satisfy myself that you are important enough."

While the others were laughing, Pauly studied his plate thoughtfully.

"Uncle, you took a long time to get here. Do you have other friends in Copenhagen?"

"But I came as soon as the boat crossed from Malmö. That is Sweden," he explained to Pauly, while Marlene said wisely, "I know."

Everyone was surprised that the matter

came up at all, but Pauly persisted, still not looking at his uncle.

"*Nein*. I mean—no, sir. I mean—after the boat docked here."

They could all see that Eric was puzzled, yet he remained patient with the boy.

"But I did come. I took a taxicab and came at once to the hotel. I read your note and went to find you. I was very lucky, I also met Gregg. That was lucky, wasn't it?"

There were murmurs from Miss Tibbs and Marlene. Pauly said, "*Ja*, Uncle. That was lucky. Only, when you called us on the telephone, you told us you would see us in ten minutes. And then, it was hours and hours before we saw you."

Marlene sputtered indignantly to think she hadn't been let in on this matter. "You didn't tell me, Pauly. You always keep secrets from me. You hateful little snake!"

"Well," Pauly defended himself, "I had to have some secret you didn't know about. And Uncle told me not to say anything. He wanted to surprise us all."

Marlene and Miss Tibbs were not particularly disturbed, one way or the other, but Gregg was electrified and sat there, neither eating nor drinking, trying not to stare, but watching Raeder intently.

He made no effort to explain Pauly's puzzling claim, nor did he seem upset by it. He brought the flat palm of his hand down lightly on top of Pauly's tow-colored hair. "When I do call you, Pauly, I will admit afterward. This time, maybe you made a mistake, or maybe someone played a joke on us."

No one mentioned the disputed phone call again while the pleasant dinner proceeded. Gregg knew that the others believed Pauly had made up the story in order to compete with his extroverted older sister. As for Eric, he was being charming, delightful to the children, nicely flirtatious to Miss Tibbs. But once in a while, as if aware that he was the subject of Gregg's thoughts—and suspicions?—he looked at her under his dark brows, without smiling.

She was a little afraid.

Something had ruined the evening, a silly little tale made up by a quiet boy who wanted some attention. Unfortunately, it had played upon Gregg's own vague, almost banished suspicions about the real Eric Raeder. *Had* he actually arrived early,

141

phoned the children, spoken to Pauly and then gone to that department store and called her own name? Why? Was he crazy? Maybe he had blackouts and did all these things in some other state, some other identity. And maybe that dark side of Eric was tied somehow to Martin Helm.

On the way back to the hotel, as they walked along the Strøget in the chilly northern night, the children and their uncle laughed, played hopping games, argued about absurdities; and Gregg, ever watchful, could not believe that Eric Raeder had lied to his nephew. If he knew of these odd events, the unacknowledged telephone call and visit to the department store, he could never have put on such an act tonight.

When they reached the Danemark Gregg said good night and would have turned left toward her room, but Raeder took her wrist and kept her with him while they escorted Miss Tibbs, Marlene and Pauly to their adjoining rooms. Gregg watched, pleased by what appeared to be his genuine caring for the children. He joked with Marlene before kissing her forehead, then kissed Miss Tibb's slightly trembling fingers and shook Pauly's hand. The boy himself avoided Raeder's eyes and ducked inside his room without a word. Gregg was disappointed, for Raeder's sake. She could see that he had noticed this attitude and seemed puzzled by it.

When they were alone in the hotel corridor, Gregg knew that, whatever her suspicions and her fears that the boy Pauly was right, it made no difference at this moment. She was still strongly attracted to Eric Raeder. His touch was exciting, his smile as he looked at her now remained intoxicating to her. She had a sudden, appalling sensation of having returned to that time eleven years ago. The years between were gone. Martin Helm was not a monstrous killer of women. He genuinely loved her. Even under this illusion, which she knew could be disastrous, she hated to shake off the mood.

As they returned to the elevators and into her corridor, he said after a minute's silence between them, "Tell me what I must do."

Taken by surprise, she almost stammered. "About—what?"

"To be interviewed by you."

Relieved that he was joking, and not sure

why she should be relieved, Gregg laughed. "I promise to interview you at your convenience. Isn't that what one says to a celebrity?" Considering today's curious developments, she added, "I'd love to ask you questions. Millions of them."

His pleasant mood, the smile that touched his deep-set eyes, seemed not to have changed, but merely to have become set upon his face.

"Naturally. Questions about my opinion of red-haired beauties. I adore them. America? I have a fondness for it. And for Europe, as well."

"Children?" she asked lightly.

"A fondness for children. How long will you be in Copenhagen? And where do you go from here?"

"I wish I knew. It depends upon whether I find subjects for some articles. All about opportunities for females traveling alone."

She stopped at her door, got out her key and he took it from her fingers, unlocking the door and letting her go past him.

"Let me help you with your research." As she looked at him, he suggested innocently, "Can't you pretend I am one of these fellows you write about? The kindl

144

old uncle? The bad-tempered banker? The lecherous scoundrel?"

Still amused, and pleased at his interest, she was caught by surprise when he went on, "And the fellow who has wanted to do this ever since he left that apartment of yours."

One arm came away from the door and caught her right shoulder. The other, taking her around the waist, caught her so tight against him she felt the hard muscles of his thighs, and her own arm moved around his back. Her fingers reached for the dark hair above the nape of his neck. His kiss was somehow primitive and violent, as if it would drain her of strength, and she responded in kind. It was the sexual response her own emotions demanded. She wondered if he knew that, or only sensed it as he felt the throb of her own pulse in her throat, her breast and loins.

As their bodies relaxed momentarily and she twisted her head away in order to breathe, the light through the open windows, from the court outside, cast gaunt shadows across his face, twisting and accentuating his features.

145

Martin Helm.

Ice water seemed to run in her veins. She broke away, backed farther into her room, heard herself whisper hoarsely, "I'm sorry. You—reminded me of someone. I'm very sorry."

It was a disastrous thing to say, and she knew it as soon as it was said. He stared at her. His mouth, which had bruised hers and still attracted her, twisted a little. He laughed and she wished he had not made that sardonic, cutting sound.

"I'm sorry, too. Good night."

He was gone before she could think of any explanation. She felt extraordinarily cold.

She closed and locked the door, turned on a lamp and, with a hunted man's fear of watching eyes, she crossed the room to draw the drapes. The windows were all wide open and several stories below she could hear dance music. Fresh air was very well, but the maids had been careless about leaving all the windows open. Surely, they knew by now that late September nights could be exceedingly cold.

9

IT wasn't until she had bathed and gone to bed that Gregg realized how tired she was. She indulged in a self-pitying, self-blaming bout of tears. It had been incredibly foolish of her to compare Eric Raeder to another man. He would, and obviously did, resent the comparison. If Eric had actually been Martin Helm, would he have shown that resentment? But, of course, he was *not* Helm.

She lay in bed, staring at the draped windows wondering what similarities, besides appearance, there were between Helm and Eric Raeder. Their approach to a kiss, for example. Helm was all smoothness and care, almost sly. Eric was direct, forceful. But he had not been deliberately cruel.

Martin Helm, in spite of all his sleek and practiced lovemaking, had enjoyed moments of subtle cruelty, sometimes taking her hand as though he would caress it and then, very slowly, turning one of her

147

fingers back until she cried out. How odd to think she had forgotten that!

She slept at last, getting several hours of dreamless sleep and only awakening to find the room stuffy, in need of air. She got up in the dark and made her way across the room, fumbled among the drapes and opened the nearest window. She slept more comfortably afterward, but still dreamed that Martin Helm had climbed in through the window and was beckoning to her with a crooked forefinger.

She awoke with a start.

A little piece of the bright northern sky, piercingly blue, was visible from her bed. In spite of the dream, she felt much better after the long rest, and rose abruptly, getting to her feet and stretching with sensuous pleasure. She could hear voices across the court as she had the previous day. She went to the window.

Marlene was there, arguing with her brother as usual, but when she saw Gregg, she left the battle in abeyance while she called across the court:

"*Guten Morgen*, Fräulein Gregg."

"Good morning, Fräulein Raeder. Did you sleep well?"

"Okay. You owe me a thank you."

"Really? Why?"

"He didn't want to, but I made him."

Gregg began to suspect that Marlene's brutal frankness was to some point. "You made who do what?"

"Uncle is taking us over to Sweden today. I told him he had to take you, too."

Gregg cleared her throat but still sounded a little hoarse when she asked, "But he didn't want me? Do you know why?"

Marlene shrugged. "Uncle likes some ladies and doesn't like others. That's how he is. He doesn't like Mama."

Behind her, Pauly screamed, "That's not true! It's not true! He likes Mama. Everybody does."

Marlene said crushingly, "You're such a child, Pauly."

Not wanting to be responsible for a family war, Gregg waved aside the discussion. She was humiliated and disappointed, but she wouldn't go where she wasn't wanted.

"Sorry. I can't make it anyway. Good-bye."

But Marlene persisted. "Yes, you are going with us, Fräulein."

"Can't. Sorry. See you again sometime." Aware of a tall man appearing in the shadows behind Marlene, she backed away from the window, turned and retreated into the middle of her room.

By the time she had showered and dressed, her breakfast had arrived, consisting of strong coffee, toast and glorious Danish pastries. As she finished the pastries and coffee she decided finally that the Raeder family had taken her at her word. She was not wanted and would not be joining the party's expedition to nearby Sweden.

When the room service waiter knocked half an hour later, she was still arguing with herself over whether to leave Copenhagen or not. She contemplated flying on to Vienna, and then back to her beloved Paris. There she had friends and could relax, while she picked up tips for another article, or even another book.

She called, "*Entrez!*" before she remembered that many Danes were just as familiar with English.

The waiter came through the little foyer

into the room. His expression seemed noncommittal, but upon examination, she saw that he looked a little smug, and immediately afterward, she saw the reason. Marlene Raeder was almost at his coattails, suppressing a fit of giggles and carrying clearly upon her freckled face the glow of triumph. Marlene always got her way.

"I told you," she sang out. "Take out your coat. You are going. I wore Uncle out. He finally agreed it was either *ja* or throw me out the window."

Aware of the waiter's interest, Gregg could not throw the tray at Marlene's insufferable uncle as she would have liked. So she did the next best thing. She laughed, and seconds later felt the real humor of it. Poor Eric Raeder! Like Pauly and Gregg, he could not stand up to Marlene.

"Very well. I'll get a jacket." She had to stop Marlene from marching into the closet and picking out what she considered an appropriate coat. To uplift her spirits, she chose an extremely fashionable, unlined jacket and strolled out into the hall, towed along by Marlene.

Waiting at the elevators were Eric, Miss Tibbs and Pauly. Only the governess looked happy to see her. Gregg wondered if it was imaginary, or if she saw a question in Raeder's eyes. Whatever it was, she liked it. As always, his presence moved her. She had not felt this way about any man since Martin Helm. And last night she had very nearly ruined everything between them because of Martin Helm.

She abandoned her pride and outrage at his disagreement with Marlene over her. From his viewpoint she had behaved like a contemptible tease last night. Gregg decided she had nothing to lose and everything to gain by sacrificing a little pride. She offered her hand to Raeder, looking into his eyes and saying, "I'm very sorry. I behaved stupidly."

His eyelids flickered in surprise, but he took her hand quickly. She made her explanation for the benefit of the others, hoping, however, that he would know she referred to their previous evening.

"I mean—Marlene told me to be on time. I'm not usually late."

His smile was warm and genuine. "It was worth it. You are looking especially beautiful, Miss Gregg."

Evidently, Eric Raeder did not hold

grudges. She put that in his plus column. It was another quality which set him apart from Martin Helm who used to magnify very small grievances. For a long time after the breaking off with him, she had feared that vengeful streak in him more than anything else.

Pauly said in a bored voice, "I'm holding the lift."

In excellent spirits, the rest of the party got into the elevator. Out in the square the children argued about who should sit in the front seat of Eric's rented Mercedes, but Miss Tibbs, intercepting a look from Eric, said firmly, "I am not going to sit in the back seat alone. Marlene, Pauly, you sit here, and here. I will be between you."

Eric helped Gregg into the front seat, a gesture she was seldom prepared for. Most of her escorts climbed into and out of their cars, galloped to whatever door was their destination and then looked around, surprised that she had not beaten them to their goal. Often, thanks to force of habit and long legs, she did beat them.

Eric said in a low voice that was pleasantly humorous, "I had better get in before Marlene decides she wants the driver's seat."

They both laughed, with a delightful sense of comradeship over a shared joke. In the back seat Marlene chattered a great deal, giving her companions information on every subject, often gratuitous facts already known to her brother, who interrupted vainly with, "*I* know that, silly!"

Under cover of all this clatter Eric asked Gregg, "Did Marlene really force you to come along today?" He was looking straight ahead as they approached the ferry named for the Melancholy Dane but ironically flying the bright blue and yellow Swedish flag. Eric's left hand was on the wheel; his right lay at his side, temptingly close to her thigh in the space between their seats.

Gregg made a droll face. "Not quite. But she used the most enticing means, telling me that you disliked the idea. In fact, you had forbidden her to ask me. I certainly couldn't resist an invitation like that."

He scowled at her, but laughter was in his eyes, and almost without knowing which of them had promoted the intimacy his right hand covered her left and their fingers were tightly locked.

When they pulled up behind a series of vehicles waiting for the ferry, Marlene and Pauly fought loudly to see who could collect the first German or Swiss license symbols. Curiously enough, Miss Tibbs did not silence them, and it was only when Gregg saw the governess smiling at her that she understood that the good lady was trying to provide a cover for the private conversation between Raeder and Gregg.

"Now, we get out and go upstairs," Marlene announced.

"Abovedecks," Paul corrected his sister with bored superiority.

"—and drink a *jus d'orange*," finished Marlene, elaborately ignoring him.

Miss Tibbs put her thin arms out, holding back both children. "Not until the ship sails!"

The governess and her two charges moved toward the stairs, still arguing. Eric turned his head, studying Gregg. She found herself surprisingly ill at ease, but not enough to release her fingers from his strong, warm clasp. When he spoke she

155

was left with her mouth open, not knowing what to say.

"Who is he?"

She finally managed a feeble, "Who is who?"

"The man I remind you of."

He would not say another word to help her out or indicate his real feelings beneath what she could see was a genuine attraction to her. Was he angry, jealous or just curious? After her first awkward hesitation, she explained carefully, "He was a man I knew a long time ago."

"Were you in love with him?"

"As much as anyone is at eighteen."

He pulled back a little, stared at her as if trying to test her face for the truth, then laughed abruptly and relaxed. "A boy in school."

She did not deny it, but he persisted.

"How could you hate a schoolboy so violently?"

"Hate?" Her first reaction was one of bitter amusement that he should be so mistaken about the great love of her life. Her second reaction was shock at the admission that she could still have ambivalent feelings about a monster like Martin

Helm. "Believe me," she lied, "he isn't—wasn't important enough to hate."

"And I reminded you of him? I'm flattered." He was smiling, but she didn't like that sardonic twist to his mouth. She looked down at their hands and, moving her thumb in his clasp, she caressed his little finger.

"I don't suppose you could forgive me for a mood. It was fright, I think." That, at least, was true. She waited anxiously for his reaction, but the ferry had pulled out into midstream and Marlene's voice shrilly broke their mood.

"That's the Kattegat on your left hand. And this way is the Baltic Sea. Isn't that so, Miss Tibbs?"

"Very true, my dear. Many waters mingle with others as the Kattegat, down from Sweden and the north Danish Islands, mingles with the Baltic Sea, which is very famous in history, you know."

"It looks cold," Pauly observed. They were lucky to catch a glimpse of the choppy blue waters behind the tunnel-like interior of the ferry.

Eric sighed, released Gregg's hand. "I

think we have kept them waiting long enough. Shall we go up on deck?"

She would like to have remained in that warm intimacy forever, or at least for the duration of the crossing, but she said gaily, "Great, though I think I'll have coffee instead of Marlene's *jus d'orange*."

They all climbed the steep stairs to the deck above and the children ran ahead to the self-service section of the restaurant counters. Miss Tibbs hurried after them, issuing orders which, Gregg was surprised to find, the children obeyed.

Eric went to order coffee for Gregg and himself while she wandered off to the far end of the deck, in the hope of getting a place at the long tables which were already filling up. Several men and women from a bus tour rushed to take the last few places before Gregg could slide in and hold them. She tried to shrug her way in, using her hips, but, failing this, looked over toward self-service, only to find Eric in the same fix. Self-service was even slower than the waiter service.

Since it would be several minutes before he made it to the counter, Gregg walked out on the afterdeck. The inky blue, windswep waters of the Kattegat—or was it the Baltic Sea?—impressed her as always. Like other great bodies of water, its power and strength, its ferocity, appealed to her, as did all of nature that never allowed itself to be conquered by man.

Behind her, a group of loud-talking German tourists approached the rail, pointing out the myriad flags on the scores of boats that dotted the busy waters between Denmark and Sweden. In the scuffle to reach the rail, two women elbowed Gregg aside, bringing her briefly to her knees. She was helped up by several in the group, and accepted their apologies as graciously as she could. But in the accident her knee was badly scraped, and, after a few seconds of numbness, it began to bleed and to sting.

Gregg limped away and, finding an empty space near a stanchion, leaned against it and took the strap of her handbag off her shoulder. She usually had a Band-Aid or two for emergencies, but as luck would have it, this time she didn't.

"Damn!"

She limped back through the eating area, waved to Eric Raeder who had two coffee mugs in his hand and was about to fill them. He looked from the mugs to the man behind the long counter and would have started after her but she motioned him to remain.

"I'll be back," she called, hoping he would stay there. He looked as though he might join her, and again she waved him back. If there was one thing she needed as much as a Band-Aid or a handkerchief, it was a cup of coffee. She looked around, saw the door to the lower deck stairs and limped across the deck. She would have to go back to the car to look for something for her knee.

The stairs were tipped with metal and plunged down at a steep angle. The lower deck was heavily shadowed, jammed bumper to bumper with autos, trucks and even two tour buses. She closed the door behind her and started down. Almost immediately, the door opened again, light from above spilling into the stairway. Greg limped on, one step at a time, then reached out to the metal railing for support.

At that second, a heavy pressure—two strong hands?—was applied between her shoulder blades. Only her frantic hold o the rail kept her from plunging down the metal-tipped stairs to the deck far below.

She heard her own startled cry and then a scream. Her body went under the rail and for a minute she was suspended over space, but she did not let go of the rail.

From somewhere on the deck below came the sound of footsteps. Rescue. In a blur, like flashes of a speeded-up movie, she thought she made out Eric Raeder's face above her as she looked up toward the door before it closed and she was alone in shadows once more.

10

ON the deck below she heard footsteps again. She cried out but it was hardly necessary. By the time the tall, blond, Swedish deckhand arrived below her, she had swung herself back under the rail and sat on a stair, hugging her shoulders and groaning. She wondered if she had pulled every muscle in her body with that mad clutch at the railing. She had saved her life, but the terror, that confused memory of Eric's—or was it Martin Helm's?—face above her remained.

The husky young Swede galloped up the stairs, taking several at a time, and bent over her. In heavily accented English he asked, "You fell? You are injured? Where is injury?"

Between her teeth she muttered, "Pulled the muscles," and asked after she could get her breath, "Did you see anyone go back through that door to the upper deck?"

He had seen nothing. She appeared to be unhurt, so he hurried past her, looking for the answer to her question, but was halted by the German tourist group heading down to their bus on the lower deck. Gregg got up with difficulty and found herself squeezed against the rail by the passengers rattling down the stairs. Among them were Marlene and Pauly, with Miss Tibbs breathlessly huffing behind them.

Marlene grabbed at Gregg who groaned but listened. "Uncle says the coffee will get cold. He says you still have time to drink it upstairs."

"Abovedecks," Pauly repeated the old argument.

Marlene pushed him. Gregg gasped and cried out, but the children were evidently used to this mutual violence. Pauly did not lose a single step but grabbed the rail and went on. Gregg stopped Marlene.

"Marlene, did you see your uncle all the time up there by the man with the coffee?"

"*Ja*. I mean, I did. There was a crowd, but he was there all the time."

"You are sure."

"I am sure. I think."

The chances were the girl would have seen Eric if he crossed the deck and came through that companionway door. Either

Martin Helm was around, or she had imagined the whole thing. Whatever the explanation, the mere idea was a horror. She let Marlene go on down to the line of cars while she made her way to the upper deck. Her knee had stopped bleeding but it was stiff as a board.

At a long table, now partially deserted, Eric sat with two mugs of coffee and several slices of cheese. When he saw her, he waved the cheese and got up to meet her. No. He was not the creature she had seen vaguely in the stairwell, perhaps only in her terrified mind. This Eric Raeder would never do such a thing. She went to meet him. Shocked at her disheveled looks, he helped her to the bench, lifted the coffee to her lips and looked at her anxiously.

"What has happened to you? You are hurt! Where have you been?"

She shrugged it off, briefly explaining that she had gone to get a handkerchief for a skinned knee.

"But why did you not come to me? I have a handkerchief." He drew it out to demonstrate, but she waved it away.

"Coffee is what I need now. Oh! How good that tastes!"

"You should not have gone out on the deck in the cold. You are shivering. Here." He began to take off his short pea jacket. She objected, but he had it around her shoulders before she could refuse it. He did not seem to need it himself, as he was also wearing a turtleneck sweater that looked very warm and suited him perfectly, showing off his lean, muscular body.

Either the hot coffee, or the jacket, or the mere presence of Eric Raeder so close beside her, effected a cure. She got over most of her fears. Even if Martin Helm *was* lurking around, and that seemed highly improbable, Eric would be more than his match.

This time they went down to the car together, with Eric helping her even when there seemed no longer a necessity for his hand firmly fastened around her forearm. Miss Tibbs and the children seemed genuinely sorry about her accident, and Pauly went so far as to offer graciously, "You can lean on me, if you like."

The ferry pulled into its slip at the Swedish port of Malmö, and Gregg's first sight of that immaculate city was a huge, ugly, gray complex looking like a cement works, putting out billows of smoggy fumes, but it was the last ugly sight she noticed in Malmö. This was the Scandinavia she had always heard about but never quite believed existed. The clean, shining, high-rise buildings were relieved from a sterile look by the addition of endless geraniums and other hardy, bright flowers on balconies and in windows. She thought it a pity that the car whipped through the city so fast, but they were headed north toward Sweden's château country. It occurred to Gregg that if Martin Helm had been on the boat, he might make himself noticeable by following the Mercedes to its destination.

She loved the autumn fields and, most of all, the wooded sectors that they came upon so unexpectedly. She had thought at first that they were on their way to visit relatives or old friends, which meant that she must be on her best behavior, for she wanted to make Eric Raeder's people like her.

On the other hand, such relations might give her more protection. She closed her eyes at the thought of going back to a hotel room alone, an easy target for the haunting Martin Helm. How had he discovered her in New York? She was sure he had been keeping tabs on her lately, but there was no real evidence, nothing she could offer as proof.

She refused to let herself believe that Eric Raeder had any connection with her fall, beyond his unfortunate resemblance to Helm. If only the two were not so inevitably tied together by their looks. As the minutes passed, separating her from the ferry accident, she built up more reasons for believing that the thing had never happened. After all, she was alive and safe, allowing for the pulled muscles, with no more damage than she had when she started down those stairs. If someone like Helm had meant to kill her, she would certainly be dead.

Gregg broke the family's unaccustomed silence to ask hesitantly, "Are we visiting relations of your family?"

Eric smiled without looking at her, as if he had some delightful secret. "It is a castle open to the public. We do this often. Miss Tibbs and the children and I. It is a *camping*."

"A what?" She wondered if she had heard right. It would be just like this wild family to take her on an overnight trip, and she totally unprepared, with no nightgown, makeup or even a coat.

"You are going to spend the night with us. We have kidnapped you."

She began to laugh, but the act of laughing made her wince at the pressure on her sore muscles. This time he looked at her with a tenderness, a warmth, that made her heart lurch with desire.

"Never did a victim go more gladly," she assured him.

A muscle in his cheek betrayed his own concern over her reply. She was enormously pleased, and excited. She wanted to play it low-key, however, not to jump and tell the world (and him) how happy all of this made her. Happy and relieved. Tonight in particular, she wanted to be with people she liked, people who were as unlike that old, remembered passion as possible.

They passed through another of the clean, neat towns, bright and cheerful with red-painted houses that loomed up more cheerful than ever against the incredible blue of the sky.

"We're coming to it," Marlene began in

a singsong voice. "I get the room facing the lake."

"I get that room. You had it last time," Pauly protested, probably with good cause. They both looked to Eric as umpire, while Gregg laughed, feeling wonderful.

"I was an only child, so I never knew what companionship there was in fighting with a sister. Or a brother."

He laughed shortly. "My brother and I fought all the time. He was a jolly fellow, brilliant and very lucky. He never spent much time studying. I was different. Everything came hard to me in school. I envied and admired him. I think I must have wanted to be Rolfe. My brother."

"I'm glad you are not."

With genuine curiosity he asked her, "Why?"

"Because perfection isn't a lot of fun." He looked at her. She added, "I like you as you are."

"So I do," Marlene put in, to Gregg's discomfort and amusement, for Marlene had heard the entire conversation.

Gregg wondered if she should apologize to the children for her backhanded slap at their father, but it seemed to her that if she called their attention to the matter, she would only make a big thing of the conversation. She was relieved when Miss Tibbs interrupted.

"This is the turnoff, I believe, Mr. Raeder."

Through the autumn woods the highway wound around thick groves of trees, strange, stark and lean, with the leaves already fallen, a witch's woods. A cold fog crept along close to the ground, and the children laughed, taking turns at wild details of former exploration. Gregg sank deeper into the warmth of Eric's coat, then glanced at him to see if he needed it. For some reason, he seemed not to mind the cold. He looked very rugged as she studied him.

Like Martin Helm. . . and yet not like him in the warm, human, unselfish ways that counted.

They came to black, wrought-iron gates, and entered the Torsten Estate. Gregg had seen castles over half the world, and stayed in many of those which currently appealed to the Beautiful People, but the château at the end of the estate road was old, vine-covered and made of some curious stone that turned gloriously pink in the afternoon fog. A three-story tower bordered a small lake north of the castle, and attached to it was a modern, two-story wing. Gregg guessed at once that the room being quarreled over by the children was the tempting one on the third floor, under the long, slanting roof of the tower.

"Camping in a castle?" she asked in amusement.

Marlene put in, "Oh, but it's perfect for camping! We have no beds. We sleep in sleeping bags."

Gregg thought that now she had heard everything. Taking pity on her stupefaction, and maybe not too sure of her reaction, Eric explained, "It is owned by the family of my aunt's late husband. They permit bus tours to visit the lower floor rooms during the day, and they serve coffee in the dungeon."

"A snack bar in the dungeon!"

He grinned. "What better place for it? The family charges four kronor for a— what you call demitasse. But in the evenings and on Mondays and Tuesdays, it s closed to visitors."

"It is when it is ours if we like," Pauly

explained. "And it's my turn to sleep in the tower."

Before Marlene could counter this, Eric went on. "The castle is no longer furnished, except for the display rooms, and so we bring our sleeping bags and cook our own meals over a fire in the kitchen yard, in the good weather. In bad weather, we eat in the dungeon at the tables where the tourists have their coffee."

"Sleeping bags in a castle. Now I've heard everything."

Eric asked with just a trace of sarcasm, "You are too civilized?"

She rose to the occasion. "Not at all. I was only thinking that, if I had known, I would have dressed correctly. I didn't even wear slacks."

"Marlene catches people like that." He added, much too seriously to mean it, "This requires thinking out. In all the cinemas of the Golden Years, the lady sleeps in the gentleman's pajamas which are too big and make the lady look very petite, very *gamine*. But I do not wear nightclothes. I wear my American sleeping bag. What to do? It is a puzzlement."

She grinned. "I might resort to the same

measures, if I were not in Sweden in late September."

Miss Tibbs spoke to her from the back seat. "He is being very naughty, Miss MacIvor. He has already arranged matters. You are to borrow one of my Japanese robes. They are quite roomy for me."

"Good. I am not nearly as petite as you are, Miss Tibbs."

Miss Tibbs was pleased, and Gregg liked the glance Eric gave her. He stopped the car in front of the gates and leaned his head back.

"Pauly, are you going to usher us in?"

Happy to have his own particular task, Pauly opened the door, jumped out of the car and ran to the gates. He stopped, looked around and then reached between the wrought-iron bars to rescue a hanging key with which he unlocked the gates. He waited until Eric drove up slowly, jumped into the back seat and announced, "I opened it myself. It's my gate."

"Who wants a stupid old gate?" Marlene taunted him sourly, ever the bad loser.

Eric explained to Gregg: "There is a caretaker Arne Olson, but we do not like to trouble him. He is old and sleeps at the far end of the property. During the rest of the week, when the tour buses come, Arne's two sons and daughter-in-law come up from Lund, that town we drove through."

This late in the season there was the look of winter in the air and this, with the bare tree limbs and the ground fog, gave a beautiful air of simplicity to the old house. The road ended in a kind of countrified parking area, an unpaved square of dirt before the ground-floor door to the tower. Beyond it was the little lake, its waters, of a blue that made one think of arctic icebergs, now blown and ruffled by the wind.

Even more interesting to the children and to Gregg was a spacious wire-fenced pen of gray Toulouse geese, honking, fussing and extremely anxious for attention. In spite of Miss Tibb's breathless injunctions, Marlene and Pauly poured out of the car and ran over to the geese, calling each of them by name.

"God help the Olsons if anyone should decide to have roast goose for dinner," Eric informed Gregg, who understood perfectly the children's excitement.

She admitted, "I never saw a live goose before. Somehow, they aren't as common on the streets of Chicago or New York as they are in this wonderful place. Please introduce them to me. And vice versa."

The children were delighted to do so, and although it had not been her first thought in proposing this close acquaintanceship with the enchanting, if rough-billed geese, Gregg noticed that Eric was pleased by her interest.

He and Miss Tibbs went over to unlock the door of the tower. Eric carried a key of his own that was not nearly big enough, Gregg thought, for such an impressive place.

Meanwhile, Marlene was introducing Gregg to each of a dozen gray geese.

"Fritzie. And Hannah. And Hulda. There. That fat, pushy one is Lars. Wilhelm is the little one by the lake. Always the last. He is Pauly's favorite. Mine is Ingrid. Ingrid is the first who comes to be fed. She will bite your hand if you let her."

"Thanks. I'll take your word for it." All the same, though her sympathy went out to poor Wilhelm, Gregg found it impossible

175

not to like the bumptious Ingrid who seemed ready to eat the wire fence in order to get to her, although it was clear that the day's food for the geese, a form of large grain, had long since been laid out for them.

Hearing Eric call her name, Gregg crossed the hard ground to the tower. Eric stuck his head out, beckoned to her, and she found herself on the ground floor of the Torsten Castle.

"The guardroom," Eric said, and identified the rooms beyond as the kitchen and stillroom. They returned to the interior stone steps, on the left of the outside door. He took her hand and led her up to the second story, which he referred to in the Continental manner as the first floor. There were a few heavy, medieval pieces of furniture, a huge chest with carved elephants, tigers, crocodiles and other exotic creatures unlikely to be found in Sweden.

In several of the rooms the glass window was set deep in a stone aperture which had probably been old even when Queen Christina was upsetting the populace with her modern ways. It was cold but Gregg knew even as these moments passed, that they were among the happiest of her life. Being with Eric Raeder, becoming genuinely fond of the children and Miss Tibbs, she found that family life could be exhilarating and wonderful.

Already, Marlene and Pauly had scrambled up the winding steps ahead of the others, so eager that they fell over their own feet. Miss Tibbs followed, a trifle less enthusiastic, but doggedly determined.

"You are not bored with all this domesticity?" Eric asked anxiously.

She said, "I don't think I've ever been happier."

He looked at her. She wondered if he had been about to kiss her when Marlene came galloping in to remind her uncle, "I'm hungry."

"So am I," Gregg added.

Eric grinned, and having enlisted Pauly's aid, with Marlene following after, went out to unpack the equipment for cooking dinner in the kitchen yard, surrounded by the lake to the north, the tower to the east and the eager, talkative geese in their pen to the west.

Miss Tibbs, who obviously knew her way around, showed Gregg the ancient clothespress, which she called an "armoire," in the tiny tower room that looked out over the cold, bright waters of the lake, bordered by stark, shedding trees.

"I can see why the children quarrel over this room," Gregg told the governess as they got the sleeping bags out of the clothespress. "It is fascinating. Look at that view." A pane of glass had been set in the ancient, barred embrasure, and it was possible to see across the lake, and even over the barren forest. Winter came early in this château area of the countryside.

Gregg returned to the sleeping bags, and Miss Tibbs, observing her expression, noted sagely, "You are wondering who has been here before and used that bag."

Gregg reddened and started to deny it. Then she laughed, and demanded, "Well who was it?"

"It has been cleaned," Miss Tibbs assured her.

"It's not that."

"Well, there have been a few others, but none were very permanent. Not quite as easy to fit in as you, if you will pardon the liberty, Miss MacIvor."

Gregg's face showed the gratitude she felt. She felt greatly reassured.

Shortly after, Eric and the children returned to help choose "bedrooms" and set up the sleeping bags. It was established that Pauly was entitled to the tower room. Marlene and Miss Tibbs would take the south room on the same level and, as the governess explained delicately, Eric and Gregg would have two of the rooms on the floor below.

"Seems most satisfactory, Miss Tibbs," Eric announced as he bundled up the bags and carried them down the spiral steps.

He had been right about the empty rooms. Gregg's "bedroom" had stone walls covered by ancient tapestries and only one piece of furniture, a huge milord chair about four hundred years old. Excellent, Gregg thought, getting into the spirit of things. I can hang my clothes on the chair.

When she turned around, she found Eric standing in the open doorway between his room and hers, watching her face. He found her expression funny, and before she could do more than change the position of the sleeping bag, he was at her side with an armful of cushions and pillows. He threw them on the floor and placed the sleeping bag on top of them.

After that, Eric brought her down to the kitchen yard where, in spite of fog creeping through the woods and a light wind blowing across the lake, Gregg found herself delighting in the charm of a big wood fire which burned her face and hands while her back got goose bumps in spite of Eric's heavy jacket.

She soon forgot about the cold, however, and the distant setting sun, the lonely, desolate surroundings; for even if she had not been stimulated by Eric's presence, the enthusiasm of the children and Miss Tibbs would have warmed her spirits. Everyone was anxious to make her feel at home, even Pauly, although he was a trifle less enthusiastic, perhaps resenting the absence of his mother, whom he clearly adored.

Marlene giggled at the sight of Gregg's face when she received her plate of the cold hors d'oeuvres, assorted tiny fish and other smorgasbord delicacies.

Gregg asked, "Do you swear that none of these flat things are snails?"

They all laughed, so she did her best and ate everything. It was surprisingly good, but then, when Pauly and Eric began to broil the thick steaks on a grate over the coals, she blamed everyone for filling her up before dinnertime. Pauly made his first little joke to her, volunteering to eat her steak as a favor to her, but Gregg ate not only the steak but also some slices of ripe tomatoes and cucumbers obtained in some mysterious fashion for this picnic.

Over dinner they told tales of former picnics at the castle, and Gregg tried to discover which of the females they mentioned had come as Eric's particular visitors. It was not until they were all eating Danish pastries for dessert that Gregg realized Eric had once been engaged to the children's mother, and that the beautiful Ursula must have been the great love of his life. Small wonder that Pauly was jealous of his uncle's attentions to Gregg. He probably wanted Eric to marry Ursula.

She tried to show everyone that she fitted in. As a matter of fact, it was one of the most pleasant efforts she had ever made. Once in a while, watching Eric with the children, she remembered how good Martin Helm had been with children. He liked to impress them, and often would go out of his way to win their friendship, as if under some compulsion which obviously did not exist in his relations with women. How Martin Helm must hate women!

The memory of times he had demonstrated this to those other women made Gregg hug her shoulders at the chilling thought, and Eric noticed at once, with concern.

"Gregg, you are cold!" He got up briskly, in spite of her protests. "Well, now, Captain Pauly, Colonel Marlene, comes the bad part. You clean up the dishes."

Gregg protested, "No, please. I want to do something myself. I'll wash. Maybe someone will dry for me."

After some polite quibbling, she was permitted to do as she wished. Marlene wanted to help her but was voted down by Miss Tibbs who reminded the girl that she hadn't made up her bed yet, and Marlene ran up into the tower to do so. While Pauly helped his uncle make up a fire in the large living room which Eric called a "solar," Miss Tibbs remarked in a low voice to Gregg, "You have had an excellent influence upon Mr. Raeder, if I may say so."

"You may, indeed," Gregg whispered. "But how is my influence good?"

"He used to be very moody and much to himself. And his temper was awful. He was jealous of his brother, about the children's mother, I used to think. You know, of course, that Mr. Rolfe more or less charmed her away from his brother. And being the heir to the Raeder properties, Rolfe had more to offer at that time. Mrs. Ursula has always been one to look out for a good opportunity."

"Yes, I've met her, and I suppose I was a little jealous, too. She's gorgeous."

"My dear," Miss Tibbs leaned over the bucket of hot water and soap suds to add in confidence, "you need not be jealous. She is no competition to you. Marlene and Mr. Eric are both fond of you. Anyone may see that."

"And Pauly?" Gregg asked ruefully.

Miss Tibbs shrugged her shoulders. "I'm afraid he is swayed by his mother's beauty. It could hardly be her attentions. She goes months without seeing the children. I don't approve of that. Not one little bit!"

After that, the time passed much too swiftly. They gathered around the huge hearth in the solar, a room that would have been barren and considerably less comfortable without the snapping and crackling of the fire, and told ghost stories.

The children went reluctantly up to bed at nine o'clcok, but even before Marlene and Pauly had gone, Gregg noticed that Eric seemed lost in his own thoughts.

He said finally, "Miss Tibbs, I am sure you are a match for any poltergeist, even the one you mentioned in your story, but are you a match for a *Doppelgänger*? A double of yourself that you might see one day—come face to face—" He broke off.

"It is supposed to be a sign of one's death, sir, but I can tell you that that belief is totally without foundation," the little woman assured him in the most ordinary tones, as if encounters with *Doppelgängers* were everyday events.

Eric laughed, reached for the governess's hand and brought it to his lips. "Miss Tibbs, you are a blessing. If I ever see my *Doppelgänger*, I devoutly hope you will be nearby, to assure me on that point."

Gregg looked anxiously at Eric, trying to

figure out his true thoughts. Miss Tibbs apologetically mentioned the time, which was midnight, and left to prepare herself for bed and, more slowly, Eric and Gregg went to their rooms. She hoped he might continue to talk about his *Doppelgänger*, about the fears that seemed to haunt him, but he hardly spoke at all until they reached her door.

He said good night, then kissed her, their bodies blending together. Then perhaps he thought of the children overhead, and he drew away from her gently. He kissed her once more, this time a "goodnight" kiss and, having recovered his composure, grinned and went into the next room.

In Miss Tibb's much too short and snug Japanese kimono, Gregg crawled into the sleeping bag, her senses having been so much aroused by that first kiss that she could not immediately get to sleep. There was an eerie silver light coming through the uncurtained window, and once the lamps were turned off this moonlight kept her awake, but eventually she closed her eyes.

Only a few hours passed before Gregg awoke. She thought it must be about two o'clock. With effort, she pulled her arm out from the entanglements of the sleeping bag and propped herself up on her elbow. She turned her head toward the doorway, wondering what had awakened her. Startled, she saw Eric walk past her fully dressed and headed toward the winding stone steps outside the doorway to her room.

She sat up, and after blinking repeatedly, decided she had indeed seen what she thought she had seen. Craning her neck, she watched him pass her room without a glance, as if he did not know she, or anyone else, was here.

Baffled, she unzipped the bag as far as possible and wriggled out silently. He had started down the steps. Consumed by curiosity, she followed. She had reached the stone landing outside her room and was wondering whether to go farther after him, when the dislodging of a pebble on the steps above made her look up.

Marlene was rapidly, but quietly, approaching her. The girl put a finger to her lips and when she reached Gregg, she whispered, "He walks in his sleep. It's very odd."

Gregg remembered a flash of his face in

the faint starlight as he had passed her. He had looked troubled, though his deep-set, dark eyes expressed very little.

"Will he be all right?" she whispered.

Marlene shrugged. "He always has been."

11

"THEN he's done this before?"

"Not for a while. He never does much. You'll see. Just walks and stops and thinks about things."

Marlene showed every sign of going after him, so Gregg retied the sash of Miss Tibbs's Japenese kimono and went along as well. There were several apertures cut into the wall as the steps descended, each long since covered by glass or shutters, but now they gave faint illumination to the steps.

Out on the grounds, Eric Raeder walked past the Mercedes, did not seem to see it, and crossed over toward the lake. He took long, easy strides, avoiding the area where the fire had been laid last night. Not far away, the gray geese, hearing his footsteps or sensing his presence, began to stir and to scratch the ground, flapping their wings with a leathery noise. One of them made a curious, cackling sound. The others would have echoed the noise but Marlene shushed them.

"Shouldn't we do something?" Gregg asked anxiously. But of course the child knew very little more than she did. They could only stand there watching him, wondering what was in his mind as he stopped before the rushes at the edge of the lake and simply stared out at the rippling water that seemed to be blowing toward him.

Gregg could wait no longer. She went across the ground slowly, trying to be silent but aware that she wanted him to wake up of his own accord. The geese obliged her. They flapped their wings frantically and by now the whole gaggle had been aroused.

There was a high wooden railing to which an old rowboat was tied. Eric moved along the shore, through some mud and rushes to the rail. By now, the geese had stirred up such a racket it was obvious to Gregg that Raeder must have been awakened. What a terrifying thing it must be to find oneself in a totally different place, having dressed without realizing it, and walked so far, without having any memory of doing so.

He leaned deliberately on the rail, with both arms crossed, and continued to watch the water. Now Gregg was sure he had come out of the unconscious state and would be safe. She did not want him to think she was spying on him and, seeing Marlene tiptoe in through the open door to the tower, she started to follow.

"Gregg?"

She stopped. For a full minute she waited in dismay, hating to be caught sneaking away after playing the spy. He had not moved toward her or spoken again. She got up her nerve, turned around and walked back across the ground to the railing where he remained, leaning on his folded arms. Looking over his shoulder, he was watching her as she approached.

He waited until she was beside him before he said with a little smile that stirred her heart, "Well, no one is perfect."

She raised her arms, rested them on the rail, touching his. "I'll be the first one to admit that," she answered lightly.

He looked as if he might have pursued the opening this gave him, but instead turned to stare out at the lake, frowning. "So, now you know."

She had it on the tip of her tongue to say something amusing, to reassure him with a laugh, but her instinct saved her. She turned his face to hers and kissed him gently on the lips. Then, still watching her, he began to explain.

"I found myself doing just such ridiculous—what you call weird—things when I was a boy. Rolfe always knew when it happened. Sometimes he would follow me. Afterward, he would tease . . . 'What is that other fellow up to?' he used to say."

"Other fellow? What did he mean?"

"The—the one who got up in the night and dressed, fastened buttons, zipped zippers, sometimes even chose a tie to wear, and went wherever it was."

"Did you go far? How long did it last?"

His face looked thin, the high cheekbones more prominent in the starlight. "I cannot know that. I only know how it is when I wake. Confusion. A horrible, haunting fear. Humiliation. To be caught like this . . ." Beside him, she stirred and he moved his crossed arms closer to her. "It is different with you. I am glad you know. I dreaded the time when you would find out. But not now. I'm glad it is over."

191

"Over?" she echoed, not sure she understood. "Do you feel that it won't happen again?"

He slapped the rail. It trembled under his hand. "You still don't see. It was you. I was always afraid you would find out."

"Why would it make a difference to me?" she asked flatly. After a long minute or two during which he studied her profile, she felt she had better explain. "I love you, Eric. How could a little sleepwalking matter to me?"

He reacted slowly. She began to be afraid he was still asleep, his eyes wide, but without expression. It seemed that he was memorizing her features, written as they were in the black and silver of the starlight. She was afraid to breathe for fear his mood would change.

He cleared his throat, asked huskily, "Do you mean that?"

She felt too shaky, too hopeful, to spoil the mood with words, and could only nod. He reached over, took her hand and brought it to his lips. She felt the pinprick of tears, both of happiness and compassion, as she reacted to his touch and to his obvious emotion. He examined her hand, turned it over in his palm.

"Were you ever married before?"

It was a strange proposal, if it was a proposal. She could see that it mattered to him and she was intensely relieved at being able to say, "No. Never." Amazed at her own timidity, she went on in a wavering voice, "Until now?"

The questioning tone made him laugh and broke the tension. He said, "Until you marry me." He took her shoulders, drew her close and kissed her. It was a kiss of warmth and commitment and unity. Their previous nerve-racking moments of truth had briefly taken their passion from them, but their need for each other seemed greater now than ever. The tenderness they shared supported each of them, glossing over past fears and failures.

With her hand against his cheek, he studied the enormous sky as it seemed to turn a trifle lighter. He murmured against her uncombed hair, "How different today is from yesterday. . . and all the yesterdays!"

Within the warm confines of his arms, she contradicted him. "But you were here yesterday. And I could look at you. And hope."

He laughed. She felt the movement of his throat muscles and was aware of how sensual his touch could be. Her mind wandered. It was as if nothing had come between her and Martin Helm long ago, she thought. They were together at last. The tortured wants and dreams of eleven years had been filled. Then, furious with her own weakness, she banished the memory and the comparison. It was not Helm but Eric Raeder she loved. Eric's needs, like hers, had been filled by the marvelous luck of their meeting.

"Thank God for Oliver Sills," he said, evidently thinking back to their meeting. She wondered if he knew Sills had arranged her reservations in Copenhagen at the same hotel as that one often visited by Eric Raeder.

"I remember. I remember every detail . . . the way you looked as I saw you in the elevator. I looked in the mirrored wall of the lobby. And the doors closed, and I remember. . ." She broke off, suddenly reliving the dread of those first moments of their meeting, but fortunately he misunderstood and took up the scene as she described, from his viewpoint.

"The most beautiful legs I had ever seen!" he said, smiling, proud of her. "I saw all this glorious red hair. Then I went on up to the office of your friend Oliver. But all the time we talked I thought of that glorious redhead. Then I saw your photograph on his bookshelf. I asked who you were. And when I came out, I met you. A miracle."

"A minor miracle. The big miracle was yesterday, when Marlene insisted that I go with you."

"Yes," he agreed, with a delightful pretense at gravity. "We certainly owe Marlene a great deal."

The girl's unexpected giggle told them they were under observation. Gregg started. She was unused to relatives or friends spying on her, but Eric Raeder made no bones about holding her as he turned and, with his free hand, motioned for Marlene to join them. The girl ran across the pebbled ground in her slippers and threw her arms around Eric and his fiancée.

Gregg found herself crying, which was

absurd. She had never been happier, and that frightened her. It wasn't natural to be so happy. Unfortunately for her own mood, the volatile Marlene began to cry as well.

"I did it. I did it. It was me. I knew you belonged together. Like in the cinema. A lot Pauly knows. As if I care what he thinks! He is so silly."

That artless disclosure made Gregg laugh. Eric smiled but probably did not appreciate Pauly's perfectly reasonable feelings. Fearing Gregg might be hurt in spite of her laugh, he raised his hand to her neck, then pulled her head in close, with her neck cradled in the crook of his arm.

"Maybe we should be careful how we explain it to Pauly. And as for Miss Tibbs, it wouldn't surprise me to know she engineered the whole affair," she said.

"I object. I think *I* had a little something to do with it," Eric insisted.

Marlene wanted to run back up every step of the tower to give her brother and the governess the news, but she was dissuaded by the practical Gregg. They all returned to their rooms in the tower together, walking on tiptoe to keep from waking the others. Marlene hugged the lovers and ran noisily upward.

Eric and Gregg stood in her room, beside her sleeping bag, and she sensed that he wanted her at this minute and would have made love to her on the stone floor with no light but the cold, silver stars outside the window, but she heard a shuffling noise on the steps and whispered, "I think Pauly is coming to investigate."

He nodded. They kissed long and tenderly, as if they would mate first with the flesh of their lips.

A sharp, gasping breath warned them that someone was watching. Gregg brushed Eric's ear with her lips, murmuring, "Pauly."

Eric grinned, agreed but did not turn around. Perhaps he didn't want to break the mood between them. All this, Gregg feared, would be held against them by his nephew. Just as Gregg caught sight of him over Eric's shoulder, the boy bolted back up the steps. She ran her long fingers over the always fascinating planes of Eric's face.

"Sweetheart, we have the rest of our lives. Let's try and make him understand first."

His eyes caught the starlight. They seemed to glitter as he looked around, missed Pauly and then gazed at her.

"I do not know why my wife should be a subject for discussion with my eight-year-old nephew. But I yield to your better knowledge of children."

He kissed her two hands lightly, glanced once over his shoulder, and saw nothing. Then he went into his own room. During the entire time since she had agreed to marry him, nothing had been said about the cause which had brought Gregg and Marlene out onto the grounds beside the chilly lake. Surely they would talk of it in future. She had ideas about it. The fact that his brother, the superior, flawless and perfect older brother, had referred to him in his sleepwalking state as "the other one" suggested all sorts of things, not the least of which was the novel *Doppelgänger* which had made Eric Raeder more famous than his brother. There were all sorts of connections, but she felt instinctively that she must be very careful in discussing such matters with him.

In the morning came congratulations from Miss Tibbs and the renewed excitement of Marlene. It also brought the deep, silent resentment of Pauly Raeder. No one mentioned Eric's middle-of-the-night stroll. Gregg spent most of the morning and their return ride as far as Malmö, trying, in Marlene's language, to "show Pauly how nice she could be."

"But you oughtn't to try so hard," Marlene advised her. "He can tell that you don't mean it."

"I *do* mean it. I want him to like me."

The females were washing up in the ladies' room of the St. Jörgen Hotel in Malmö. They had worked their way through the midday smorgasbord and now been promised the sight of some rare, live black swans in the local park.

The pragmatic Marlene said, "Well, if the swans don't cheer Pauly, you certainly can't hope to. Let's go and see what the swans will do."

"Let's," agreed Miss Tibbs.

Marlene went out arm in arm with both women, but though Eric was glad to see them and complained that they had just spent hours apart, Pauly still had nothing to say to Gregg. They went down the stairs and out to the street, the children quarreling about who should walk with Eric.

Hearing the problem, Gregg tried to step aside and offer her place beside her fiancé to Pauly, but Eric held her fast, refusing to let her go. Perfectly audible to Pauly, he said, "You are going to be my wife, and the children know it. You mustn't start wrong, *Liebchen*. Self-sacrifice is not good."

She could think of no way to please both Eric and the children, so she could only go along with Eric's solution.

They all enjoyed the two black swans who, like Marlene, appeared to be spoiled, opinionated and much used to being the center of attention. Learning more about the children seemed extraordinarily important to Gregg now. They were not Eric's children, but his success with them showed what a superb father he would be. She found it strange but increasingly wonderful to picture Eric as the father of her children. She reverted mentally to those ecstatic days of her eighteenth year when she pictured Martin Helm as the father of her children.

Marlene chattered on, giving names to

the swans, and they all followed them around the lake. Then, far too late, Gregg looked around and saw that Pauly had disappeared. She did not want to worry Eric who was explaining the origin of the big black swans to Miss Tibbs, so she walked over to Marlene.

"Where did your brother go? He shouldn't wander too far away in a strange city."

Marlene shrugged. "It is all right. He speaks a little Swedish. He will find us."

"Find us? *Where is he?*"

"He's such a silly little boy, he's probably off sulking, making as if he has disappeared, so we will worry. We mustn't let him know we do worry. Not that *I* do!"

"I know it is only a joke. But, Marlene I—we depend on you to help us find him." Gregg was getting worried. She could not see the boy anywhere in the park. "How can he have gotten so far away? I just saw him a few minutes ago."

"No," Marlene disagreed, her smooth forehead wrinkled in a frown. "It's been longer than that. He had thirty Swedish kronor, so he probably wanted to spend them before we get back to Copenhagen.

Maybe he took an autobus back to the Hotel St. Jörgen. There were a lot of shops around there. He is sure to be there."

Gregg backtracked to Eric who was listening interestedly to Miss Tibbs. She touched his arm. Seeing her face, Miss Tibbs broke off in alarm.

"What is it, Miss MacIvor? What has happened?"

"Marlene and I were talking about Pauly. He seems to have wandered off."

Eric swung around, away from the fence and the long, black, serpent-like neck of the male swan.

"What the devil? Pauly?. . . Pauly!"

Several other visitors to the park turned to stare at him and then to look anxiously for their own youngsters. Miss Tibbs began to blame herself, in spite of Marlene's insistence that it was all Pauly's doing.

"He only wanted to make us look for him."

"And so we are," Eric chided her sharply. "Where has he gone, Marlene? Tell me!" There was no mistaking the authority, or the anger, in that voice.

"I don't know, Uncle. Truly! I don' know for certain." The girl was a little frightened and Gregg felt that she was telling the truth partially, at least.

Eric strode off, away from the women, toward the car.

Gregg put her arm around Marlene, and, with the nervous Miss Tibbs in tow, they hurried after Eric.

It was soon evident that Pauly had not lingered around the park. At the park entrance, a young blond artist was sketching a general view of the park. He did not look up from his sketch pad when Eric spoke to him in German.

"Have you seen a boy pass you in the last few minutes? A boy alone, eight years old?"

The artist waved airily with his pencil. He seemed to understand German, as so many Swedes do.

"Passed me. He liked my work."

"What did he do then?" Eric asked. To Gregg, who shared Miss Tibbs's nervousness, he sounded more anxious than he would like them to believe.

"He waved a thumb at passing cars, so. A Volvo took him up, that way. Toward the center of the city. After that it was not my concern." The artist went back to work.

Marlene made a muffled sound. Gregg, who was closest to her, was sure she said, "I think—" and broke off. Probably, she did not want to betray her little brother whom she nagged and tried to dominate but whose welfare was a deep concern.

"Marlene," pleaded Gregg, "if you suspect anything, please tell us. Is he just running away because he is unhappy and doesn't like me?"

"Oh, no. It's not you. It's anybody. Except Mama. He always wanted Uncle Eric to be our father after Papa died. I told him Uncle wouldn't be so silly. Who would want to marry Mama except that awful Heinz Albrecht?"

Gregg smiled. "But then, you think Pauly had another purpose in running away."

"But, of course. To send a cable."

"A cable! A boy of eight send a cable?"

With patience, Marlene said, "He's seen me send them. And I've seen Miss Tibbs He will ask a grown-up to help him. H may be silly, but he is not stupid."

Gregg began to think that both childre

were prodigies, probably because they spent so much time with adults, and precious little time with children their own age. It was sad, but it hadn't hurt Marlene very much, in any case.

Eric, who had helped Miss Tibbs into the back of the car, returned to Gregg and Marlene.

"What do you think, darling?" he asked Gregg.

"Marlene wonders if he might have gone into the center of the city, back to the St. Jörgen Hotel."

He put his hands out, took Gregg's hand and Marlene's. On their way to the car he asked the child, "Why would he go there? Did he leave something at the hotel?"

"I think he went to cable Mama to come home."

"I see. Yes. It sounds like Pauly." He ruffled Marlene's hair. She wrinkled her nose, but clearly did not mind the friendly gesture. He explained to Gregg, "It's just as well. I was going to write, but we will let Pauly announce the best news I've ever had to give anyone. I'll telephone to Aunt Alex tonight from Copenhagen. I want you to love her as I do." He smiled. "And vice versa."

She wished to believe him, but wondered if Pauly's dislike would rub off on Baroness Alexandra de Lieven. They piled into the car, with Gregg beside Eric. He pulled her closer to him.

"I feel better when you are near me," he said.

But she was lost in thought. As they drove away, Gregg suddenly realized that it had been a long while since she'd last thought about, or feared, Martin Helm. Maybe Eric's presence in my life has canceled him out for good, she told herself with a smile.

12

GREGG learned a great deal about Pauly Raeder that day. He was matter-of-fact, deliberate, stubborn to the point of intransigence. They found him exactly where Marlene said they would, in the lobby of the St. Jörgen Hotel. He did not look in the least surprised to see his family, and, to Gregg's annoyance, he showed no sign of affection for his sister or his uncle. Only Miss Tibbs received his infrequent and really beautiful smile. The others, on the other hand, seemed to find young Pauly's attitude a normal one.

All the way back to the dock area of Malmö, Eric and Marlene tried to get Pauly to reveal the details of his cablegram. Gregg kept slipping farther down in her seat, wishing they would talk about something else. She could see in this argument the difficulties of understanding among such assorted personalities.

At dusk they drove onto the ferryboat *Ophelia*, and everyone seemed to be upset, angry or resentful except Gregg, who was merely ill at ease, very much aware that her engagement to Eric Raeder was the real cause of the trouble.

When they got out of the car for a walk around the deck above, Pauly hung back, and Gregg was sure he hoped to walk up the steps with his uncle, an "accidental" encounter during which they would make up. Unfortunately, Eric was behaving in his most stubborn way. These qualities being revealed so early in their relationship did not change Gregg's own feelings, except to make her aware that she loved him as much for his faults as for his virtues.

He put his arm around her, firmly ignoring Pauly, and started up the steps. She felt his attitude was a mistake, but did not think a stubborn man could be won over by a blunt statement, or even by wheedling, so she kept her opinion to herself. There were other ways to bring about a reconcilation.

"Sorry, Eric. I'll be along in a minute. I forgot a handkerchief." She laughed. "Just in case I have another accident."

He saw through that, pulled out a handkerchief of his own and offered it to her with one of the smiles which she found too endearing to ignore. Marlene promptly pushed her brother between the shoulder blades.

"Get on, Pokey-Pauly!"

Gregg cringed at Marlene's roughness. She and her brother climbed up the steep steps ahead of the grown-ups, leaving Gregg disgusted with the failure of her own first attempt to play "understanding mother."

She knew a few minutes later that Eric did care about his nephew's feelings. At the drink bar, he offered the boy a bottle of bubbly orange juice, and when Pauly shook his head and moodily walked away, Eric's troubled gaze followed him. Gregg wanted to urge him to make the first step in regaining the boy's good humor, but she wondered if that too might be a mistake. Maybe things would work out without her interference.

Marlene believed that salt was the best salve for old wounds. She advised her brother crossly within the hearing of the grown-ups, "Why don't you stop acting like a brat? I'm your friend. You needn't be mad at everyone. You're such a silly child! A baby!"

Miss Tibbs began to make peace between them, while Eric and Gregg exchanged wry grins. "God help the man Marlene marries!" he whispered.

Moody or not, Pauly seemed to find his sister's nagging perfectly understandable. He kicked at an empty paper cup on the deck and started to talk to her. The two of them wandered away to the afterdeck and began to count the many foreign flags flying from the crafts on the water.

Eric offered Gregg a cup of coffee and then, over the lip of his own cup, he murmured, "To our future!"

"Our future." She added then, trying to hold onto a cheerful mood, "Is is *prosit*, or *sköl*?"

"In these waters, perhaps it should be *sköl*."

He looked at her for a long minute. Then he asked where she preferred that they be married. She was startled at the suddenness of the question, but pleased and touched that he wanted to marry so soon.

She confessed, "I haven't thought."

That was the wrong thing to say. She

saw it at once. He looked upset, annoyed. I've hurt him, she thought. He believes I'm not eager, but I want him more than anything in my life.

He said coolly, "I don't suppose it matters. Do you think it's too soon? You want to know me better, of course."

She breathed deeply, banished a small annoyance at his sensitivity and blurted out the truth. "I want to marry you this very day, darling. Well, this very night. Now, are you going to turn me down?"

He pushed away her hand and kissed her under the interested gaze of other passengers. She was slightly flustered and suspected she had blushed, which seemed ridiculous for a woman of her experience.

"Would you consider being married in Geneva? Very soon?"

"Can I have my Uncle George over, to give me away?"

"You may have the President of the United States, if you like."

"When?"

He was watching her face with intense concentration, like Martin Helm used to when he would repeat, "Do you love me better than your life? Better than your god?

Better than. . ." She was afraid Eric was about to say something similar but instead he asked with a little hesitancy that stole her heart, "Would a week be too soon?" As she began to smile and he read her answer, he added, "A week from today. In Alex's garden, within sight of Lac Leman."

"Lac, oh, Lake Geneva." It sounded too close to the future Raeder in-laws but she didn't consider New York her home, and the idea of marrying him in Chicago was horrifying. It would be like carrying out the original marriage to Martin Helm. Geneva sounded ideal. She said so.

This called for another kiss, to which Gregg fully contributed her share. Pauly witnessed this with the scowl of most children at such "unseemly" public behavior. But Miss Tibbs and Marlene called him out to the afterdeck again to count the flags and Gregg muttered, "Now we've done it! Do you think he will ever come around?"

"Shall we cancel all plans to make Pauly happy?" He sounded less humorous than ironic, and that posed problems, too. She had wanted to gain the children's friendship, and only succeeded in causing a rift between two people who loved each other.

If it was simply a case of childish jealousy, all would eventually work out. But if Pauly genuinely depended on Eric as a father, there might be many future problems.

However, she loved Eric Raeder too much to let young Pauly ruin her own, and what she hoped would be Eric's, happiness. She tried to banish the prickling doubts, the submerged but not dead memories of her first love, and mentally to plan her upcoming marriage, aware at the same time that Eric was watching her constantly, with a love, and yet a little thread of doubt, that haunted her.

Some minutes before the boat pulled into its Danish ferry slip, Miss Tibbs came to ask Gregg, "Would you go into the ladies' room with me, my dear?"

"Of course."

Eric let go of her hand with a reluctance that she could not miss. "Be right back," she assured him.

Gregg was sure the governess wanted to speak to her alone, and as soon as the two of them were away from the others, Miss Tibbs said, "Miss MacIvor, you must forgive Pauly and not let this splendid new happiness for the family be ruined for you by worry over a little boy's loneliness and jealousy."

"I won't, Miss Tibbs. But thank you. I do understand. I thought it was just a little boy's sulking and that he would forget it in a few hours. Is there any way to win him over? And please call me Gregg."

"Well, you see, Miss—Gregg, Pauly likes to think he is special. Different. As we all do. He thinks he is the only one who loves and must protect his mother. And for a very long time he has tried to pretend Mr. Eric was his father, who will always be partnered, if I may say so, in his mind with his helpless and dainty mother."

"Ursula Raeder? Helpless?" Gregg realized the implication of her quick remark and tried to explain it tactfully. "Mrs. Raeder is lovely, and a beautiful woman. I only meant that she need never be helpless. Any man would be delighted to protect her. A friend of mine named Duane Colt was very attracted to her, the last time I saw them."

"Any man but Mr. Eric." Miss Tibbs lowered her voice to a whisper. "He's never forgiven her for jilting him. It's true that it was a long time ago, and so many things have happened in the meantime. But I feel that one of his reasons for pretending to dislike her is that he has never really forgiven her."

This annoyed Gregg. "Forgive me, but I doubt that." Her voice sounded sharper than she had intended.

Miss Tibbs was upset by this unexpected result of her attempts to soothe Gregg. "Oh, please don't misunderstand, Miss Gregg. I didn't mean anything. You've been so nice to me, and wonderful with the children. And you are certainly the answer to a prayer, as regards our dear Mr. Eric."

Gregg patted her shoulder. "It's quite all right. I know that you're only trying to help me—and Eric, and the children. But, come on now. We should be getting back. We must be nearing the docks."

"Yes. You are right."

Gregg opened the door, holding it while Miss Tibbs ducked under her arm and stepped out on the deck. Gregg followed, but lost her in the pushing, elbowing crowd. Fortunately, she saw Eric's tall figure across the deck. He was striding toward the steps to the car deck. She called to him, and just as she reached his shoulder, he turned.

She had forgotten how deep and terrible Martin Helm's eyes could be, like pits of ashes where the coals still glowed when a breath of air stirred them. In the shadows, she saw that he wore a raincoat that completely covered his clothing and even the lower half of his jaw and neck.

Her throat was parched. She knew her tongue flicked over dry lips, but for once in her life she lacked the strength even to scream. She saw his grin, the flash of teeth.

"You! Is it you?" she heard herself whisper hoarsely.

A hulking male passenger shoved his way between them and plowed on toward the steps to the deck below. Gregg was whirled around and groped to find security against the coffee counter. She recovered her balance, tried to stand on her toes to see where the man—Martin Helm?—had gone. There was no sign of him.

The horror he inspired in her was so great that she could only be glad she had lost sight of him. Holding tight to the rail, she hurried down the steps to find Eric's hired car. Not until she wound her way between several small cars and reached the blue Mercedes did she take a deep breath. She had one desperate prayer, to find Eric himself waiting there for her. The children and Miss Tibbs were already in the back seat, but there was no sign of Eric. Before she could say a word, Miss Tibbs leaned out the open window to ask, "But what have you done with Mr. Eric?"

"What have *I* done?"

Marlene informed her brightly, "Pauly saw you talking to Uncle Eric a minute ago."

Gregg looked in at Pauly. She was so serious, so white-faced and tense, that the sight of her shook him out of his sulky mood.

"Pauly, did you see your uncle wearing a raincoat?"

He was very small in the far corner of the car, but he sat up, stared at her and then admitted, "It looked like it. But it couldn't be, could it? Did Uncle have a raincoat on? I don't think he took one with him."

Gregg did not know either. She had no idea what to think.

"I spoke to someone. I thought it was

your uncle, but apparently it wasn't. He—frightened me a little."

"Dear, oh, dear," Miss Tibbs murmured. "Was the gentleman unpleasant to you?"

Marlene said, "You needn't worry now, Gregg. If the man comes here, we'll fix him."

"Then, if it wasn't Uncle, where is he?" Pauly asked.

Gregg kept clutching her arms, chilled to the bone, wondering. . . I did see Martin Helm! It must have been. He really has followed me here. I must report him to someone . . .

What if he really was Eric Raeder, after all? What if that tortured, sleepwalking man actually did see his *Doppelgänger* in the looking-glass? And had the *Doppelgänger*, which was only another persona of Eric Raeder, always been Eric, even when he called himself Martin Helm? This might explain those blackouts which he attributed to sleepwalking.

While the children and Miss Tibbs looked out, trying to see who would catch a first sight of Eric, Gregg knelt with one knee on the front seat, trying to remember

218

every detail of the face of the man she had run into on the upper deck, but of course much of his face had been in shadow.

That face with the terrifying eyes and the hideous grin—was it possible Eric Raeder could ever look at her in such a way?

What am I getting into? Do I want to take the enormous chance of marrying him? But I love him, and I can cope, even if he should prove to be—That's ridiculous! There is every difference in the world between Eric and that other one. But how odd! Here I am talking about "the other one" just as Eric's brother did in their childhood. I must banish it. What I saw just now was the real Martin Helm, quite distinct from the dear and kind man with whom I have fallen in love!

"He's coming. There he is!" Pauly shouted. He looked as if he might cry in his relief. Gregg wanted to hug and reassure him, but she knew better than to intrude until he showed some sign of accepting her. Even an eight-year-old might feel that his friendship had to be earned.

Eric Raeder came striding along through the crowds. Gregg thought Eric looked as tense as she herself felt. Was he ill? Or—

He burst into angry German, then abruptly changed to English for the benefit of Miss Tibbs and Gregg.

"You were all gone. I could not find any of you. I've tramped over the whole damned boat!" As everyone in the car looked at him, he apologized. "I am sorry. I suppose we must have missed each other."

He got into the car, reached for Gregg's hand and squeezed it. Then he looked over into the back seat and saw the three gazing at him anxiously. He relaxed, smiled at them in the way that won Gregg's heart, and she could see the others relax and return his smile.

"*Bitte*, I am not angry. I only have a headache. It happens now and then, to us all. It may even happen to you one day, Pauly."

The boy reached out, locked his arms around his uncle's neck and clung to him as Eric rubbed Pauly's back comfortingly.

"Here, here, young sir. We are good friends again, aren't we?"

The boy nodded, sniffing back the shameful tears.

Miss Tibbs and Gregg looked at each other with enormous relief. As for Pauly's sister, she said cockily, "I knew it all the time. Grown-ups worry about nothing."

Marlene was like a dash of cold water in the face; she brought everyone back to normal. Gregg laughed, much relieved, and when Eric felt for her hand while they awaited the sharp jolt of the docking, she wondered how she could ever doubt him.

They drove back through the bright evening air to Copenhagen, where Marlene made such a fuss about wanting to eat dinner in the glamorous hotel restaurant that the tired little group yielded.

A dozen times during dinner Gregg furtively watched the man she loved, and knew quite well that she wanted to live with him and be his wife, in spite of any lingering questions she might still have about the similarities between Eric and Martin Helm.

It was Helm I saw! It had to be! she told herself, and admitting this, she admitted also that Martin Helm was somewhere nearby, probably laughing at the fright he had given her.

Why hadn't he killed her, a woman with a dangerous knowledge of his real self?

In the lift, after dinner, she looked at

Eric again. He was rubbing his forehead, his eyes closed. She could almost share the pain herself and glanced quickly at Miss Tibbs on her other side. The little governess had also noticed his pain.

"Migraine," she whispered. "My poor father had it. A dreadful thing."

Gregg wondered if it had anything to do with his sleepwalking the night before. His worrying about it might trigger the headaches.

He needs me more than ever, she decided. It was another strong bond between them.

13

TWO days later, having canceled the rest of his personal appearances in northern Europe, Eric Raeder rounded up his family, this time including Gregg, and flew back to Geneva. So far as Gregg could tell, there were no more headaches for him. There were also no more sightings of Martin Helm. What was he waiting for? If, of course, he actually existed, in Copenhagen or elsewhere, why didn't he make a move to get her?

The family was picked up at the Geneva airport and driven into the city. Gregg herself had only visited Geneva as a tourist, and then very briefly. Her favorite Swiss city was Lucerne, a town Marlene dismissed as "even more touristy."

Gregg kept turning to admire various vistas, pointing out the balconies of the Richemond Hotel. "I stayed there two years ago . . . Wonderful meals . . . I loved my room . . ."

"Tourists always do," Marlene retorted loftily.

Pauly said, "I got good cake there when Mama took us."

It was Marlene who disturbed Gregg, however, with her cool remark. "It'll be nice to come home. You aren't going to be looking around all the time after we get to Great-Aunt Alex's house, are you, Gregg?"

"Looking around? Why should I do that?"

"I don't know, but you looked in the face of every person that got on the plane at Kastrup Airport."

And did not see Martin Helm, thank God. But she said aloud, "You've got a keen imagination, Marlene."

Marlene scoffed, "Ha!"

All the same, it made Gregg nervous to notice that Eric had glanced at her after the child's penetrating remark.

The Baroness de Lieven's grizzled, haughty chauffeur rushed the black Bentley past prominent city landmarks and famed hotels and, before Gregg could grasp the fact, they had turned inland toward the profusion of shrubs, woods and abundan

224

flowers that was the home property of the baroness.

Gregg asked Eric in a low, noncommittal voice, "Are you sure your aunt was not upset by our news?"

He drew her closer to him. "She was delighted. If you think otherwise, it is only because you haven't met Alex. Isn't that so, Miss Tibbs?"

"Indeed, indeed, yes. The baroness is, I think, the finest lady I have ever known."

"Always excepting present company," Eric put in, with some amusement at the governess's flustered state.

"Oh, I never meant to imply—I'm sure, I did not mean—"

Laughing, Gregg assured her, "I understand perfectly, Miss Tibbs." All the same, it had long been her experience that the more a stranger was built up to her as a paragon, the less she liked that paragon when at last they met.

The car drove between elegant, lacy iron gates, and on between lawns and rose bushes, approaching a small château hardly larger than a French pavilion. The car drove straight under an archway into a rectangular court.

There were several faces in the windows on the right side of the house. Servants, Gregg thought, suddenly relieved to remember that this was not Eric Raeder's household. Servants, in Gregg's experience, were people like herself, hired by the day to do a job, as she did hers. But to have them underfoot all the time seemed a real horror. She didn't know if she could get used to them.

Luckily, only one person came out onto the cobbled courtyard to greet the travelers. It hardly seemed possible that the white-haired, slender lady, with a sky-blue sweater thrown around her shoulders, was anything but a genteel-looking house-keeper. The children piled out of the car before the chauffeur could help them, and ran to throw their arms around the woman, who received them with affection but an indefinable air of grace and elegance that Gregg knew must have been passed down through generations. So she was the Baroness de Lieven, after all. Gregg liked the look of her, but as the lady watched her coming across the cobblestones, Gregg suspected those handsome blue eyes could be uncomfortably penetrating and not easily deceived.

Well, I don't intend to deceive her, Gregg reminded herself.

Smiling, the baroness held out both hands and made a rather charming gesture of ignoring Eric while in English she tried to make Gregg feel welcome.

"My dear Gregg—may I call you so? I am delighted. You are exactly as you were described. Beautiful and charming. I despaired of my nephew these past few years, but I see he was searching for you. Come in. Meet my other guests . . . Ah, Eric, *Liebchen*, I approve." She had let Gregg go on to join Marlene and Pauly who, nudged by Miss Tibbs, waited to escort her into the house.

Gregg, who was being hurried away from Eric, looked back to see that the affection between him and his aunt, the baroness, was deep and sincere. She barely had time to note this before she was seized in a bear hug by two masculine arms. She did not have to crane her neck far to guess that, through some astonishing circumstance, her old friend Duane Colt had arrived for her wedding.

He buried his lips in her hair and murmured, "You're breaking my heart! You know that, don't you?"

"Duane, stop it!" She knew how much Eric would resent the attentions paid her by this handsome Hollywood hero. She broke away from him, but not before the sound of a trilling feminine laugh made her aware that Duane had apparently accompanied Ursula Raeder to Switzerland. Pauly's cable had reaped more results than he intended.

The children, meanwhile, had gone to their mother, Pauly more quickly, hugging her; but Marlene held back, waiting to test the warmth of her mother's greeting. White-blond hair, perfectly styled, hung down to her shoulders. She looked as glamorous as ever, and twice as beautiful. Watching Ursula Raeder, Gregg could not understand how Eric had been able to resist her.

Evidently he had. He came in with his aunt, whom he called "Alex" and, nodding curtly to Duane Colt, he approached his sister-in-law. He let Ursula kiss his cheek, then looked around for Gregg.

"I'll take you up to your room, sweetheart. I wanted it to be *my* room, but it seems that Alex is a stickler for propriety; so you will have your room practically at the opposite end of the house from mine." He grinned at the baroness, adding in German, "Dear Alex, the halls may be very active at night."

"Only until the service, my child," she replied calmly in the same language. "Meanwhile, luncheon will be ready in less than an hour. I suggest you do not be late."

For the first time, Gregg felt that the whole thing was real. She, who had always been free and alone, would now belong to someone else, a dear man, no matter what his faults. She hugged herself in anticipation. She had never realized before just how lonely her life had been, or how remarkably well Eric suited her own needs.

Without going into the large drawing room opening beyond the hall, they went up the center staircase arm in arm, and on the upper floor, which smelled lightly of roses everywhere, Eric surprised her by shifting her around to face him, pulling her body suddenly to his.

"Now I can really welcome you, darling."

Her fingers went around his neck,

bringing his head closer. They kissed, and she was aware again of the naturalness of their union. More than brief, burning passion—and she felt all of that—there was the exquisite sense of belonging, a sense she had shared with only one other person and for such a short time: Martin Helm.

"After the ceremony tomorrow, where shall we go? Someplace far or near?" he asked when they moved apart.

"Near."

He was happy about that. "We agree. You see? We agree on everything. My darling, I need you . . . How I need you!"

Thinking rapidly about that evil pursuer, wherever he might be, she said, "Let's not tell a living soul where we go. We'll just drive off in the car and stop wherever we want. Maybe even Lucerne. But don't tell anyone, please. That is, can the baroness keep a secret?"

He assured her with a smile, "She has kept endless secrets in her life. She wouldn't fail us at this stage. And I would like one person to know how to reach us, in case of illness to the children, or to Alex herself."

She understood and agreed. It was only

natural. And she could not tell him that it was his double, his *Doppelgänger* named Martin Helm, that she was afraid of.

After these few minutes alone, they had no more privacy that day. The children had dashed off to check all the things they loved in Great-Aunt Alex's home. Marlene had a flower bed whose roses, she proudly boasted, decorated the long dining table. "And I'm paid for them, too, the regular market price."

Pauly raised rabbits. These had to be counted and examined to be quite sure none had disappeared during his absence.

Between Duane Colt and Ursula Raeder there was no escaping company for Gregg. She had enough to worry about with Duane's ridiculous conduct without finding herself increasingly jealous of Ursula Raeder every time she tilted her head in front of Eric to speak with him. Down tumbled her hair, which she would switch back out of her own and Eric's eyes with elaborately impatient gestures.

Duane finally pinned Gregg down that evening in a corner of the huge, comfortable eighteenth-century salon which had been adapted to a sort of living room.

"I wish you wouldn't act like this," she told him sternly, as one would speak to a child, trying to be reasonable and dictatorial at the same time. He had boxed her into a corner behind the faded love seat, and her chief fear was that Eric might think the worst.

"I've got to, Red. God knows I don't want to get your boyfriend down on me, but I came clear over here to look after you." He did seem surprisingly earnest.

In another place she would have been inclined to laugh at the idea of Duane Colt protecting her. She had always felt slightly maternal about him and not at all in love.

"Look, Duane, I don't want him to see us like this. He doesn't understand our way of being so familiar with each other. He doesn't know this means absolutely nothing!"

"Speak for youself." He correctly read the frown this brought to Gregg's face, and said hastily, "Okay, okay. But let me tell you something, Red. Something that Ursula told me."

Gregg had a sinking feeling that this would be unpleasant. "I don't want to hear any recycled garbage, if that's what you have in mind."

"He was madly in love with Ursula and his brother took her away from him."

"Isn't that a bit dramatic?"

"Well, he bribed her away," he amended. "Eric was just starting out then, working for a newspaper. Ursula admits she was wrong to marry Rolfe, the brother. She says she always loved Eric better."

"And you believe her?"

"Now just wait a minute. Now comes the best part. I mean the worst part. Eric went north on assignment for his newspaper, and when he was leaving Denmark the plane crashed. He was laid up for a year or two. They had to practically remake his face."

"Don't!"

"Well, when he left the hospital, he wandered around Europe, wouldn't go home for ages, and. . ."

She became aware of a stiffness in her bones. Even her fingers felt numb. "How long ago was this?"

"Ten years—no. Maybe eleven or twelve years."

"And they didn't keep track of him during those years?"

Duane shrugged. "None of his family did."

"When did he recover and come home?"

"It must have been years after the accident. That little kid, Marlene, was already born. He came home for her first birthday party."

She said, "Someone's coming," and pulled herself free of him. "I don't want to discuss this again. Do you understand me?"

Looking hurt, Duane watched her cross the room to the hall and the staircase.

But in spite of her quick dismissal of Duane's secondhand tale, and a long, tender conversation with Eric that night before their wedding, she slept badly. She did not dream, but even in her sleep seemed aware of the enormous step she was taking. It did not really bother her to live in Europe until her husband made other plans. She had spent part of each year in Europe since her affair with Martin Helm. And being a writer, Eric would surely understand the importance of her own work, and give her time to do it.

Finally, she came to the most haunting of her worries: that story told secondhand by Duane Colt. Was it a coincidence that Eric Raeder was out of touch with the world while Martin Helm was commiting his terrible crimes? When she came face to face with Helm on the ferryboat, she had known at once that he wasn't Eric; so why the doubts?

She got up at last, took some aspirin and eventually fell asleep.

In the morning she was driven out to the airport to meet Uncle George, having insisted she preferred to go alone, that it might be bad luck for Eric to see her before the ceremony. Marlene had been harder to shake, but was home at the château now, carefully choosing the flowers for the intimate family ceremony to be held in the lovely music room.

Uncle George was his jolly, ruddy-cheeked self, and before he even greeted his niece he carefully shook hands with a good-looking, middle-aged woman who had been his seatmate on the plane, remarking at his first greeting to Gregg, "Nice woman. A widow, too. Gave me her address in Bern. Is that hard to get to from here?"

Gregg laughed, assured him it wasn't and led him to the car.

The old but ever-impressive Bentley and its grave chauffeur took Uncle George's breath away. Nevertheless, when they were returning to the château, he took Gregg's hands, examined the engagement ring Eric had given her, whistled at the diamonds fanned out around a strange, milky opal and reminded her:

"Opals are bad luck."

"Not if they're my birthstone. I want to show you something. Whatever you think, don't speak too loudly. I took a Polaroid of Eric and the children yesterday. Here it is."

Her fingers shook a little as she gave him the stiff-backed picture. To her surprise, he looked at it with the requisite interest and said, "Good-looking family. You say they don't belong to him? I don't like the idea of you marrying a guy with half-grown kids."

"No, no. They're his brother's children. Very precocious, but I like them enor-

236

mously . . . You didn't see anything else? Any—similarity?"

"Between him and the kids? Not particularly. He's dark and they're light . . . Oh." All of a sudden, he realized what Gregg had meant. "There's a resemblance, all right. You thinking of Helm? You probably go for the same type all the time. They say it's natural."

She settled back in relief. "Then you would never mistake Eric for Martin Helm?"

With a short laugh, he handed the photo back. "Good Christ, no! Helm was thirty-five if he was a day. And that was about fifteen years ago."

"Eleven."

"Well, whatever. And you can't tell me this guy of yours is any forty-five. Honey, what's got into you? If you have any doubts, you'd better cut your losses right now and give him back his damned opal."

"It was his mother's."

"Bully for his mother. But what's that got to do with you loving him? The thing is, are you marrying him because he reminds you of that cutthroat? Because if you are, I've a good motion to thrash you!

237

It's a rotten trick to play on a guy who sounds pretty nice, from the way you've described him."

"Don't be silly. I'd be more likely to run away from him because of the resemblance. It's just that I think I've seen Martin Helm in Europe. I think he's here somewhere. Wherever I go, I feel as if he's right around the corner and he'll pop out any second."

He did not laugh as she hoped he would. "You think he wants to murder you like those others?"

"I think he has to, eventually. But why the cat-and-mouse business? And do we have any evidence at all, so we can turn him in if we do meet him?"

"Funny," he mused, looking out the window. She found his thoughtful expression unpromising. He appeared much too indifferent about the matter now, and she began to suspect that he was hiding something. "Forgot what I was going to say," he muttered.

"You said . . . 'funny.' What were you thinking of?"

"Nothing. Can't think why I—Look here! You think I'm holding something back? You calling me a liar?"

She glanced up at the chauffeur with his proud, straight back, and hoped he wasn't paying attention to their conversation.

"Uncle George, please . . ."

He gave in. He had always cared greatly for his niece, the only child he and his wife had known. "Honey, it's little enough. I had to change planes in Zurich, you know—"

"I know."

"And when I was climbing those damned steps into the plane, I looked back—haven't the foggiest notion why—and there, I saw a fellow on the field, watching me as if he were an old buddy. And I thought: Who the hell is he? I knew, and yet I didn't. Gray hair. Kind of German-looking, with a gray, wispy mustache."

"Uncle George, *who was he*?"

"Probably a nice Swiss banker waiting for his own plane to Bern or some such place."

She watched him. She knew. "Somehow, he reminded you of Martin Helm."

"But I didn't place him then. I don't now. A gray-haired old dog with a Fu Manchu mustache? It couldn't be Helm."

"Anybody can put on a mustache and

dye his hair. Besides, it might be gray by this time. Don't you see?" She began to perk up. A marvelous idea had occurred to her that would end all the ridiculous suspicions and feelings once and for all. "It couldn't possibly be Eric. Eric was here. In Geneva."

He looked shaken. "Kid you really are crazy. Why the hell would your boyfriend watch me in disguise, in Zurich? Besides, you know where he was this morning. He was with you, wasn't he?"

"I haven't seen him this morning," she said quietly.

He shook his head at her impossible suspicions, and they said no more until the car turned into the de Lieven grounds and she stirred herself to point out charming little picnic grounds, a gazebo, Marlene's flower garden and other sights which would take their minds off the subject of Martin Helm.

Before the car reached the archway leading to the inn courtyard, they saw Eric, looking lithe and rugged and strongly sensuous to Gregg. Obviously, he had not yet dressed for the wedding. He had no jacket on, not even one of his now-familiar turtleneck sweaters. The sleeves of his shirt were rolled up, and his dark golden arms made Gregg long to feel their power and warmth.

He waved to them. The chauffeur slowed. Eric caught the door on Gregg's side, leaped in and, under the observant eyes of Uncle George, he took his fiancée in his arms. Never had Gregg's wishes been so quickly fulfilled. During the playful tussle that followed, his enthusiasm, his obvious and immediate desire for her, should have assured her of the vast gulf between this man she loved and the other she had never forgotten.

What a ridiculous thing her uncle had suggested, that she loved Eric because she had failed to win Martin Helm!

Uncle George's slight frown thawed to a smile as he watched Gregg fending off, while urging on, Eric's joking and determined kiss.

"I told you it was bad luck. I'm not supposed to see you until the ceremony, Eric! This is Uncle George. You haven't said a word to him."

Eric looked over her shoulder, gave one

hand to Uncle George and begged his pardon.

"Good morning, sir. Excuse me. She makes up these superstitions about weddings, but I don't believe in them. I haven't seen her since last night. Do you know what I was afraid of? That she might see a plane at the airport and take off for New York. On the spur of the moment, as you say. She is like that, you know."

Uncle George took his hand, clasped it and, looking him in the eye, said, "How do you do? You can see that she came back. Maybe she's met her match in you. I certainly hope so."

"So do I," Eric said firmly, glancing at Gregg. Both he and her uncle were waiting for her to assure them.

She said nothing . . . Two hours until the ceremony. Had the minister arrived yet? Thank God the time was close at hand! Once the ceremony was over, nothing could go wrong. Eric would belong to her and she to him. Martin Helm—if there was a Martin Helm pursuing her, haunting her throughout Europe—could do nothing.

14

HEINZ ALBRECHT, the friendly suitor of Ursula Raeder, had driven in while Gregg was at the airport and from the minute he arrived was constantly underfoot. He managed to do everything but read the Reverend Kurmann's service at the wedding.

In honor of the day Eric wore a white shirt and somewhat out-of-date and very European black business suit. Lean and tall though he was, Eric looked too muscular, too athletic for the suit, and Gregg could harldy wait until he changed into his far more suitable sport clothes, the sweaters that gave his movements an easy grace. Yet, curiously enough, she loved him better than ever when she thought that he looked just a trifle awkward and out of place, as in that wedding suit.

Her own dress was a buttercup-yellow raw silk, sleeveless, with a simple thread of a belt. She carried a prayer book brought by Uncle George, belonging to her mother, and through the middle of the prayer book, as a kind of placemark, lay one of Marlene's long-stemmed yellow roses. The ceremony was interrupted twice by Ursula, all in virginal white, shushing her daughter who persisted in the whisper, "I gave her the rose . . . the rose was mine . . . See it?"

Almost before Gregg knew what was happening, she and Eric were exchanging their vows. And when, after the blessing, Eric kissed her, she felt that this was the most joyous moment of her life. The past was dead.

On the receiving line, Heinz Albrecht tried to outdo the bridegroom's embrace, and Ursula did as much for Eric. In spite of Albrecht's bear hugs and his anxiety to kiss her on the mouth, Gregg's attention was diverted to another scene going on within an arm's length of her. The mail had just arrived, and Marlene and her brother were examining the stack of envelopes and parcels.

"Look at all the mail, Pauly. Someday I am going to have many letters and packages, just for me. I like packages. Will you send me packages?"

"Maybe. You always want presents.

Greedy!" This incurred a kick in the shins and his furious retaliation, but the bickering was conducted without raised voices, and no one except Gregg paid any attention. After the exchange of kicks, the children went on amicably sorting through the mail.

"These are for Great-Aunt. And see how much fan mail Uncle Eric gets. And Gregg, too. . . from Oliver Sills. What a funny name!"

"See this? Marly, look. To Gregg from. . . Timothy J. Me-haffey, private inves. . . investigator . . ."

"That's a policman."

"I know!" he cut her off impatiently. "Gregg has funny friends."

Uncle George came through the group, gave Gregg a big kiss and wished her happiness. They held onto each other for a long moment, until the baroness came up to Gregg.

"My dear friend, it has been less than two days, but we have come to know each other, I think. I wish you and Eric well."

Gregg hugged the woman whose bones seemed so fragile under Gregg's strong hands, but her poise and the look in her pale eyes suggested that the Baroness de Lieven was far stronger than she appeared. Ursula came to congratulate Gregg charmingly and was succeeded by Duane Colt, to whom Marlene had taken a great fancy. He whispered as he kissed Gregg, "Happiness, anyway, no matter what."

Following Duane came Marlene, her usual enthusiastic self, and then Pauly who gravely took Gregg's hand and wished her well. She had taken the liberty of hugging him in return, and though he did not respond, neither did he recoil from her. By the time Eric slipped his arm around her waist and piloted her out to his British MG parked in the courtyard, she was still looking back and blowing kisses. Duane, Marlene and Uncle George followed them, throwing rice while the baroness sighed, shrugged and smiled at their goings-on.

Eric kissed Gregg as she got into the MG. He had no sooner climbed into his seat than he asked with one of his wry smiles, "Did Duane say anthing about the movie test?"

"Well, not today. But I've been thinking that he might not be bad."

"I wasn't thinking so much about his

suitability, but about the fact that if he was in Hollywood, he could not be here."

He seemed to be teasing, so she laughed, but could not help reminding him, "I'm afraid I couldn't get rid of your sister-in-law so easily."

He looked at her, obviously surprised. "Darling, are you jealous of Ursula?" Though playing it lightly, she nodded, and she could see that he was pleased. Nevertheless, as they drove out through the rose-bordered estate road, he assured her, "I stopped loving my featherheaded sister-in-law long, long ago. Before my accident. If I weren't so fond of the children, I would never have occasion to see her. She is a nuisance."

There seemed a thousand confidences, a thousand chances to make love, though they promised each other to drive straight across country to Lucerne before they stopped for their wedding night; and of the two of them, Eric seemed surer of the future, of their own contentment. They held hands as they rapidly covered the kilometers between Geneva and Lucerne.

There had been so many good-byes at the last minute that no one had thought to give Gregg her mail, and she kept wondering about Timothy J. Mehaffey. Why should a private investigator write to her? And who could he be? Maybe Uncle George had something to do with it. Could he have hired the man to locate Martin Helm?

When Eric asked her what she was thinking, she lied easily.

"I was so glad you changed your clothes. When you wear these sweaters it gives me a better chance to admire your muscles." She ran the fingers of her free hand over his chest and smiled playfully.

They both laughed, but she did not indulge in any more such teasing while he drove.

They reached Lucerne at dusk, caught glimpses of the Lake of the Four Forest Cantons, as Eric called it, and avoided the great, lakeside hotels which were familiar to Gregg, choosing instead a hotel facing a tiny square in the town. The River Reuss, with a view of endless bright flowers, bordered the hotel terrace, the old covered wooden bridge and the inn's grassy grounds.

As luck would have it, Gregg's little

velveteen tote bag was not brought up with them, and Eric had to go back after it. She could hardly wait until he returned.

"You're a magician!" Gregg whispered, spellbound. "I've been here half a dozen times and never saw it like this. Look! There's Mount Pilatus. I love the little cog train thing that takes you up there. To see all this. . . with you! It's wonderful!"

They stood together at the window, Eric behind her, pointing out the enchanting architecture, the scenes, the beauty of the Alps beyond, and all the time she was becoming more and more aware of his body against hers, his hard, muscular strength, and yet, the tantalizing coolness of his cheek as his face brushed hers before he kissed her.

She was a tall woman and not used to being lifted of the floor, nor had she been used to making love even before her dress was unzipped. She found his force and persistence, his sheer strength, far greater than that of the men in her past, and she welcomed his body as she had never welcomed any lover in her life. Her memory of Martin Helm's lovemaking became blurred, retiring into the dim past.

Afterward, he asked her as they lay together in the huge Swiss bed, "Did you find me brutal? I've wanted you for—How long is it since that day in Oliver Sill's office?"

With her lips touching his ear, and her fingers lightly playing over his shoulder and then across his lean abdomen, she murmured, "A strong man. There is a difference. You could never be brutal."

"I hope not. What are you doing to me? You must like to be assaulted."

"Only by you, darling. Only by you."

From their room, they could see the light shining across the river, and they told each other they should get up and dress for dinner. Neither of them moved for a few minutes. Each knew, with a deep, unquestioning knowledge, that the other was perfectly happy.

The sharp buzz of the phone shattered their mood, and Eric reached over for it while Gregg turned on the bed lamp.

Eric spoke impatiently in German. He looked over at Gregg, ran one hand over her cheekbone and mouth and, while listening to the voice on the phone murmured tenderly in his best English, "What a beautiful creature you are!"

She leaned across his body and kissed his neck, lingering there. He returned to his guttural German, then broke into English, trying to keep his mind on the telephone conversation:

"We did not call you for dinner. You are mistaken. I made no such arrangements. I came down to collect my wife's handbag. My name is not Halversen. It is Raeder. . . Well, then, you are mistaken. My wife insists that there is no one else like me, isn't it so, darling?"

He did not wait for her to sit up straight and stare at the telephone in a curious, furtive way, but returned his attention to the phone. "We will eat dinner on the terrace over the river if it is not too cold. Please reserve for us a table in an hour. Understood?" He set back the telephone, and then laughed at the management's confusion. "They insist I ordered dinner in the room. Dinner for one, if you please. A honeymoon dinner for one?"

She forced an answering smile. "And they thought your name was—what?"

"Halversen, I think. Sounds Danish. Or

Swedish." He cupped her chin with his hand. "Sweetheart, would you prefer to eat here?"

She wanted to stay hidden from all strangers, especially this "Halversen" who had been mistaken for Eric Raeder, but they could not run away forever. If Martin Helm—alias Halversen?—was still around, better to meet him head on, and have it over with. Unfortunately, her husband was more observant than she suspected. He stopped teasing her suddenly.

"Sweetheart, are you cold? You are shaking."

"Nothing like that. How could I be? No. Tell me, what was that about you bringing up my tote bag?"

"They claimed I had given them the instructions at that time. It is ridiculous. I did nothing like that. Come, we will dress for dinner. And forget these stupid mistakes they make."

To change the subject she asked, "What shall I wear? What would you like me to wear?"

He grinned. "If you wore nothing but that body God gave you, you would be better dressed than all of those hausfrau we will see . . . and how the men would envy me!"

She tried to concentrate on this raillery and forget the fears, the endless haunting by either her own imagination or a very real and dangerous enemy. Perhaps tonight would be the time to tell Eric the whole story of Martin Helm . . . No, not the whole story. But the fact that she had intended to marry him, and that she and Uncle George had discovered the other facets, the many identities, of the man she had once loved. She knew she must be very careful in telling Eric. No man would want to believe he had been married because he reminded his wife of another lover.

Nor was that even true now. Her relationship with Eric was far different from the one she had shared with Martin Helm. Martin, the arrogant superior, the "teacher" of a silly young virgin! Even if he had been normal, decent and unselfish, he would never have been the true partner, physically or emotionally, that she found today in Eric Raeder.

She wore a blue-violet dinner dress, and her husband whistled in a very American way as he zipped her up and kissed her between her shoulder blades. When the honeymooners went down to the lobby, whispering their shared amusement at the "alpine look" of the painted stairs, the lobby, the indoor dining room, they also found the cast of characters perfect, and this gave them fuel for more shared jokes.

By the time they were seated on the narrow terrace annex of the dining room, with the lights of their own and other hotels reflected in the river only a few feet below, they were both so happy Gregg felt that this might be the time to tell him about Martin Helm.

It was after the white wine had come, and they were making absurd toasts "to the most remarkable man in inner and outer space," to the "beauty who reduces Venus to a hausfrau," that he mentioned the reason for his bad temper on the telephone, earlier in their room. He seemed to find the plain little wineglass fascinating as he twirled it slowly in his fingers, not taking his eyes from it.

"It was not the mistake, you understand. Not the fact that they accuse me of saying what I did not say. It is because I remember what used to haunt me. The face like mine.

254

Which is me? I asked myself that when I was in the hospital after the accident. There was much plastic surgery necessary. And I had suddenly this fear from my childhood which came back. What if I walked in my sleep and did not remember who was the person guiding my brain, the person who controlled my movements? For my real self was asleep. Do you see?"

She looked across the table at him. From her heart, she murmured, "Yes, I do see." And at the same time she knew she could not tell him about Martin Helm.

He startled her by asking suddenly, in light, almost joking tones, "Do you love me, Gregg? You haven't said so for—can it be a full hour?"

She wanted to ask, "Do you doubt it? What about today? What about now—minutes ago?" But she knew some deep and terrible insecurity, rooted in his boyhood, was the source of that question.

"I do love you. Do you know how much?"

He smiled. He had known quite well what she would say, yet he had needed to hear it. She knew that a few people on the little terrace were listening but they were unimportant, so long as Eric understood.

"In my whole life, darling, I loved my parents and my aunt and uncle, and friends. And I love you more than all of them put together." It sounded so like a child's reasoning that he laughed, but she said soberly, "I mean it. I do!"

"Don't mind my foolishness, darling. It is just that I like to hear you say it." He caught the sympathetic smirk of a woman at the next table, and reddened, then broke down and laughed at himself. But Gregg did not share their amusement. She whispered, "I'm not very hungry, are you?"

That pleased him but he insisted, "This has to be a very special dinner. I'll not have Oliver Sills saying in years to come that I starved you."

"Who cares what Oliver says?" She held out her glass. He poured the bright Swiss wine.

They left much of their dinner uneaten, but enjoyed each other's company immensely. Even the occasional silences between them were comforting. As Gregg looked around at the tables behind Eric, she saw that one little man at a table against the far wall looked out of place. He was alone, unlike the others, and he seemed to be trying to catch her eye. His own eyes were small, twinkling, yet curiously unattractive. Malicious, she thought, and wondered if she imagined the sinister quality.

Partly because of this little man's persistent stare, Gregg had more than one reason to be glad when Eric suggested with elaborate and amusing casualness, "Have you finished your brandy, *Liebchen?*"

She hadn't, but she drank it hastily and pushed back her chair before either Eric or the waiter could get around to help her. Under the interested gaze of several remaining diners, Eric and Gregg strolled into the lobby and toward the heavy staircase. Below the wide, square banisters was the concierge's desk where the night concierge had just answered the telephone. He exchanged words with the room clerk at the next desk and then raised his head.

"Herr Raeder? The long-distance telephone for you. Would you care to take it here?"

Gregg and Eric looked at each other. She knew he was uneasy at the sound of this, and had jumped to the conclusion that something was wrong at home, perhaps with the children or the baroness.

"Darling," she suggested, "take the call now. I'll be waiting for you."

He hesitated, but when she hurried on up the stairs, he leaned over the banisters, studied the telephone and then gave in and went back down.

Gregg had just reached the top floor, two above the street, when she saw a man waiting in front of the door next to the Raeder room. It was the little man with the evil, twinkling eyes. She stopped. He had made no menacing move toward her and was scrawny enough so that she felt she could defend herself if he gave her any trouble. But still, she did not want to pass him. She waited a couple of seconds, then, resenting her own cowardice, she stalked along the corridor, hearing the creak of ancient timbers underfoot.

She had almost passed him, and was conscious of great relief. Then he spoke. His brogue reminded her of something. A letter. A name pronounced with difficulty by Pauly Raeder.

258

"You'll be wondering, ma'am, what my business may be."

"I am not wondering at all. I don't know you. Excuse me."

He put out a hand, vigorous and strong below the striped sleeve of his black coat. "Now, now, you'll not be telling me you don't know the name of Timothy J. Mehaffey."

"Frankly, I'll not be telling you anything. My husband is just behind me on the stairs there." She moved on.

Sticky-sweet, like the paper that traps the fly, Timothy Mehaffey stopped her, insisting, "Oh, no. He'll be talking on the telephone until I get in my say up here. A friend of mine, newsman in Berlin, he's talking to your husband. An interview-like."

"What is it you want? Make it quick. I'm not a patient woman."

"You should've read my letter," he insisted, gently chiding. "Tells you the whole megillah. Now, here's my thinking . . . How'd you like to be hiring me to leave someone be? Not report him, like. I'm awful good at tracking, I think you should

259

know. Awful good; so it's hard to stop, since I've the scent, you might say."

Her thoughts were in far greater turmoil than the even tone of her voice indicated. "I don't want you to leave someone alone. I don't really care whom you are tracking."

He cocked his head on one side and regarded her. "Ah! So that's the way of it, now? Well, then, how'd you like me to find someone for the police, without your having to say a single word? Point of fact, nobody need know you'd ever had so much as a hint of what he was about."

"You aren't making any sense. You must have me confused with some else." She reached for the old-fashioned doorknob in the center of the door, but was stopped by his next challenge.

"Didn't you know the truth then? That Herr Marek Helmer tried to kill you a few days ago on the *Hamlet*, bound for Malmö?"

That shook her. "What are you talking about? I was with my husband's family."

"And what about when you were pushed down the steps to the lower deck? Come, ma'am, it was painful. You couldn't have forgotten it."

"I caught my heel on the step and nearly fell, yes. Go about your business. I am not interested." She stuck the huge key into the lock as if she were stabbing this sinister little man. He did not move but called after her:

"Your mistake entirely, ma'am. It's in my mind to track him down and turn him over to the police in Hamburg. But I'm needing a bit of help-like. Costs money, following criminals, so it does. And it's a danger. Don't you be doubting that, ma'am."

He knew she had become interested. She pushed open the door but looked back, trying to make her face a blank.

"Now, wouldn't I be a fool to believe such a cock-and-bull story?"

They both heard the elevator pull noisily to a stop. Mr. Mehaffey showed nervousness for the first time.

"You'd better think it over, Mrs. Raeder. I'm not a killing man. That wife butcher is. I want to catch him in the act, but it costs money, this tailing business."

"Is there a reward?" she asked ironically.

A man and woman get out of the elevator, and Mr. Mehaffey lowered his voice.

"There'll be that, all right. But only if it's proved he's the lady-killer. Thought I might catch him in the act, like I say, and save the next lady. But he's liable to kill you. You want to be the lady he maybe kills?"

Nice fellow. He probably didn't care whether the victim died or not. Meanwhile, the man and woman went into a room down the hall. Gregg said, "How can you keep him away from me? He isn't going to listen to you."

He said smugly, "It'll take a bit of doing. But I can be that convincing; you'd never believe how convincing. It's my native charm. I'll befriend him, talk about my rich lady friend that's headed for Hamburg. I'll say she's bound to die an old maid, with all that money, too. He'll stop following you and try for the old maid. A little innocent planning ahead. I'll catch him in the act. There's a sizable reward if there's proof against Marek Helmer."

She refused to understand. "I'll report him myself then, when I see him."

"And speaking of seeing him, I'm sure you see the resemblance between Helmer and your husband. Perhaps it's more than a resemblance—"

"My husband is *not*, and never was, this killer you're dreaming up!" she gasped, losing control.

"Well, let's just say I'm not as sure as you are. And if you are wrong, I wonder how long you'll be safe with him—"

It was the one thing above all that she did not want to think about.

She went into the room in which she and Eric had been so happy, and idiotically, locked the door from inside. She felt sick and desperate for a minute or two. But then she looked at the bed, its huge, comfortable surface carefully remade by the *femme de chambre*, the pillows shoved back into the bolsters, and felt a sense of belonging and comfort.

Still, she was worried. She began to wonder if Timothy Mehaffey could actually make trouble for Eric. Did he really suspect him?

It was not so much that the police could be made to believe Eric was Martin Helm, or Marek Helmer, whatever the criminal's real identity. But Eric, with his inner doubts about the sleepwalking side of himself, must never even know there was a criminal who looked so very like him. She wished now that she had made a deal with Mehaffey to keep away from Eric.

And meanwhile, Eric was downstairs on some faked telephone call. Gregg's courage came back, fed by anger. She unlocked the door and went out into the corridor again wih her fists clenched. No sly little Mr. Mehaffey was waiting this time. Her angry features and the white knuckles of her hands swinging in march time astonished an elderly pair of ladies who had just made their way out of the elevator. She rushed down to Eric at the concierge's desk.

15

"**D**ARLING, I'm sorry. It was an idiotic call. Somebody from Berlin, wanting me to write about our honeymoon. Who told them? Where did they find out about it? Stupid business! And I thought—so much hemming and hawing at first, I thought it was someone from Geneva trying to tell me about a calamity. Now, then—Herr Kummler, I take no calls except from the Baroness de Lieven. Understood?"

She knew as they went on to their room hand in hand that even the alarming Mr. Mehaffey could not spoil their relationship. She loved Eric Raeder more now than at the moment of their marriage vows, more than she had loved him even in their first glorious coupling after their arrival at the old Reuss Hotel.

During the hours that followed, and in the next days and nights of their honeymoon, they both felt, with each new discovered facet of the other's being, that their original meeting had been destined in some way. They laughed together, yet they knew when not to press a sore spot, not to pursue something painful, like the possible subject of his next novel. They learned tolerance, and even love of each other's differences. So much happened between them in their growing knowledge of each other, that with the disappearance of Timothy Mehaffey from her life, Gregg could almost imagine he had never existed.

It was impossible for Gregg to believe, one brisk, golden morning in October, that this was the two-week anniversary of their wedding.

"The second week," Eric explained, as he draped a delicately carved wooden Lion of Lucerne on a gold chain around her neck.

She turned her head to kiss him, but felt the delightful touch of his lips on her bare shoulder, and enjoyed the sensuous pleasure.

They decided to celebrate the momentous occasion by strolling over to the nearest stadtkeller where they spent the early hours of the evening spearing bread cubes and twirling them in the cheese fondue warmer, and sipping an excellent beer. They had a great time feeding each other, losing bits of bread in the melted cheese and laughing. It was one of those glorious times when everything they did seemed funny, and Gregg thought she had never really seen him so devastatingly attractive as when he laughed.

They had not intended to attract so much attention, but as Gregg dropped her napkin and Eric reached under the table to pick it up, she noticed that a few faces had turned their way, and amused smiles abounded. She glanced around casually.

Across the floor which served as a stage for the charming young Alpine enter-tainers, she saw a face that had begun to seem part of a half-forgotten nightmare. Timothy J. Mehaffey was back, and watching them with his thin little smile. She pretended not to see him and looked away quickly, but she was too late. He was getting up, and she realized with dread that he would be coming past their table.

Just as Eric raised his head and handed the napkin to Gregg, Mehaffey appeared beside their table. While Gregg held her breath, the little man addressed Eric in

English, or at least Mehaffey's version of it.

"Excuse the liberty, sir. You'll be Herr Eric Raeder?"

Gregg's fingers began to twist the napkin.

Eric did not seem too surprised, however. He smiled, agreed.

"Thought as much, sir. I was in the big shop in Stockholm when you went at autographing your book about the *Doppelgänger*, and I found it that fine, I thought never to put it down."

Gregg breathed again. Mr. Mehaffey gave her a mischievous glance before returning to his pursuit of the celebrated author. "There's a question I've always wanted to ask a man like yourself, sir."

"Yes?" His tone was not encouraging, and another man would have realized that he was interrupting something, but Timothy Mehaffey did not appear to be easily rebuffed.

"Well, then, sir, where *do* you get your ideas?"

Even Gregg recognized that as the oldest and most hackneyed question of all, but in this particular case, she found herself anxious to change the subject.

"Eric, I hate to interrupt but if we are going to get there, we really should be leaving."

He took up her cue promptly. "Very true. As to your question, Mr. —?"

"Mehaffey."

"As to your question, the idea for *Doppelgänger* came from a simple look in the mirror. That is all." He rose, pushed back his chair and spoke significantly to Gregg. "Ready, darling?"

He took her arm, but Mehaffey trotted along beside them with ridiculous persistence.

"Sir, you say a mirror? I take it you saw this creepy fellow and thought he was somebody else. A monster, a murderer, maybe? But Herr Raeder, is it possible then, that a man like yourself could be a murderer and not even know it? In the book, I mean. Because I thought, in the book, the man in the mirror was the author."

"Heavens!" Gregg cried loudly. "I had no idea it was so late. Sweetheart, we'll never get there at this rate. Excuse us, Mr. Haffey."

"Mehaffey, ma'am . . . *Güten Abend*, Herr Helmer—er—Raeder."

Gregg glared at the man and took Eric's arm, heading toward the exit. They were out in the street before Eric stopped under the blue-white streetlight and asked, "What did he call me?"

He was clearly puzzled, and Gregg could not see any sign that he had ever heard of the name Helmer before. Thank God, she thought, and dismissed Mehaffey's mumblings with the carelessness they deserved. They walked briskly in the opposite direction from the hotel, and had gone at full speed for about a block before Eric grabbed her shoulder to bring her to a halt.

"Where are we going? Or are we just—going?" he asked.

"I thought maybe we'd go to see the Lion of Lucerne? The monument looks much better all lighted up at night."

He startled her by a sharp look, and the remark, "You really didn't like that fellow did you? But why?"

"Pushy. I want you all to myself."

That soothed him. In excellent spirits they started through dark, narrow streets toward that monument in the park dedicated to the Royalist Swiss Guard massacred in Paris during the French Revolution. They passed a lighted beer garden and then were in darkness again. Gregg felt herself drawn closer to her husband as they reached silhouetted shapes buzzing and talking around the spectacular sandstone carving of the lion, crouched upon the Bourbon shield in mourning of the Swiss Guards who had given their lives in defense of Louis Sixteenth and Marie Antoinette. The brightness of the illumination made the surrounding night all the darker by contrast.

As the crowds milled about the great monument and Gregg stood on her toes to see over a pair of tall, male heads in front of her, she heard Eric exclaim something, as if he were startled, or shocked. She glanced at him anxiously. He stood absolutely still, staring at the people around them.

"Eric! What is it? Someone we know?"

He shook his head. She did not dare to pursue the matter. In the light of the monument, his face looked pale and drawn. She couldn't imagine what had affected him so, but if he wouldn't speak of it, she would have to let it go.

"Have you seen enough?" he asked somewhat harshly.

"Yes. I only thought if we walked this far that annoying little man wouldn't bother us."

They started back toward the ring of lights around the distant lake. Others were strolling ahead of them, enjoying the clear night air in spite of the frosty nip of early October. Eric did not say anything, and Gregg felt a little put out.

That's the way it is, she thought. The honeymoon is over.

As they reached a streetlight and she looked around, she saw Timothy J. Mehaffey pattering along behind them. He had slowed when they did, and it seemed clear that he was following them. It occurred to Gregg suddenly that the sight of him might have upset Eric for some reason. Seeing her attention caught, he now looked back. He surprised her by his laugh

"All our efforts to escape that pest were for nothing. I see he is still around."

It seemed clear from his casual reference to Mehaffey that it was not he who had startled him at the lion monument. What then? Gregg wondered.

They said very little during the rest of the walk back to the older part of the town. But worse than the silence itself, Gregg thought, were the carefully impersonal remarks he made now and then, as if to keep her from guessing what really troubled him.

"There must be a wind tonight. The lake seems to be ruffled." And then, "I always liked these little streets. Quaint, aren't they?"

How Marlene would have scoffed at such "tourist talk"!

Because of the curious moment at the lion monument, she had a premonition that his sleep would be troubled that night. His lovemaking seemed desperate, furious, as if he could not believe that she would respond; yet she shared his feelings. She understood without knowing why he felt so desperate. And she found she did not love him less for that.

But late in the night when the world outside the windows began to take on the blue cast before the predawn gray, Gregg felt the mattress in the great bed yield on her husband's side, as he got up. Trying not to make a sound, she pulled herself up against the pillows to watch him. He began to take his clothes off the chair, and to dress.

Was he awake?

Should she rouse him? She had always heard that this was a dangerous thing to do. She waited, hearing her own noisy heartbeat, terrified for him. What if someday he did not wake up? What was he thinking during these ghastly minutes?

Dressed now, he stuck his feet into the hauraches he kept by the bed, and walked to the window, looking out through the two inches between the long window drapes. His eyes were open and she would have sworn he was awake. In every way he looked normal.

He turned from the window, walked deliberately past the foot of the bed toward the hall door. Gregg thought: I've got to *do* something!

She slipped out of bed and, standing there in her filmy gown and bare feet, unaware of the numbing cold, she asked very quietly, "Why are you going out?"

In the most matter-of-fact way he said, "It wasn't a mirror, you know. I saw him."

Putting together all she knew of his imagination, the childhood teasing by his brother, and tonight's startling development, she said, "You faced him tonight, didn't you?"

His fingers tightened on the metal doorknob. It may have been this touch of cold metal, but she knew suddenly that he had awakened. He raised his head, did not look at her for a few seconds. She felt an aching pity for his humiliation, but was aware of an even stronger emotion for him. The real horror in his life, she suspected now, was not that he walked in his sleep and imagined things, but rather, that he, too, had seen Martin Helm. Tonight. At the lion monument.

She laid her hand on his arm, said gently, "You saw a real person, you know. He simply looks like you."

With an effort, he smiled and looked down at his hand on the doorknob. "Out for my usual night stroll, I see."

"Not alone this time, darling. That's all over and done with."

He studied her for a long minute before taking her in his arms and murmuring, "I'll adore you always for that."

"And for other things, too, I hope," she came back pertly, trying to get him into a happier frame of mind.

He lifted her into his arms, insisting, "You are like ice, no matter how much you say you love me. I'll have to warm you up."

"Please do," she said, and then added slowly, "because I need you so very much . . . you will never know how much."

It was the truth, but it was also what he needed to hear.

One thing had been accomplished by the confrontation between Eric and Martin Helm. Since the detective, Mehaffey, had been following Eric at the time, he must now be aware that Eric was not the criminal he was after.

Gregg had still not made up her mind whether or not to tell Eric about Martin Helm (leaving out certain details of her own love for the man), but she did want very much to get Eric out of the vicinity of the hotel and another possible encounter with him. The next morning she approached the idea obliquely by admiring Mount Pilatus from their window. Eric suggested that they make a visit to the mountaintop and take a lunch along. She fell in with the plan at once. They had the hotel prepare a picnic basket with a bottle of the local wine, cheeses and foie gras for the chewy dark bread, and various fruits, plus a carefully wrapped, highly caloric piece of chocolate cake for Gregg.

She saw no signs of Mehaffey or Helm as they left the hotel. She didn't know whether to be relieved or to keep looking, wondering—If Helm was not here, where would they find him?

They drove around the end of the lake and on to the foot of the mountain where one of the bright-coloured little cog trains was just creaking and cranking to a halt. Half a dozen people waited to take the cog up to the peak. No one looked familiar to Gregg, but she was disturbed when she saw Eric looking around, examining each face as she had done. It hurt her to see his apprehension and the angry glint in his eyes. In spite of all her efforts not to make the comparison, she remembered Martin

Helm's furious eyes when, in some small way, she had displeased him.

But the difference was there for her to see the minute he turned back, with his sudden warm smile at sight of her.

"Of to our picnic on top of the world. It is one way to get privacy."

She laughed at his European notions of "the top of the world," reminding him, "We have peaks in California and Colorado almost twice as high. You European chauvinist!"

He wasn't angry, as Helm would have been at her contradiction. "It is the highest peak we can reach for lunch, at any rate."

They climbed into the last cog car and sat very close together, with the lunch basket on Eric's knees. Several children with their red-haired mother crowded in around them, and Gregg marveled at their good manners. She almost wished Marlene and Pauly were there. But it was just as well that the sharp-eyed, curious Marlene could not be here. Nothing would remain a secret around her for very long.

Gregg stole a glance at Eric, caught him looking at her with a loving gaze that positively demanded her response, even in public. She pretended to reach over him, to look into the picnic basket, and in doing so, kissed his cheek. He reddened a little but didn't look displeased.

The car gave a pull and a jolt, throwing two of the children and their mother onto Eric and Gregg. There were shrieks and laughter. The group above them on the cog likewise fell against each other, and in the scuffle Eric found himself with the children's mother practically in his arms. There were apologies all around, the confusion caused in part by the fact that the children's mother and Gregg were both wearing nearly the same shade of green, as the young mother was quick to explain. Her hair was much lighter than Gregg's but it was red, and the mistake aroused more jokes.

Several German tourists also enjoyed the scuffle and seemed to find Eric's predicament, with two pretty women, a huge joke. Gregg wished she could understand their German, which was much too rapid for her to get more than a vague sense of their conversation. But their presence and the sound of his native accent had lightened

Eric's mood, and she was relieved to see him perk up so quickly.

By the time they reached the top of the cog's tracks and joined the other visitors brought out by the perfect weather and the breathtaking scenery, Gregg and Eric were laughing as loudly as the other tourists. Watching the cog cars start their grinding way down the mountain, Gregg wished she and Eric might remain at the top, safe from the problems waiting several thousand feet below them.

She had forgotten that there was a big building where they might have gotten refreshments, and that this was not precisely a single sharp peak on which they stood, but a very civilized and busy series of leveled-off corners, including a lookout leveled at the end of a little path to the left of the main building.

To escape other tourists like themselves, Gregg and Eric wandered off to the least populated spot, where he pointed out various Alpine peaks, arguing with himself, to her amusement, over whether an almost unseen point was the tip of the Matterhorn or not. He was quite sure he couldn't make out Mount Blanc, but he showed her half a dozen others that might or might not be famous peaks. Gregg took his word for all of them. The sky seemed very near, very blue, and the geography below far enough away to be part of another world.

They were still debating about whether or not they should break open the picnic basket or wander around first, when the German tourist group came along the path toward them, making loud requests of Eric in their own language.

Eric swore under his breath, saying, "Shall we run for it?"

"No, please, Not run. Make it a fast walk," she laughed, thinking of the steep, rough terrain.

Pretending they had not guessed that they were the object of all that running and waving, Gregg and Eric strolled, ever more rapidly, in the direction of the lookout, but they could not outrun their friendly pursuers. As they gave in and stopped, the latest group of tourists climbed out of the cog train, wandered past them and along the path toward the distant Mount Pilatus lodge. Headed in the same direction were three children. Gregg recognized them as belonging to the other woman in green who had fallen into Eric's lap on the cog train.

The German tourists surrounded Eric, apparently wanting him to snap pictures of them. Gregg wished him luck and, waving to him, went over to the three children who were evidently looking for the rest rooms, and she pointed them toward the restaurant in the building beyond them. She went on toward the lookout, stopped to let a youthful, running group pass her and glanced over at the southerly view, wondering if she could make out lakes Thun and Brienz and wishing Eric were there to identify the peaks and lakes in this direction.

By the time she started back on the path to the lookout, the children's mother was now there, her red hair gleaming in the sunlight. A tall man in an old safari jacket and peaked green Alpine hat was behind the woman now, about to surprise her by seizing her shoulders in an embrace. As Gregg watched, sharing the woman's enjoyment of what seemed to be a moment of pleasure, they suddenly began to struggle. The woman shrieked and lost her balance, as she tried to look back over her shoulder.

Alarmed, Gregg cried out a warning. The woman fell to her knees, and other tourists converged on the path near the lookout, attracted by her scream. The tall man in the safari jacket mingled with the crowd and slipped out toward the main lodge.

Gregg ran up the path and almost collided with the three children belonging to the woman in green. They had come up just in time to see their mother fall to her knees. The younger girl was crying, and the older girl and boy were in a state of panic. Gregg took the little one's hand and led them all between the chattering groups to find their mother who was sitting on the ground in the middle of the lookout, being patted and consoled by two indignant American women.

"Masher!" the older of the two insisted. "Tried to kiss her, and she lost her balance and nearly fell over into the valley. . . and she didn't even know him!"

There were murmurs and questions throughout the crowd, but no one seemed to suspect anything worse had been attempted. The woman was recovering from a brief bout of hysteria and now surveyed the practical damage. She felt as if she had pulled several muscles, and her right nylon stocking was torn to shreds.

Suddenly, Gregg saw Eric pushing his way through the crowd. He reached her, took her aside and looked her over. There was fear in his face and the tightness of his grip.

"My God," he whispered harshly, "I thought it was you!"

She moistened her dry lips. "What do you mean? Where were you?"

"Over on the path. Toward the west. I'd dropped the picnic basket while I took pictures for those fools, and when I went to pick it up I saw you struggling—that green dress—then you seemed to disappear. Down the mountainside, I thought. God! I thought that—" He began to kiss her, to reassure himself that she was real.

She felt as tired as if she really had fallen. She could not respond for minute.

He thought she was the woman in green. Had someone else made that same mistake, catching a glimpse of a red-haired woman in green, and tried to destroy her? One more push, the way Martin Helm had always gotten rid of his witnesses. She swung around frantically, trying to catch a glimpse of the man in the Alpine hat and the safari jacket. He was gone.

16

THE women were asking the victim to describe her assailant, and Gregg stopped, motioning Eric to silence as the woman in green hugged her weeping children. The mother herself seemed between laughter and tears. She began in German, but the Americans looked around, asking for translation, and the young woman repeated her description in English.

"He tried to kiss me, I think. It seemed as if I knew him. Then I saw that he was not—the one I thought."

"Describe him, my dear," one of the Americans pursued the matter.

"Tall and good-looking. Dark eyes. Not unlike that gentleman." She pointed to Eric.

Everyone looked at him, and those nearest began to back off. Gregg held his hand more tightly, but her effort at moral support was unnecessary. The woman waved away the crowd's suspicions.

"*Nein. Nein.* It was not that gentleman.

A man older. A lined face. Not so hand-some."

This time Eric was genuinely embar-rassed. He muttered to Gregg, "Shall we find our picnic basket? I left it back there," he pointed.

"Yes. Let's go, please."

Meanwhile, several in the crowd ex-changed comments about the young woman's assailant. Gregg heard snatches of their remarks as she and Eric started back toward the lodge.

"I saw the fellow . . . He said the lady had fallen down. He was going for help."

"That one in the pale jacket and the hat? He took the cog down. He went from here to the cog. Very fast."

So Martin Helm—if it were Helm—had managed to get out of a dangerous spot, Gregg thought. The police would have to know now.

When they were beyond the edge of the crowd, Eric asked in a puzzled voice, "Why the excitement? He only tried to kiss her, didn't he? What did the Americans call him? Masher?"

"It's an old-fashioned word. Trying to

make time with her." She laughed shortly. "That's old-fashioned, too."

"But it was only that, wasn't it? They don't suspect anything else?"

"I suppose not. How could they? They don't know him."

He looked at her sharply. "But we know one thing. The man resembled me."

"Well, it wasn't you. It was someone older." She tried to coax him out of that worried look, and the memory of his sleep-walking and haunted dreams. "Someone not so handsome, darling."

Eric said after a minute or two, "I know who the fellow must have been."

She stared at him, unable to say a word.

"Don't you understand, darling? The fellow I saw last night at the lion monument. He is real. He was here. Others have seen him, too. I suppose it is too late to go after him now."

She hugged him, happy that he didn't know anything more about his horrible look-alike.

"What is all this?" he wanted to know, taking her around the waist and examining her face. "Are you *that* anxious for your precious chocolate cake?"

"I am. Believe me, I am!"

He laughed at her appetite, and they walked up the path toward the spot where Eric had left their picnic basket. Then he and Gregg moved to a little hollow near the mountaintop, partially shielded from the other tourists by an outcropping of rock, to enjoy their lunch.

Gregg's relief and happiness overflowed into her manner, her quick reaction to his touch, the joking conversation between them as they ate their lunch. She was particularly happy because now, if ever, there had been the clearest evidence that Eric Raeder and Martin Helm were two very different men. Eric's lightheartedness came from a similar reassurance. There was a real man somewhere who strongly resembled him. The *Doppelgänger* theory had been disproved.

After lunch, when Gregg stretched out on the ground with her head across Eric's thighs, she wondered if there was some way that she could tell him about Martin Helm. But there was always the strong probablility that he would suspect her reasons for marrying him. As if she could possibly have married Eric just because he reminded her of that murderer, that sinister creature who was hounding them now!

She turned her head and kissed Eric's wrist, the thin, vulnerable spot above his hard-boned, brown hand. After only two weeks of marriage, she found it impossible to believe she ever loved that other one, who had called himself Martin Helm.

She could tell that her little demonstration of affection had touched him far out of proportion to the gesture itself. He caressed her hair tenderly, but afterward pulled one long strand and she cried, "Ouch! Beast!" and then laughed. The sweet mood with its faint, bitter worry passed away.

When they got to their feet, gathered up the remnants of the picnic and returned to the cog train, Eric glanced over toward the lookout where several tourists stood pointing at the various Alpine peaks, and the miniature movie-set appearance of Lake Lucerne and its man-made surroundings.

"Flirting?" Gregg demanded, with a slight edge to her question.

Belatedly, he noticed the red-haired woman who had just rounded up her children and was signaling madly for the cog train to wait. They all settled themselves on the train, the woman and her children close behind Gregg and Eric.

The heart-stopping little jerks downward had hardly begun when the woman started to joke about her romantic encounter with the stranger.

"He was so like you," she marveled to Eric. "Older, but then, in the sunlight everyone looks older. And if he had not worn a different jacket, and that Austrian hat, I would have believed he was you." She fluttered a little. "What a ridiculous thing! He was so anxious, I thought he would knock me down into Lake Lucerne."

One of her children pointed out that she would have fallen into a valley, but aside from topography the woman was very sure of herself.

One of the young Germans teased Eric, "Was it for this then that you left your picnic basket on the hill? So you could run and kiss the *gnadige Frau*?"

Everyone thought this was highly amusing. Gregg laughed, too, but with a strong sense of discomfort. She wished they had not been so busy stressing the absurd idea that Eric could have done that thing to the woman. Someone here must have seen Eric and the man in the safari jacket at the same time! But they were all too bent upon playing up the unfunny joke, making it appear that Eric had been the culprit after all.

Beside her, Eric was growing more and more tense. He shared her dislike of the subject and tried to change it, pointing out the sheer drop and the terrific angle of their descent.

"Are there accidents on the cog?" he asked. But no one knew about accidents or danger, or if they did know, they did not wish to discuss such subjects. Eric gave up in disgust and tried to ignore the company.

By the time they reached the ancient MG and drove back to Lucerne, Gregg was nearly certain that Eric had gotten over his irritation and they could at least pretend to forget the episode on the heights of Mount Pilatus. But the first thing he said when they reached the hotel was, "I'll leave you here, darling, and be back soon. I want to go for a short walk, just to stretch a bit. Will you be all right?"

"Of course." She wondered if he hoped

to meet the man who looked like him, and the idea of such a confrontation frightened her. "Please be careful. If you should see that man, he might be dangerous."

"What man? Darling, you are dreaming. I've no intention of meeting anyone."

"Eric, the man is a crook. He could be violent."

He started to turn away, seemed to have second thoughts and kissed her forehead. Afterward, he looked into her eyes. "How do you know?"

"I don't know, exactly. But he tried to attack that woman. He can't be exactly a boy scout."

"I'll be back before dark. Don't worry. This is Switzerland, not New York."

She wondered if she should force him into taking her along, but pride and common sense stopped her. She went into the lobby of the hotel, swinging the picnic basket, but with her anxious thoughts confined to matters far away, wondering just what Martin Helm's game was. She heard her name called in a rich brogue that made her want to hurl the picnic basket in the face of the man who approached her.

"Mrs. Raeder, did you have a pleasant day?"

She couldn't help saying, "Until now."

Undeterred, he skipped along beside Gregg, trying to keep up with her long strides. "Ma'am, are you after saving your husband?"

She passed the elevator, but stopped at the bottom of the stairs. "If you really want to capture Martin Helm, forget my husband. Go through town tonight. I saw Helm today on Mount Pilatus." He had an odd look on his face and he had lost the usual lying smirk. Maybe, just maybe, he would admit now that Eric Raeder was not Martin Helm. She said sharply, "Last night you followed us. You saw the real Martin Helm when he came face to face with my husband. Or are you playing ball with Helm now?"

His ingratiating, false grin had faded to a hard stare, but she stood up to it. He shrugged then, "Well, now, if you want the truth, he's not nice, this other one—if he is the real Marek Helmer. I knew that after I'd been five minutes in friend Helmer's company. But I found a way to gain his trust, as you might say. You'll be surprised to know I'm now working for him." She opened her mouth. He held up a hand. "Unwillingly, to be sure. I'm supposed to keep you suspecting your husband. I think Helmer wants to spread the suspicion that he's crazy, capable of anything."

"But why?"

"For some nasty reason. Who knows?"

"What!"

Back came the ingratiating grin. "But if I had the money, I think I could lure him into Germany. Set up his approach to the rich old maid in Hamburg I mentioned. It might work."

"If you had the money." Her cynical tone escaped him.

"Pre-cisely."

"Why can't he simply be arrested and delivered to Hamburg for trial on the old charge?"

"On what evidence, ma'am? It's getting the evidence that's going to cost me."

"How much?"

For the first time he seemed genuinely hesitant. "I'm needing, say five thousand Deutsche marks to do the job properly."

"Well, just don't try your tricks on my husband. And if you want further proof of his innocence, ask someone what happened on Mount Pilatus. Both men were up there. . . . Now, please leave me alone."

Still, he managed to interpose his body between her and the stairs. "Well, ma'am, there's the matter of finances. My plan. First, remember, you'd have me in your corner, so to speak, to tell you all I learn from Helmer and whoever he's working with . . . But to get back to my plan. If I could just be turning over this Helmer to the police, all's well. The proof, that's the key. You know the law these days. They'll let him off the hook if he's not caught in the very act of murder."

It would be worth anything to get Martin Helm and Timothy Mehaffey out of Eric's life and her own. She was so afraid that Eric might learn the whole, ugly truth. But could this persistent little man actually maneuver Martin Helm back to a situation where he might be captured?

"I can't—and won't give you five thousand Deutsche marks. You may as well face it. If you put through this Hamburg business, you'll have the reward you were talking about. However, I am willing to give you a smaller sum. And I'll want results." She pushed her forefinger hard against his chest. "I'll want to read about those results, not see them. Do I make myself clear?"

"Clear, good lady. Very clear. How . . . what was the figure you had in mind?"

"Five hundred dollars seems adequate. You must remember the dollar has risen in value recently."

He appeared distressed but not despairing. "But that would hardly see me to the borders of West Germany. It's true there's a lot of blank area in what's known about Marek Helmer, but my studies show me that he began his nefarious career there. His mother abandoned him during an air raid. Left him among the ruins, as it were. Later, when he'd done a bit of all right on the black market, she was after coming back, demanding his support. The Hamburg police have a theory that he thought she died in the bombing. Then, to find her a tramp and a sponger turned him sour on females. But you can't condemn a man because he's soured on females. It's evidence that does it. They were that sure Helmer had committed the Hamburg murder, but there were no prints. No proof they could nail this fellow with. Nor even your husband, when it comes to that. Though friend Helmer (he calls himself Helm, as you know) claims that, with a picture of your husband, and your husband's 'criminal actions' against you and others, they'll identify him quick enough in Hamburg."

She was inclined to believe him. Helm had never spoken of his family except to make remarks about the blond divorcées and widows he saw on the cruise ship with Gregg. And unfortunately, eleven years ago, this sort of gossip had been common enough.

"Very well. I want you to keep my husband and this man from meeting, so let's not haggle. I have an account in a French bank. I'll give you a check on a Paris branch. You can cash it anywhere. Five hundred now—" He started to speak. She held up her hand. "And another five hundred when you have something to report, some proof, from Hamburg. And by proof, I don't want you to send me anything direct. Here is my French agent's card. Whatever information you send, make it to her office in Paris."

"I get the picture."

She wrote a check to "cash," leaning on the stair banister, and held it just out of his hands. "If I see you again, or if my husband sees you again, the deal is off. Frankly, your nuisance value is only worth so much. No more."

"You may trust me, ma'am." He folded the check lengthwise and carefully slipped it into the slit pocket of his vest. He seemed to have no fear that the check would not be honored.

"I don't trust you," she told him. "And if either of us sees you again, I have no reason to make that second payment."

He surprised her by assuring her seriously, "If I get Helmer nabbed, I suppose I won't be needing more than what you've agreed to pay me. There was a woman in Hamburg, his first victim, I'm thinking. The family's offered a bit of a reward, but there's got to be proof of him caught in the act, so to speak."

"And still you need my thousand?"

"Sure now, it takes a bit of money to live while I'm working to nab him."

She closed her handbag with a sharp

click. "Good-bye, Mr. Mehaffey. Not *auf Wiedersehen*, but good-bye."

"Exactly so, ma'am." He tipped two fingers to his forehead in salute and went trotting across the lobby to the street doors.

She had no belief in his integrity, but felt that he might have inducements to pursue the arrest of Martin Helm. Meanwhile, there was the worry over Eric's possible encounter with Helm. She had gone up to the landing before second thoughts occurred to her and she went back down. She walked out to the street, stood on the cobblestones for several minutes, staring toward the busy, narrow streets of the town where long, attenuated shadows told her it was late in the day. There was nothing she could do. She knew that. After a little while, she went back into the hotel and to the bar which adjoined the lobby.

She was too depressed, and too anxious about her husband, to pay much attention to the interior of the wood-paneled bar which looked more like a London pub than a comfortable, continental gathering place for both men and women. She took one of the ladder-back stools at the bar and ordered a vermouth cassis without looking around. It was a minute or two before she became uncomfortably aware that a man at the end of the bar had moved up to take the stool beside hers and had begun to watch her. She turned around.

Duane Colt sat there with a full stein of German beer in his hand. His smile flickered, faded. He was like a child with a present that he thought she might not like, but she was delighted to see him. He represented home and a curious kind of self-absorbed innocence that appealed to her now.

"Surprised?"

"Thunderstruck."

"Are you sorry?"

"No, of course not." She hugged him and received his cheek-to-cheek embrace. "Delighted. But how on earth did you find us?"

He was triumphant. "I've been sent. Well, I wanted to see you, but the children—Marlene—sent me. She thinks something's going on."

"Going on? Between Eric and me? I should hope so."

"Don't be an ass, Red. Ursula's kids have been doing a little snooping. Nice kids

301

when you get to know them. Anyway, Marlene made Pauly tell me about it. The kids think this guy, Heinz Albrecht, Ursula's boyfriend, is plotting things against Eric. And you."

She received her drink from the barman and felt for it without taking her eyes off Duane's face.

"What kind of things?"

Seeing that she took him seriously, he brightened.

"Phone calls, mostly. You know Pauly. The kid adores his mother and she's not the most motherly woman in the world. He hangs around her and hears funny things. Not from her but from the boyfriend, Albrecht. Like calls to somebody in Lucerne. He mentioned something about a doorman, back in New York. A kind of threat. Or reminder. The fellow he keeps talking to used to be a doorman. They're in some deal together, and it involves you and Eric."

"How? About what?"

"That I wouldn't know. But the fellow he talks to used to be this doorman in New York, and—"

"My God? At Ursula Raeder's apartment." Suddenly, she remembered the conversation at Mrs. Raeder's cocktail party. Some mysterious new doorman. Could he have been Helm? The man was missing when Gregg and Oliver Sills left the building. Was it because he feared Gregg would recognize him? She and Oliver had talked for several minutes in the lobby while they waited for a cab. Hadn't they mentioned Martin Helm and the dead woman who recently had fallen out of a window?

She thought back. She was sure there had been a discussion about the resemblance between Eric and Martin Helm. Even if there were no discussion for Helm to overhear, Albrecht might have noted the resemblance himself. If Martin Helm actually had been working as doorman at the apartment building, then he *was* in New York when Alys Lane died. It was all coming together.

"I think it adds up. I knew he was following me around New York those last few days. I felt it! And he kept right on following me to Denmark, trying to make it look as if Eric were crazy, forgetting things he had done, people he had talked to."

This was all too confusing to Duane, but he asked, "Then it makes sense to you?" He ventured to take her hand and squeezed it so hard her wedding and engagement rings cut into the flesh. "I swear, Red, I really want you to be happy. This isn't some blackmail scheme, is it?" She hesitated. He added, "It's nothing you've done, I know. But I couldn't help thinking they have something on Raeder."

"They don't. The man Albrecht has been calling on the telephone is a criminal."

"Red! What're you mixed up in? Look here," he went on anxiously, "I admit I wanted Eric Raeder to put in a good word for me with the studios. But I sure as hell don't want to get mixed up in anything that would—that they could blackmail me for later on. You know how it is in my business, when you really get on top."

She laughed so hard she had to wipe her eyes with a cocktail napkin. She felt a trifle hysterical. "Poor Duane! How transparent you are!"

He had a feeling he was being insulted. "What do you mean, transparent?"

"Honest, Duane. Just honest."

Mollified, he murmured, "Does it mean trouble for you, this business about Albrecht?"

"It explains a great deal. Albrecht is the one who is in trouble. He's dealing with a very dangerous man, and he may not even know how dangerous."

"I don't know, Red. Pauly says it sounds like whatever they are doing is Albrecht's idea. He made threats, said to this guy: 'You couldn't even put the plan into action without me. You need me.' Something like that."

"Did he sound afraid?"

"Not so you'd notice. He said, 'No threats. You need me alive.'"

"Alive! Good God!"

"Scary, isn't it?" He looked around the room. "Where is this Wonder Man of yours?"

"He's in town. I think he's looking for the man Albrecht is dealing with. A man named Martin Helm, among other names."

"What? You let him go?"

Her hands were trembling. She set the drink down. "I couldn't stop him. Besides, Helm wouldn't want to hurt him. He plans to use Eric somehow. If there's anyone in the world he really would want to get rid of, it's me. I've a suspicion he would want it to look as if Eric had killed me. Then Helm could blame all the crimes of his past on Eric."

He was aghast. "And you haven't called in the police?"

"And have him slip out of it? He tried something today against another woman. And that woman believes the man tried to kiss her, not kill her."

That stopped him. He raised the beer stein, drank a long draft and made a face. "Beer's not my speed. Anyway, I can certainly see why you are so nervous."

"I've got one hope. I sent a private investigator out to find out what Helm is planning, if he can. He's quite a bloodhound . . . I hope. Now, if only Eric would get back safe and sound!" She was still shakily using both hands to bring her glass to her lips.

Duane Colt set his stein down and turned on the stool to signal the barman. Suddenly, he nudged Gregg.

"How do you like that? You've got a

quick answer to your prayers. Isn't that Raeder out in the lobby?"

She jumped off the stool. A man and woman had come into the bar through the open doors, but behind them, Gregg saw a tall man cross the lobby to the concierge's desk. He asked a question.

Watching him move, seeing his brown corduroy coat, the faint graying of his hair, Gregg caught Duane's arm. Terror weakened her entire body, and she could hardly get the words out.

"Not—my husband. I think that is the other one."

17

"WHAT the devil, honey!" Duane got off the stool so quickly it spun crazily for a few seconds. "Hadn't we better do something? Call the gendarmes, or gestapo, whatever?"

"And accuse him of looking like my husband? He does, you know." Yet he could see her panic. She whispered, "He mustn't be here when my husband returns. If only I can keep them from meeting until I tell Eric the truth about him! *If* I can tell Eric."

"Someone else may do that for you. Look. Who's that?"

Timothy Mehaffey had come in from the street, and now tapped the tall man's shoulder. They exchanged a few words and, a minute later, they went out together toward the street.

What was that all about? Gregg thought. But whatever the reason, Mehaffey was taking Helm out of the hotel. That was the answer to a prayer. Maybe Mehaffey had been on the level with her after all. She watched Martin Helm's movements, the slightly overblown swagger in his stride, the seedy arrogance of his mannerisms. He hadn't seemed seedy eleven years ago, but she was very young then, and easily impressed.

"Was I ever really that young?" she murmured.

Duane looked from the departing men back to Gregg. He understood her comment. "So that's the criminal Albrecht's been dealing with? He looks like Raeder, and yet he doesn't. He seems much older. You know, he's like someone trying to play a younger role. I still feel we ought to report him. Warn people. That is, if the guy is dangerous."

"Yes, we ought to do something. Anything." She pushed between surprised newcomers on their way into the bar. Duane reached for her, then came after her to the door where she stopped. He tried to calm her, aware that his own words had triggered her outburst.

"I'm sorry, Red. I know there's nothing you can do. But if that joker is so dangerous, you ought to get out of here—out of Lucerne—as soon as you can."

She saw that people were beginning to look curiously at her and Duane. At the same time, she knew that there was nothing to be done while she counted on Timothy Mehaffey. If she interfered now, she would lose the chance that Mehaffey might serve his purpose. Besides, in a cowardly way, Gregg wanted to avoid facing Martin Helm. She wondered if the man might still have some sinister power over her.

"They've gone," she discovered with relief. "It didn't seem possible, but Mehaffey may be honest, after all."

"Mehaffey? Oh, the little creep who looks like a mouse. You trust him?"

Suddenly, she remembered Martin Helm's brief talk with the concierge, and asked Duane, "Would you mind just looking out into the street? I'd like to know if they are waiting in the square. Meanwhile, I'll find out what he asked the desk."

Duane obliged her good-humoredly. He looked his immaculate and dashing self, actually more glamorous than the big movie and television stars she had known; his very perfection made her smile. He was at the opposite end of the spectrum from the evil Martin Helm, yet there was about him that same suggestion of the attractive, artificial creation.

She went to the concierge's desk, but the man only shook his head at her question. He was polite, but definite.

"Yes, one gentleman inquired for you, or for your husband. But Herr Raeder's instructions were very strict. The desk said nothing to the gentleman."

It was as bad as she had thought. "The gentleman who just left here with the little man?"

The concierge was surprised. "No, Frau Raeder. The young gentleman who inquired for you is over there in the doorway. You were talking to him a minute ago. No one else asked for you."

"Not a tall, graying man in a brown corduroy jacket? He spoke to you just now, and then left the hotel with the little man. Didn't he ask for my husband or me?"

"No, Frau Raeder. The gentleman in the brown coat asked for Herr Mehaffey only. And as you see, Herr Maheffey came in and they left together."

She didn't know what to think at that

disclosure. Was Mehaffey still lying to Helm, working for her, and for the reward he would be paid in Hamburg if he brought Helm to justice? She wanted terribly to believe that. But he was taking a dangerous chance if he hoped to fool Martin Helm for long. What was going on?

"Is all well with you, Frau Raeder?" the concierge asked, more curious than solicitous.

"I don't know," she said honestly, and motioned to Duane who reported that Mehaffey and Helm were at the far end of the street. Mehaffey seemed to be talking with animation.

"See here," Duane said, noting signs of panic in his usually confident friend, and apparently not anxious to have it rub off on him, "you'll be wanting to see Raeder alone. Maybe we can all meet for dinner. Meanwhile, why don't I just wander back to the bar? Would you believe it? An old lady tourist—attractive, actually, real class —recognized me and got my autograph."

"Marvelous, Duane. You do that." They embraced briefly, and she left him in a hurry, hoping to head off Eric before he had a chance to meet Helm.

She walked up to the square and looked everywhere along the streets that emptied into the square, but saw no one who looked familiar. Strange, prickling thoughts occurred to her during the long twilight hour while she killed time trying to find her husband.

"Just suppose—" an insidious voice suggested, "just suppose you cannot find Eric Raeder because you saw Martin Helm a few minutes ago. And a man can't be in two places at once."

There was a simple reassurance. The man in the lobby had been graying, and different in many ways. She now knew her husband well enough to be certain that the only way Eric could ever be Helm was during some blackout, some sleepwalking episode. And he would hardly go about powdering his hair and lining his face during such a blackout. Also, another positive note. Albrecht was up to some crookedness with an acquaintance who had been a doorman. So there was another man involved. Who else but Eric's look-alike?

She had talked herself into a more confident mood by the time she saw a tall man striding toward her from the direction of the lake, and this was unquestionably her husband. She ran down the narrow sidewalk toward him, noted his surprise at the sight of her, and then he pleased her by holding out his arms, a gesture he was usually too reserved to make in public. Within the comfort of his arms she thought for a disastrous moment that she might cry. He removed one arm from around her, reached in his pocket and brought out a package which, unfortunately, had been crushed by their embrace. Inside the paper bag she found a chocolate pastry which had been squashed but still looked delicious.

"I remember the shops have them in their windows in spring," Eric told her, enjoying her pleasure as she began to eat it. "I was lucky to find a shop which still makes them, but now you will spoil your dinner."

"It's worth it! I wish I had a present for you, because we have a visitor and I don't want you to be impolite."

He tightened his grip around her waist. "We will think of some present. I can think of several ways you may humor me. Who is the visitor?" He stopped in the square and looked at her, frowning. "Not tha fellow who looks like me. Not the other one."

"No, no. It's my friend Duane Colt. He came to tell us something the children have discovered." She explained about Heinz Albrecht's telephone conversations overheard by Pauly. She hurried through the story, pointing out the possible damage that could be done by a man deliberately attempting to look like the well-known Eric Raeder, who was presumed to be a rich man. "As I see it, this is the way Albrecht and your look-alike can try and blackmail you. Please don't be angry, darling. We can work it out, now that we know about Albrecht."

His quick, unexpected laugh made her stare at him. She couldn't believe his reaction.

"Sweetheart," he explained, "they couldn't have done me a greater favor. Do you think I do not go out of my mind with the thought that I might have called to you as you said, at the Magasin du Nord in Copenhagen? Or that I made the telephone call to Pauly before I arrived at the hotel? This afternoon, as I walked, I knew the man who looked like me was the best gift

315

in the world. His presence proves that the other one is real, not some hideous part of myself unknown to me."

"Of course. Eric, it's so obvious!"

They stopped and kissed. Two evening strollers snickered as they passed, but Eric and Gregg couldn't have cared less. She said just before they reached the hotel, "Then you won't be rude to poor Duane who really has helped us?"

"Just as long as he has not been one of your lovers."

"I can assure you he hasn't."

"Not for want of trying." But he didn't look too cross, and she felt that they had overcome that hurdle.

"What are we going to do about Albrecht and the other one?" she asked.

"Prison would be ideal for both of them, but the scandal would upset Aunt Alex." He considered the crisp, cold, twilight-blue sky. "I suppose the best punishment would be to let them try their blackmail and then laugh at them. After all, they aren't physically dangerous. Albrecht is only a hanger-on, and my look-alike can hardly be more than that."

She thought of those women who had

died. She thought of poor Alys Lane who had kept Martin Helm's secret for eleven years. But in the end, she, too, had gone the way the of the others. *Not dangerous?*

He felt the sudden tension in her body, and consoled her cheerfully, "They can't hurt you, you know. They've nothing at all to hurt you with. They hardly know you. They might have gotten to me mentally, made me believe a lot of ridiculous things about myself. But not now. I suppose Albrecht got the business of my sleep-walking from Ursula. She is one female who sets my teeth on edge."

Gregg couldn't help saying, "Yet she almost ruined your life by marrying your brother."

He took this calmly, and she felt he was honest when he remarked, "I can't think how I could ever have loved her. But you must not mind that. It's different with me. See? You smile. But I confess it. I am more jealous than you. I couldn't stand to know you had been really in love before me. Here, now. Haven't I reassured you? Don't be so tense, darling."

With immense effort she relaxed. She could hardly tell him that his assurance had only added to her fears. But this meeting on the street, aside from giving her the warm, pulsating pleasure of having him beside her, had at least bridged the difficult problem of Duane Colt's presence in Lucerne. She would concentrate upon that, and not worry about the other problem until the matter came up, and then pray that Eric never would find out the full extent of her relationship with his look-alike, Martin Helm.

"I think poor Duane is a little afraid of you," she explained as they went into the hotel.

"Of me? Why? I'm a harmless fellow."

"But he is constantly afraid he will make an enemy of you, and then you won't recommend him for the movie."

"Good God! Is that all? I'll recommend him then, before he becomes any more of a nuisance. And by the way, my darling, I hope I never hear you call me 'Poor Eric.'"

She laughed at that. "Believe me, I can't imagine it ever being necessary. But you can be a little frightening at times."

"Not to you, surely."

Since he appeared ready to take her seriously, she dismissed the subject with a quick wave of the hand.

"Not to me. Would I adore you if I were afraid of you?"

. . . I adored someone once, her thoughts reminded her. . . and I was afraid of him . . . Forget that? Banish it! Thank God for this, the one person I do love.

Eric saw Duane Colt looking young and hesitant in the doorway of the bar, and motioned to him. The actor came obediently, after a questioning glance at Gregg. Eric shook hands with him, asked how Marlene and Pauly were doing and whether the Baroness de Lieven was well.

"Very well, sir. She drove Red's—I mean Gregg's uncle to the airport herself yesterday. Your uncle is quite a man, Gregg. He made a big splash with the baroness."

Gregg was amused. "He managed to flirt with another lady, a total stranger, on the plane into Geneva."

Eric asked the actor, "How are you coming along with your career? Have you tested for *Doppelgänger* yet?"

"I read before Buzz Ballenstein in New

York," Duane said eagerly. "The sale went through, you know, and Buzz is likely to direct it."

His enthusiasm for Eric Raeder's book was contagious, and it proved impossible for the author to resist the subject when Duane began to question him about motivations, characters and Eric's own feelings, whether they differed from those of his hero or not. It was a subject Gregg found fascinating, for it would illuminate Eric's own private life and especially his sleep-walking.

The two men moved out to the empty dining terrace where waiters were just setting up the tables, although the air was too chilly to make the terrace popular that night. Duane, who was obviously sincere in his admiration for *Doppelgänger*, asked if Eric thought his hero believed in "The Other One."

"The other one *is* different," Eric insisted. "When I was a child I knew a boy who—" He hesitated, did not look at Gregg but kept on: "This boy walked in his sleep. His brother, who was a humorous sort of fellow, made up stories about what he had done, where he had gone during these times that he could not remember. It was all lies, but for a long time the boy didn't know that. When I wrote the novel I changed the sleepwalking other self to a real second self. The image the hero sees in his mirror."

"But this image person doesn't behave like the hero," Duane Colt put in. "When I—I mean the hero—stands in front of a mirror he sees his image moving differently, smiling when he's puzzled, moving a foot when he moves a hand. Things like that. So when I read the lines I play it for horror; isn't that right?"

Gregg watched her husband who shook his head.

"Only in retrospect. At the exact moment these things happen, they are puzzling. You—that is, the hero—want to understand the trick. Who is doing this to you? What is the reality of the thing? Does this other self commit acts you are incapable of?"

"But, darling," Gregg protested gently, "your hero doesn't react that way in the book. At the end, this creature in the glass comes to possess him. The man who now understands it is all a trick, that malicious human beings are back of it . . . that man isn't in your book at all. He is someone you understand now. But he isn't in the *Doppelgänger*."

Eric caught himself and agreed. "I suppose in the light of day the *Doppelgänger* is drivel. I am frankly surprised it has done so well financially."

"Don't say that. Don't even hint at it, sir. Believe me, it's the finest commercial piece of writing I've read since *Love Story*," Duane insisted.

Eric grimaced, but accepted the praise graciously. As far as Gregg was concerned, she could have blessed the actor for bringing out the change in Eric Raeder's view of his sleepwalking. Little would Martin Helm suspect that the very fact of his existence erased a fear with which Eric Raeder had lived most of his life! Considering the evil of Martin Helm's life, it was ironic that he should now be responsible for some good.

She caught the two men grinning at her and realized that in her anxiety over the conversation she had been repeatedly licking chocolate off her fingers like a sloppy child.

She suggested, "Why don't you two men

stake out a table in the bar, and I'll join you as soon as I wash and drag a comb through my hair?"

Duane said gallantly, "No need. You always look gorgeous, Red," and as Eric glanced at him, he added, "While Gregg's prettying up, we'll have a little more talk about that hero you've created, sir."

Leaving them, Gregg caught her husband's amused look and was glad that Duane Colt's interest in his own career was so transparent. She went up to their room and washed, deciding at the last minute to change the dusty green outfit she had worn to Mount Pilatus for a rust-colored skirt and matching top. She was giving her hair one last brush when the telephone rang.

I'm late, she thought, and they are getting impatient. Has Duane run out of questions about his dream role?

She took up the phone, said lightly, "Yes, darling. I'm all through fooling around. I'll be right down."

"Now, that'd be a kindness indeed, Mrs. Raeder," came Timothy J. Mehaffey's voice, all syrup-of-shamrocks. "But could you be giving me a minute, if you please?"

Badly shaken, Gregg took a few seconds

to recover before laying down the law. "If this is a report, get it over quick. If it's more money you want, forget it."

"As a matter of fact, ma'am, things haven't been going so well. This Helmer is not so dumb as I'd like. I caught up with him a little while ago and he's—see here, ma'am—he's liable to be along any minute. This call was his idea. I'm to needle you about the danger to you from your husband."

"I'll *bet* it was his idea! His, or Heinz Albrecht's!"

He surprised her by the nervous rapidity of his answer. "I don't know Heinz Albrecht in person, ma'am. And I'd not have you thinking my plans are changed. They're the same. What I told you earlier, that's the same. Hamburg, you know. But I do need more money. I have a friend there, a female who's done me favors before. I'll get her to help me bring the fish into the net."

"Speak louder. I can hardly hear you." She certainly had little faith in his scheme to trick Helm into capture in Hamburg. Why should Helm let himself be trapped there? Was Helm just leading Mehaffey on until he could figure out what the little blackmailer was up to? "Your two asssociates must have been surprised about your Hamburg plans."

"Please, ma'am, that's between you and me. But here's the thing. All I know of the German chap, Albrecht, is what Helmer says. I needled him. Said he'd not be able to involve your husband in anything. He swears Albrecht's going to show a snapshot of your husband to the witnesses in Hamburg, them that's left after all these years. And your husband fits the description. We both know that."

"Because he happens to look a little like a killer named Martin Helm. But even so, how will it benefit Helm and Albrecht to have my husband suspected, or even charged?"

"That I don't know, ma'am. There's more to it than arresting your husband. I don't know what it is yet. But it's bad. I'm thinking it's deadly." He lowered his voice again. "Meanwhile," he went on, "I'll be trying to put through our little plan, yours and mine."

"Very likely! I'm going to hang up, so I

advise you to spread the word among your gang. We don't pay blackmail."

He grew excited, as if his very life depended upon her paying what he already knew she wold not pay. "Only for now, ma'am. Helmer thinks he can get money from you to hold off. I was to tell you he'd lay off hounding your husband. But I didn't believe him. He just sent me to tell you that, for some reason. Maybe to test me."

"You are a fool, Mr. Mehaffey. And so is Heinz Albrecht. You can't play with a murderer like Martin Helm."

He hesitated. "There's only one thing in Helm's favor, ma'am. The family didn't know where your husband was twelve years ago, when he had that plane crash. There's a period when there's no record this Albrecht can find on your husband's doings, after he left the hospital. Even Albrecht's woman, this Ursula Raeder, she didn't know where your husband went. And it may've been that time when the thing happened in Hamburg. That's how I get it from Helm. What I'm telling you is worth five thousand Deutsche marks now, wouldn't you say?"

She finally lost her carefully controlled temper. "I always knew you were a fool. You can't trust Martin Helm, even if all that rigamarole is true."

"But he thinks we are friends, in a manner of speaking."

"Friends!" she cried. "*I loved Martin Helm for ten years*! And I wouldn't trust him for a minute. Five hundred dollars is all you get. I don't care how many people saw Eric in Hamburg twelve years ago. Tell that to my loving Martin Helm!"

The sharp click of a closing door made her swing around in panic to see Eric standing there. He looked as if he had been there for several minutes. She had never seen him quite like that, the hard lines of his face stiff and cold, with none of the warmth or understanding she had come to know in him. How much had he heard? Undoubtedly the worst part of her conversation, the frequent mentions of her old love for Martin Helm.

18

AFRAID, but angry still, Gregg tried to compose herself. She offered the telephone to Eric.

"Darling, this is our blackmailer, representing Heinz Albrecht. Do you want to talk to him?"

His eyelids flickered and he did not move for an instant. In the silent room Gregg heard Timothy Mehaffey's voice coming to her frantically over the phone.

"What's up?" What're you doing to me, ma'am?"

Eric crossed in front of her, took up the phone and listened to Mehaffey's nervous plea. Then, still silent, he set the phone back on its cradle. She watched him.

Without looking at her, he said, "So much for blackmail. I take it you've already paid this ex-lover of yours five hundred dollars. I'm afraid that won't go far these days."

"Ex-lover! It's that weird little man who followed us around Lucerne. I gave him the money for a plane ticket and enough to keep him going for a little while. Just to get him out of our hair. He's Timothy Mehaffey, a private investigator."

Of all quarreling habits, she hated silence most, and, not knowing what to do with him in this mood, she ran the comb through her hair again and calmly asked, "Did you leave poor Duane down in the bar alone with all those females begging for his autograph?"

He caught her arm, not very gently.

"After ten years, was it 'poor' Martin Helm?"

She gave up all pretense and turned to him.

"Eric, you want the truth? I've been terrified of Martin Helm for eleven years. I was engaged to marry him when I was eighteen. Remember how you felt at eighteen, the woman who now leaves you cold? With him, it was worse. I lived in constant fear that this monster would kill me after the engagement was broken."

"Why?" he asked, smiling faintly, in a way that seemed more sad to her than a scowl. "Merely because you would not marry him? It must have been an earth-shaking love."

"Not quite. Uncle George and I discovered that a man exactly like Martin, with his description, using his initials, had been involved in the deaths of two rich women. God knows why he had picked me. I was far from rich, but there was a substantial inheritance from my parents; I suppose he knew about that."

He stared at her. With a deep sense of relief, she felt that he believed her. She only hoped the one truth she was most afraid of would not occur to him, that his similarity to a vicious murderer had drawn her to him in the first place. She spoke quickly.

"A month ago Alys Lane fell out of a window. She was the witness who saved Martin Helm from a murder charge eleven years ago. Her landlady said she lived on a small cash income, rather mysteriously. The landlady reported that a man whose description could be that of Martin Helm visited her occasionally. And on the day she died, neighbors heard a man quarrel with her. I'm convinced if we knew more about that quarrel, we'd know why she died. But she was apparently alone at the time of the 'accident.' I think he probably met Albrecht and saw me at Ursula Raeder's apartment house the same week Miss Lane died. The coincidence is too great. I believe Alys Lane and his getting the job in New York are somehow connected. Maybe she knew his plan and threatened to warn someone. Me, for instance? Who knows?"

His grip tightened on her arm. It hurt, but she scarcely noticed the pressure. She could tell by the look in his eyes, the bodily tension, that he recognized the truth.

"Eric, he and Albrecht are after you now. I think the little detective may be on our side. Anyway, he told me it was something about Hamburg twelve years ago. I suppose Helm must have killed a woman there, too. They want to frame you, or scare me about it. Some scheme or other. What can we do?"

"You forgot to remind me of one important item, my darling."

The panic returned. He did not mean to forgive her, then. "I've tried to tell you everything about the past, Eric. Everything."

"All but one thing, *Liebchen*. You forgot to tell me that this Martin Helm, the man you loved, is so like me that you marry me when he fails you. *Is that how it was?*" He shook her a little to punctuate the fury and hurt and the fear in that last remark.

The worst had come and she was almost relieved. There was nothing left now to fear. She had never begged, but she did so now. "Eric, think! I was afraid of you when I saw you in the elevator that day. At a distance you appeared to be a man I hated. I was terrified of him. When you came to my apartment, I was afraid before I let you in. If I loved him, would I feel like that?"

His fingers slowly released her. Though the physical pain ceased, she was still unsure of what he himself felt. He let her go, but the suspicion was too deep.

"You believe I was capable of killing someone in Hamburg?"

"No! I only said—"

"You paid that detective because you were afraid. *Liebchen*, I know why you married me. I reminded you of your first love." His anger was a cover for something else, an anguish which she longed to dispel.

"Mehaffey says they hope to make the authorities believe it was you in Hamburg

332

years ago during that time in your life when you had been—ill"

He said grimly, "But there is one thing Albrecht and his friends are not aware of. You see, I do happen to know where I was twelve years ago. It is not something I'm proud of, but it can be proved, if necessary."

"Darling, what are you going to do?" Bewildered, she thought he must be walking out on her and their marriage.

"First, I'm taking you home to Geneva. After that, I am going to prove, once and for all time, that my brother lied to me about my sleepwalking, that he lied in spreading these tales to Ursula and indirectly, to this Albrecht. Where I went, what I did, how long it lasted . . . Albrecht is building his little scheme on empty air. Now! Your poor Duane is probably biting his nails, wondering what has happened. Let's be grateful he is here. I'm sure there is nothing more you and I want to say to each other tonight."

She felt a little cheered by the idea of returning to Geneva. Surely he wouldn't take her back to his own home if he was through with her. But this was her first experience with a smouldering, brooding anger since the days of Martin Helm, and she didn't know quite what to expect.

As they walked to the elevator, he remarked, "If I read young Colt correctly he has placed himself in a position where he has to depend on us for his transportation."

She could not stifle a quick laugh, and her spirits rose mercurially when she saw that his eyes looked less forbidding, almost as if he, too, were amused, but he made no effort to take her arm as they walked, and she did not dare to touch him, for fear he might think she took this matter between them too lightly. Besides, there was the matter of her pride, which matched his.

Duane got up to meet them, and before Eric could do so, pulled out Gregg's chair.

"Sorry," Eric said, "but it appears that I must be in Geneva tomorrow morning. That means driving all night."

Duane could not help seeing Gregg's shock at this, but he pulled himself together and behaved charmingly.

"Well, at least Mr. Raeder and I had a drink together. Good vibes between us, I think, don't you sir?"

Eric's eyebrows went up at the extreme

respect shown him and said, "Such respect denotes great age. Why not make it Eric?"

"Oh. Sorry, sir. I mean Eric. Well! So the honeymoon is over. Had to happen, I guess." He waited for their laugh. When he got only a flicker of a smile from Gregg and nothing at all from Eric, he began to move away from the table awkwardly.

"Well, again, so long."

Eric glanced at Gregg, then with a sudden clearing of his throat, he said, "See here, Colt, where are you going from Lucerne?"

Duane was too casual. "No idea. I flew here from Geneva. A local flight. Guess I'll fly back to the States eventually."

"Why not drive back with us to Genva? You can keep Gregg company while I am away."

Duane tried not to appear too eager, but his acceptance was so quick that Gregg looked up to see if Eric remembered his prediction. She thought he had given her a side glance, but she could not tell now. However, she remained hopeful. At the same time she realized how spoiled she had become during her adult life. She had never before cared very much at the breakup of a romance. Now she found herself desperately hanging onto any clue that would show her he still loved her. His slightest motion meant everything to her, and she tried to read into these motions some hopeful sign. So far, they appeared to be at a stalemate.

What did he intend to do? Where was he going after they reached Geneva? She knew she would be even more terrified if she thought about Eric going off to do battle against a creature like Martin Helm and possibly the ferret-like Mehaffey.

"Do we eat now, or on the road?" Duane wanted to know, adding sociably, "My treat."

Eric agreed that they could have dinner in the hotel, and then drive through the Alpine passes by moonlight. Duane and Gregg were both relieved at what seemed an improvement of his mood.

They had a few drinks before the excellent dinner, so it was not surprising that when they started out in the little MG, with Duane Colt buried among the luggage in an extraordinarily small space behind the front seat, that neither Gregg nor Duane cared too much about how fast Eric drove.

Duane, who had no serious problems beyond the question of whether he would play Hans Pogge in *The Looking-Glass*, went off to sleep almost before they had passed the environs of the lake, but Gregg was much too worried to let a few iced glasses of white wine soothe her. She did feel relaxed enough to move nearer to her husband, even attempting once to let her head drop unobtrusively against Eric's shoulder.

The humiliating truth was that his shoulder muscles were hard, the tweed of his jacket was rough, and he made absolutely no effort to welcome her close proximity. She pretended the gesture had been accidental and sat up straight, willing herself to stay awake, to make small talk. She got little response, but she chose to believe this was routine when a man drove rapidly across a mountainous country, no matter how good the roads might be.

Duane roused himself after sunup and began to make conversation with Gregg. They tried to include Eric, but his answers were brief and to the point.

"I say, sir, I mean Eric, can I use your

name next time I connect with Buzz Ball-enstein?"

"Ballenstein?"

"The Trades say he's set to direct the movie."

"The Trades?"

"Trade papers. About Hollywood." From Duane's tone, he could hardly believe that a civilized man needed an explanation for so obvious a matter.

Eric was no longer listening. He had glanced out at a big blue Mercedes rushing past them, heading northeast. Gregg looked around after the speeding car and asked nervously, "What is it?"

"It looks like Albrecht's Mercedes. I thought I saw Albrecht at the wheel. Going to meet your friend Martin Helm, probably."

His chilly manner spoiled any hope Gregg might have had that he had forgiven her. Nothing remained but to be grateful, at least, that Helm's gang had not followed them back to Geneva. She wondered what Eric planned, and she found herself absent-mindedly clasping and unclasping her hands. Eric stopped this by closing his fingers over hers so tightly she grimaced.

She hoped the gesture indicated a peace offering, but he said immediately, "Don't. It's very annoying."

Duane, the peacemaker, put in, "It's been mighty good of you to take me along. I'll be off for New York right away."

Eric asked in businesslike tones, "Will you oblige me, Colt?"

"Anything you say. Just name it."

"Do not leave Geneva for a few days. Until I return from a short trip."

Duane leaned forward. "You mean that? I'll look out for Red. That is, Marlene told me she and Pauly are on Gregg's side, too. They haven't any use for Albrecht. And it wouldn't surprise me if your aunt threw him out. Maybe that's why he's on the road like a bat out of hell."

"Thanks, gentlemen," Gregg put in. "I appreciate it, but I really can look out for myself. I'm much more concerned about Eric trying to tackle Albrecht's friends alone."

As if she hadn't spoken, Eric addressed himself to Duane. "I imagine Gregg will be returning to New York about her articles when I get back. She would naturally prefer company on the flight, wouldn't you, Gregg?"

His question triggered the temper which she had controlled for hours . . . I am not some brow-beaten little hausfrau, she told herself. Her fair complexion was almost as red as her hair.

"Yes. That sounds ideal," she said icily. "Duane," she leaned her head back to address him more closely, "if you are in a hurry to see those people about the movie, we can leave tomorrow. Or today, for that matter."

The little MG gave a lurch. Eric muttered, "These damned roads!"

Duane was too nervous about the undercurrents of the conversation to say anything. And not another word was spoken until the car pulled in under the porte cochere of the de Lieven château.

The Baroness de Lieven was out in the windy courtyard to greet them, surrounded by Marlene, Pauly and Miss Tibbs. The girl was jumping up and down; the boy looked anxious and kept glancing toward an open window of the great hall where Ursula Raeder looked out, her fingers spread lightly over her golden hair to keep its perfection from being rippled by the cold autumn air.

The baroness greeted Gregg with a light kiss on each cheek, afterward joking with Eric. She treated Duane Colt with a charming informality which showed Gregg just how effectively the young actor had ingratiated himself with his hostess during the last two weeks.

But it did not take long for the baroness to see that something had come between her nephew and his bride. The party all went in to breakfast, everyone else talking with great animation, to cover the awkwardness between the newlyweds. The baroness did not have time to inquire into Eric's problem, but contented herself with a brief word to Gregg.

"My dear, is he being difficult already? You mustn't mind. He sulks briefly, but he will come around. He loves you very much."

Gregg felt a strong inclination to cry out the truth; she smiled instead, but did not manage to hide her doubts. The other members of the family were still at breakfast when Eric came down to say good-bye, carrying nothing but a battered Swissair flight bag. He kissed the baroness, Marlene and Gregg on the cheek, waved casually to Ursula, Pauly and Duane. Then he left in a taxi, refusing to be driven to the airport. Gregg did not go to the window to see him off; she felt numb after the indifference of his kiss.

The Baroness de Lieven came in after the cab had gone. To Gregg she said gently, "He looked back. He very much wanted to see you," which did not raise Gregg's spirits.

"I do wish someone would tell me whatever is going on," Ursula complained as they all left the table. "I know Heinz has done something stupid. I've told him I don't want any more to do with him. But still, Eric has to run about, being very rude and cold to me. I've done nothing."

"Perfectly true, my dear," the baroness agreed in her calm way. "Gregg, when you have recovered from that wild midnight ride, I wonder if I may show you over the estate?"

"Thank you. You're very sweet. I would enjoy that."

Marlene put in, "And we'll show the grounds to Duane, won't we Pauly?"

But Ursula had her own designs on the actor, and Gregg was not surprised at his answer when she turned in the hall to ask him, "Are you leaving tomorrow?"

Duane felt a little awkward under all this attention, although he obviously enjoyed it.

"Well, Red, I thought we should wait until Eric gets back. He asked me to."

Gregg went up to her room, closely and rather anxiously watched by the baroness.

In the afternoon when she had roused herself with a brisk shower and rubdown before getting dressed for the expected walk, she found the Baroness de Lieven pacing up and down in the hall, clearly having waited some minutes for her. Gregg's apologies were brushed aside.

"All unimportant. What is of consequence is that you understand and forgive my nephew."

"Forgive him?"

"For his mood. He has his insecurities. I feel certain he was sorry he has behaved so abominably. I was quite frank and asked him if it was your fault. He said no."

Gregg saw that the baroness, though sympathetic, was curious, and as they went out across the courtyard, beyond the small, inquisitive ears of the children, she said briefly, "I was engaged eleven years ago when I was eighteen. Eric discovered that the man resembled him. He seemed sensitive about it."

The baroness nodded. "Eric has had his problems. I thought the writing of his book had eliminated the doubts and fears. He used to have—difficulty sleeping."

"He walks in his sleep."

"Ah, then you know. He never understood what happened during these phases." She sighed. "The ridiculous thing is, he went nowhere. Did nothing. The phases only last a few minutes. He always woke up. But his older brother, Rolfe, had a great sense of humor. He teased him without mercy. Made up dreadful jokes. I remember one time he pretended Eric had killed a little frog in the pond out there. Of course, it was not true—Eric loved animals —but there were dozens of episodes like that. I did what I could, but brothers— well, one does not like to interfere."

"How horrible! Forgive me, but I don't think I would've liked Rolfe."

The baroness frowned up at the milky sky. "I thought Eric made his brother the villian of his novel. But no matter . . . Rolfe was very jolly, quite stout toward the end. He looked like his German father, and he was a delightful fellow when he wanted to be. He tried to keep Eric in good spirits after Eric's accident."

"I'll bet!"

"But I'm afraid that unpleasant fellow, Heinz Albrecht, may be behind Eric's present troubles. When I heard about his telephone conversations—they certainly sounded like a blackmail scheme—I tried to learn more. Instead, the cowardly creature ran away, even from Ursula."

"Albrecht is only the tip of the iceberg. What I don't understand is where Eric went today."

In the distance behind them on the estate road, they heard Marlene and Pauly running toward them, laughing, waving a newspaper. The baroness touched Gregg's hand quickly.

"When Eric could be moved after the plane crash, he was taken to a hospital near Basel. I'm the only one in the family who knows this, and that he has gone back several times since. Much of the money from his book will go to help other confused souls there. Several of the doctors are close friends of his. And Dr. de Vries treated a good many accident victims who, like Eric, suffer emotional traumas. Dr. Vandemeer, too, is an old and valued friend. I am sure Eric has gone to see them."

"Gregg! Great-Aunt!" Marlene called, interrupting any further confidences.

Pauly tore the newspaper out of her hands and thrust it at Gregg. There was a hopeful plea in his eyes and his voice.

"I found it. She didn't. I found it for you."

Gregg was delighted at Pauly's offer of friendship.

"Thank you, Pauly. That was very kind of you. What is it?"

Marlene put in, "It's Great-Aunt's newspaper. It's about the German-speaking part of Switzerland. Look, from Lucerne: 'Eric Raeder, author of the international bestseller, *Doppelgänger*, has chosen this city for his honeymoon with the beautiful American writer, Gregg MacIvor.'"

Gregg took the paper. She was aware of a quick excitement at seeing Eric's name. The baroness read the lines over her shoulder. A minute later, as Gregg's gaze shifted from the "honeymoon" story to other items from the Lucerne column, her eyes spotted an all-too-familiar TIMOTHY J. MEHAFFEY.

With a finger that shook in her panic, she pointed to the brief item.

"My German is not very good. What does that say about Timothy Mehaffey?"

Noticing her excitement, everyone peered at the words. The baroness looked at her with a sympathy, which told Gregg her first rough translation had been correct.

"I hope he was not a friend of yours, dear. He seems to have drowned. Evidently, he fell into the River Reuss. His body was found among the greenery below the dining terrace of a hotel."

19

GREGG made a remark her friends found senseless and mysterious. "He really was helping me and I didn't believe him. But they obviously did, so they killed him."

"What?" the baroness asked, shocked. "My dear, what can you mean? Did you know this man?"

Gregg indicated the children who showed signs of extreme interest. The baroness understood her gesture and changed the subject, suggesting that the children go to get their American friend, Duane Colt, who would be interested in seeing Marlene's flowers, as well as Pauly's pet rabbits.

It was hard for Gregg to think of anything after that, except her anxiety to tell Eric of the horrifying end to her deal with Timothy Mehaffey. Mehaffey's murder—and it couldn't be anything but murder under the circumstances—demonstrated that Martin Helm remained as ruthless as ever.

A downpour of rain struck them on the way back to the château. By the time they had turned the children over to the anxious Miss Tibbs to dry out, Gregg knew it was vital to reach Eric and warn him. Still puzzled, but thorough and efficient as always, the baroness rang through to the hospital on the outskirts of Basel. She asked to speak with Eric Raeder. While Gregg waited, looking down at her fingers which felt dry and rough due to her nervousness, she heard the report. Herr Raeder had arrived but had gone into town to look for a doctor. Weather conditions in Basel were extremely bad; a thunderstorm was raising havoc with plane service.

Shortly after the household had gotten to sleep that night, Gregg was awakened by the barking of dogs. After a few minutes of this racket, she went to the windows and, pushing the heavy drapes aside, looked out to see the Baroness de Lieven in a long coat over her nightgown, her white hair in one thick braid down her back. She held a black umbrella over her head. She was speaking to a gardener in the covered doorway to the courtyard. The gardener, a sturdy little man the baroness's age, had all he could do to hold the leashes of three water-soaked, nervous German shepherds. He inclined his head politely, and trotted out toward the porte cochere, almost dragged along by the three dogs.

The baroness looked up to find Gregg at the window. "Either a prowler or the storm has upset the dogs, my dear. Nothing to trouble about, but I am going to call the police. The estate is so large, sometimes one needs a little outside help."

Gregg at once suspected the worst. She leaned out, said in a low voice, "Please come into the house, madame. It may be the man who is threatening Eric and me."

The baroness picked up the damp skirts of her nightgown and scuttled into the central hall while Gregg, throwing on a heavy, quilted robe, hurried out to meet her at the foot of the stairs.

"I had no notion things were so serious," the baroness began, slightly breathless. "I don't believe Heinz Albrecht presents a physical danger."

"No, but his friend does. I'll wait with you while you call the Geneva police." She took the arm of the older woman, who accepted her help gratefully.

"Thank you. Heavens! I wish all these drapes on the ground floor had been closed. I cannot help wondering who might be looking in at us."

They felt safer in the baroness's cozy morning room. While the baroness made her phone call to an official in Geneva, whom she addressed as "Puppchen," Gregg closed the drapes. A great deal of cold air smelling of rain and wet foliage had poured in from somewhere, but Gregg was in no mood to investigate every window on the ground floor.

With the call completed, they started back through the great hall to the staircase, only to be jarred by the buzzing of the telephone. The baroness sighed, then returned to the nearest telephone extension in a corner niche of the great hall. She had no sooner heard the voice at the other end of the line than she signaled to Gregg, who was studying the various windows. It was almost too much to hope this might be Eric, but Gregg asked in a tremulous voice, "Is is you? Is it really you?"

Her husband's laugh was the most welcome sound she could think of. "I hope so. Darling, what is it?" The pleasant, warm chuckle had faded. "Are you all right? You aren't actually going to New York with that actor, are you?"

"No, I never intended to. But, darling, listen. I saw a Lucerne paper today. You remember that man who was working with Albrecht and Helm? He was found dead in the river, below our hotel terrace."

There was a moment's silence. Then he took the answer for granted. "They killed him? Why?"

"Because he was going to trap Martin Helm some way. Helm must have found out. Don't you see? He is a murderer. He may be after you next."

He was irritated at her blindness. "*You* are his natural target. I'll take the first shuttle plane out. Damn! The weather here is terrible. I was late getting in. And then I couldn't locate Dr. Vandemeer. I've found him though, and I have the affidavit. I'll be home before you know it. Meanwhile how well protected are you? Look, darling, let me speak to Aunt Alex. But first, do you love me?"

"More than ever. Oh, please, Eric, take care of yourself. Don't fly out if the weather is bad. Here is Madame."

"I love you, Gregg, darling . . . Oh, Aunt Alex!"

"This is Alex, dear boy. We have sent for the police, just to be certain. Call when you are leaving Basel and we will send Thibaut to the airport with the car. And I expect Gregg will want to go, too."

Gregg put in loudly, "Yes. Be sure and tell him."

"No, dear. Eric wants to take a taxi. He says it will make it easier for us. He doesn't want you to leave the estate."

They left this matter in abeyance. When the connection was broken, the baroness set back the telephone, put her arm around Gregg and they walked upstairs together.

Gregg said, "Thank God Eric isn't angry anymore."

"He is like that. You must be patient. He's worth a little patience, my dear." She stopped and listened. "You know, I have heard nothing since the dogs were leashed. I believe our alarms were all imaginary."

This optimism proved to be well-founded, but it did not console Gregg, who had to wait until the telephone rang at six-thirty the following evening to hear from her husband. She was so excited she cried,

"He must have arrived at the airport! I'll go and meet him."

At the baroness's nod she went to the phone. A woman's voice spoke in French, a language Gregg understood a good deal better than German.

"Madame la Baronne de Lieven? This is the Hôpital Française Etrangère. I have been asked by the nephew of Madame to call upon Madame Raeder, his wife."

"Speaking." Gregg felt she had known it all the time. It was bad news. "Is he hurt? What happened?" Frantically, she motioned the baroness to listen also, whispering to her, "Is there a French Foreign Hospital?"

"Yes. Who is speaking? I recognize your voice, Sister Magdalen." She looked at Gregg, covered the speaking piece briefly. "I know her . . . Is my nephew ill, Sister?"

"We are told it was a small accident in the taxi from the airport, Madame la Baronne. A few facial cuts and a blow to the back of the head. He wishes to see his wife."

Gregg cut in, "I'll go at once, Madame, would you come with me?"

Sister Magdalen cleared her throat, as a

hint. "You are always welcome, madame. But Monsieur Raeder has only just been admitted. He will need quiet. Only one visitor at a time. After Madame Raeder, then you will be most welcome, if Monsieur is not too tired. You understand?"

"Perfectly. I will go tomorrow."

Gregg asked urgently, "You are sure it is not serious? You are sure?"

"Quite, madame. But he is badly shaken. The taxi was struck from the side. The driver received a whiplash."

Gregg dropped the phone into the hands of the baroness. "I must go. Excuse me."

Duane Colt moved in on them. "I'll go with you. I'll wait for you while you visit him. You can't go out alone. And he did ask me to look out for you."

Miss Tibbs and the children met her with assorted messages for the patient. In twenty minutes, Gregg and Duane arrived at the three-story stone building on a side street within sight of the lake. They rushed up the steps which still ran with rainwater, though the storm itself was blowing over and any minute the stars threatened to come out. The hospital's main floor reminded her of a gloomy church interior, with its archway and severe, undecorated stone walls, and she shivered. Duane pulled her coat collar up, trying to be helpful, but she scarcely felt his touch.

At the desk, lighted by dim globes that cast everyone's face in sinister shadow, a small nun with humorous dark eyes and a strong jaw came out to meet Gregg.

"You are Madame Raeder. How charming! Yes. An American. One can see that. The young gentleman may wait in this little room. I will show you. Monsieur, perhaps these magazines will entertain you."

Anxious as Gregg was, she had to smile at Duane Colt settling down to religious magazines in French and German.

"I'll go out and look at the lake," he said.

Gregg hurried after the bustling little nun. They took the lift to the third floor.

"Monsieur Raeder asked for a room over the courtyard. I think he believes he may see the lake from his window. He must crane his neck to do so, however, and that poor headache he complains of will not let him crane his neck just yet."

"I know he is fond of the lake," Gregg

356

murmured, reflecting that there was still so much she did not yet know about her husband. She wondered if she would be permitted to embrace him, or was he too shaken up? "Is he safe here? There are some unpleasant people who might not wish him well. Could they reach him?"

Sister Magdalen's eyebrows raised slightly, but she assured her, "We like to believe we screen our visitors. We have some foreigners here who are incognito, so we are most careful. Ernst Bosch is employed by us. You did not see him, but he saw you. He is a powerful man and he serves us in many ways. Then, there is Louis de Saulx. I believe you call him an orderly. He is here tonight. Of course, our patients have calls on the telephone. Your husband has just received one, but it was brief."

"Probably the baroness, asking if I have arrived."

When they walked out of the lift on the third floor, the first person they saw was a powerful blond young man in white, unlike the bilious green that Gregg was used to in certain hospitals at home.

"De Saulx," whispered Sister Magdalen.

Two nuns passed. Gregg eyed them suspiciously, but no disguised male could have that fragile, transparent look. She was enormously relieved. All the same, she thought it quite possible that the car which ran into Eric's taxi had been driven by Martin Helm.

"*Ici*, madame." Sister Magdalen made a sweeping gesture toward the last door next to an old stairwell.

Gregg asked, "Who uses that staircase?"

"Only those inside the hospital. A court-yard door opens outward only." The nun looked at her, but asked no more questions. She opened the door to Eric's room.

A single globe of low wattage hung high above the bed, illuminating a crucifix but not giving much help to the patient who had been reading a Geneva newspaper. He dropped the paper as the door opened, and Gregg gasped when she saw him across the room, holding out one hand to her.

His face looked as if someone had played tic-tac-toe with it. There were half a dozen adhesive strips plastered haphazardly over his face.

"Glass broke, sweetheart. Side window of the cab," he explained as best he could.

There was an adhesive patch at one side of his mouth as well.

Sister Magdalen chided him, "Do not talk more than you must, Monsieur Raeder. Now I will leave you alone with your wife for a few minutes. Only a few. Monsieur must get his rest." After that, she withdrew into the hall, closing the door.

"Darling, I was so worried!" Gregg started across the room. He held out his hand to her again as she approached the bed. A gauze bandage was bound loosely across his palm and the base of two fingers. There seemed to be no painless part of him that she might kiss, so she took up the injured hand and touched the gauze bandage with her lips.

At the same time they were startled by sounds outside the long, curtained window, the breaking of bottles, as if garbage were poured out.

"In the courtyard. Been moving trash ever since I got into this place," he murmured, after wincing painfully at the sound. "Sweetheart, would you ask them to be quieter? After all," his chuckle was faint but real, "this is a hospital zone."

Frowning in the dim light which allowed

her to see only the bright, feverish look in his eyes, she went over and pushed open the drapes to the long, floor-length window which opened upon a minuscule balcony with a protective rail about two feet high.

"No wonder it's so noisy," she told him. "The window is open." She could not see any activity in the courtyard below. Everything looked deserted.

"Better close it, in case it rains again," he suggested.

She started to reach out for the window catch. Into her mind came a flash of memory: Alys Lane cleaning her windows. The earlier fiancée who jumped out of a hotel window. Martin Helm always had great success with windows. She thought: I haven't really seen the face of that man in the bed behind me. Panic welled up instantly inside of her.

She clutched the window frame so hard her knuckles ached, while she tried to speak with exactly the same tone she had previously used. "The damned thing keeps blowing out of my hand. I'll get something to—to reach the catch."

He knew. In spite of her effort to show no emotion, he knew.

Before she had finished speaking, it was as if an enormous cloud had hurled itself at her. He was standing behind her, fully dressed, with the hospital gown loose over slacks and a sweater. His body pressed hard against her back as he murmured in her ear, with his hands moving softly over her shoulders toward her face.

"My little girl disappointed me once. Not again. I loved you then. Did you know that, my sweet? How I suffered when my little girl ran away and left me, practically at the altar! How different from good, faithful old Alys! Poor girl. This whole masquerade about Raeder was her idea, though she didn't know it. She saw his picture in the paper early Sunday. Pointed out the resemblance. A millionaire and he could have been my twin."

"Not quite!" she put in tightly. "And you murdered the woman who protected you."

Just for a second he hesitated. "Too bad. She guessed my thoughts the minute after she'd shown me the picture. Started giving me orders. Actually threatened to expose me. Her precious conscience wouldn't let her cover for me again! All that fine middle-class morality. Well, I agreed and left her. I waited in the garbage disposal room. I can smell it yet! Then, she began to wash her windows, as I knew she would. It was fate, playing into my hands. I took the opportunity it presented. Fate has always been my friend."

She shuddered, trying to maneuver him into further betrayal, hoping someone would hear him, would come to see why she hadn't come out of his room yet. Anything to gain time. "So you went right from murder to murder."

"No, my sweet, I changed my appearance a little, got that doorman job. I hoped to study Raeder, but he didn't show up there. I didn't know how I'd work my idea. I had to think and plan. Then—I told you fate always helps me—Albrecht noticed me. His idea was better than mine. We'd make Raeder and the whole world think he was mad. Albrecht wanted to have Raeder locked up. Then that empty-headed Ursula would handle his estate. My idea was more secure. Raeder must die. Suicide, driven by his 'crimes.' One of which was the murder of his wife in this hospital. You may imagine how I loved that part of it. It was almost the crowning moment for me."

"I can hardly blame you." She wet her lips which were dry and stiff. "But you can't count on Albrecht. He'll cheat you."

His mouth against her ear was warm and made her flesh crawl. "He can't. He's involved in every step. To betray me he must betray himself, and he's too much of a coward to do that. He was with me when that miserable little liar Mehaffey died. No. Albrecht isn't going to betray me . . . But as for you, my faithless sweetheart, you betrayed me for that cheap carbon copy, that mirror image. I could hardly believe my luck when I saw you that night. Two debts to pay. One to give myself what was coming to me. The other, to pay you off. I heard you and the old lady on the phone last night, you know. I was almost close enough to touch you. You must admit, I think of everything. Fate and I!"

"Martin," she began, rambling in her desperation, "Eric knows I am here. Your game is over. There can't be two of you in the same place."

She could see the twist to his mouth. The

little adhesive bandage flapped ridiculously from a corner of his lip.

"How right you are, Mary Gregg. I got word just minutes ago from the airport. Your precious Eric hailed the nearest cab, but he didn't notice friend Albrecht, the driver, with a flowering mustache and a billed cap. I'll give the devil his due. One small tap on the head did it, and now he's at my disposal."

"How inconvenient! Two Eric Raeders!"

"Not at all. Tonight Eric Raeder will push his wife out the window. Then he, too, will be found in that courtyard. A suicide, after the horror of his act." His voice purred softly. "I don't suppose it will ever be known why he did this monstrous thing, or where he hid the money everyone assumed he had, but with his mental history, well . . ."

Far away in the night air she heard traffic calmly passing on some avenue. She was aware of kitchen workers rattling dishes in a building beyond the courtyard. Even the hospital room clicked and cracked behind them, as if it were alive with ghosts of past patients. With his hands so close to her throat, did she have a chance to scream?

His face was so close she might have bitten him, but she poured out the greater hurt, hoping to throw him into shock for a second or two by the unexpectedness of it.

"When I saw you in Lucerne you looked so pitiful. Now, all this tape and gauze—Poor Martin! It doesn't hide that shabby, seedy look. No wonder you had to try blackmail. You certainly couldn't get another woman."

His eyes glittered, dark against the white tape. He looked as if he were stupefied. Perhaps no woman had ever before told him the truth about himself. She began very gently to push away his hand.

"Poor Martin! The way you've changed . . ."

She felt his body, stiff and motionless, and thought that one quick twist would free her, but with her move he recovered, his fingers closing about her throat and squeezing. She scratched at his face, tried vainly to kick him, and to her own astonishment, the pressure on her throat weakened. His eyes looked enormous. She had never seen such horror. He was staring over her shoulder as if he had seen a ghost.

Painfully, she forced herself to turn her

head and saw the ghostly vision that had sent him into shock. Eric Raeder stood there, motionless. A heavy German Luger in his hand was aimed at her assailant, but she doubted if Martin Helm even noticed it.

For several seconds Martin Helm remained in that stupor, then he backed away. Through the gauze and the bandages his face seemed to wrinkle, to stretch and twist with abysmal terror.

"I thought it was—a mirror." And then, in the voice of a lost child, "Don't, please don't hurt me . . . Don't shoot. . . ."

He backed against the half-open window, which flung out wide under his weight. Still screaming, "Please, please don't . . ." he stumbled over the rail behind him. As Eric Raeder reached out to catch him, Helm's flailing arms knocked Gregg against the wall and, unable to regain his balance, he hurtled outward, down to the dark courtyard below.

The corridor door had opened. The room seemed to be full of people who rushed to the window to look down. Eric helped Gregg to her feet and held her close, but she managed to see Sister Magdalen's graceful hand move to cross herself as she murmured a prayer for the fallen man below. Even Duane Colt was there, looking down with great interest, trying to study the exact position of the dead man's body, sprawled on the paving stones.

20

GREGG, Eric and Duane returned to the hospital's reception desk from the now bright-lighted and busy courtyard where the dead man's body was being transferred to the morgue.

"Did he really look like you?" Duane asked.

"He didn't look in the least like Eric," Gregg insisted shakily before Eric could answer. "He was revolting. And funny-looking, too. Horribly funny-looking with gauze and adhesive sticking to him." She began to laugh. Sister Magdalen offered her a glass of water which Eric held to her lips, watching her with anxious attention.

"Are you all right, darling?"

"Of course she's all right. But tell us what happened," Duane demanded. "Tell us everything."

"Is she really all right, Sister?" Eric was asking, only to be reassured by Sister Magdalen in her calm way. "God!" he burst out, betraying panic for the first time.

"I forced Albrecht! I forced him to call Helm and say everything had gone off as planned. If I had known it would trigger the attack on my wife—" He looked at Sister Magdalen. "It's my fault she was almost killed."

The nun dismissed this with her customary good sense. "You behaved quite sensibly, monsieur. As one would expect." Then she had to quiet Duane, whose endless questions might disturb the patients, as she reminded him.

To ingratiate himself with these busy people who were ignoring him, Duane reminded Gregg, "I was out on the sidewalk, you know. I saw the taxi that brought Eric. Albrecht was driving. Eric jumped out with this big gun, practically a cannon, against Albrecht's head. Was I flabbergasted! He said to call the police, that Albrecht and this other guy were up to something but Albrecht wouldn't say what, just that he was supposed to call Helm at the hospital and then take Raeder to the rear entrance. What do the police think?"

Eric had borrowed some of the nun's stoic calm. He shrugged.

"I imagine Albrecht suspected Helm

would kill us, but I doubt if he would have had the guts to help in the butchery."

Duane ended on a note of triumph. "So I got an orderly to hold Albrecht, and then I called the police. In French. Myself. And I don't even know French!"

"How very brave of you, Duane!" Gregg praised him, with a side glance at Eric, but her husband had not noticed anything humorous. He was too worried over her near-miss, and was almost as annoying as Duane with his persistent questioning.

Sister Magdalen agreed that it had been quite hectic. "Especially when we told Monsieur Raeder his wife was in that room with—with the other Monsieur Raeder."

"We all wanted to barge in and rescue you, Red, but the sister reminded Eric how dangerous that would be. Hey, Raeder, wouldn't this make a good novel for you? And I might play my own part, maybe."

Eric put his arm around his wife, got her on her way to the front door and said firmly, "We are going home to bed. No one is going to write anything tonight. However, since we are sure to be visited tomorrow by every official in Geneva, you will have plenty of time to tell your tale. Good night, Sister. Good night, Colt."

"Darling," Gregg reminded him in a low voice, "Duane is staying with all of us at the château."

Eric said, "Damn!" but managed to persuade Duane to sit in the front seat of the Bentley, with the incurious Thibaut who had arrived upon orders from the Baroness de Lieven.

As they drove back to the château with their hands interlocked and their bodies very close, Gregg asked Eric, "How far is Heinz Albrecht really involved in all this killing? Helm said he helped to murder the little detective. They found out Mehaffey was betraying them to me."

Eric considered the story Albrecht had already confessed to the police. "He insists the violence was all Helm's doing."

"Albrecht wanted you locked up as insane, so Ursula would have your power of attorney. Wouldn't it have been funny if the courts had appointed the baroness instead?"

She closed her eyes for a minute. She would always regret that she hadn't believed Mehaffey when he told her he intended to turn Helm over to the Hamburg police. He was simply playing two games, and Helm caught him at it.

"Who will claim Helm's body now?"

"The police say someone is flying in from Hamburg to identify the fellow." He laughed for the first time since he had arrived that evening in Geneva. "A lot of good it would have done them to blackmail me. Reach in my pocket there."

She did so, touched the big heavy Luger and her fingers jumped. He said, "Sorry, but the Luger is actually your fault. After your phone call to Basel I borrowed this from Vandemeer. Rather glad I did!" He took a sheaf of papers and a snapshot from the other pocket. "There. That picture was taken by Madame Vandemeer in their gardens on Lake Locarno in May, twelve years ago. No one knew where I was, except the Vandemeers and Aunt Alex. I wanted it that way. I had to examine my own feelings and fears about myself. Well, I did. I recovered, but while I was in the hospital, Helm must have been wooing and murdering the woman in Hamburg. Anyway, I also got an affidavit from

Vandemeer, stating that I never left Locarno during my stay."

Gregg stared at the snapshots of the group, a middled-aged man with a neat, well-kept mustache, several children and one young man, all arms and legs in a pair of swim trunks, but with the strained, tense look of someone who has suffered. The scars across his forehead were still unhealed; but except for the vague similarity of contour, and perhaps the deep-set dark eyes, no one would possibly have confused this Eric Raeder with Martin Helm.

She thought of all her doubts, the fears, the frantic hope that Eric Raeder was not that killer. She said, "If only I had known from the first. If only I had seen these pictures!"

He countered with just a slight edge to the words, "If only you had come to me directly, with what you knew about Helm!"

He still didn't know the worst, the things she had suspected him of, and she knew she would keep that one secret from him forever. She loved him too much to risk losing him again.

She changed the direction of her

thoughts quicky, as he asked, "Do you suppose Ursula knew about any of Albrecht's schemes?"

She laughed shortly. "I doubt it. She isn't the kind who keeps secrets. Besides, Helm wouldn't trust her. I think poor Alys Lane must be the only one he trusted, and in the end, he murdered her."

"Here we are," Duane's voice boomed at them from the front seat. "Here's the archway."

Eric murmured to Gregg, "I wonder why I feel as if we had adopted a stray."

Duane said with great satisfaction, "Ah, home at last!"

GUIDE
TO THE COLOUR CODING
OF
ULVERSCROFT BOOKS

Many of our readers have written to us expressing their appreciation for the way in which our colour coding has assisted them in selecting the Ulverscroft books of their choice. To remind everyone of our colour coding—this is as follows:

BLACK COVERS
Mysteries

★

BLUE COVERS
Romances

★

RED COVERS
Adventure Suspense and General Fiction

★

ORANGE COVERS
Westerns

★

GREEN COVERS
Non-Fiction